Praise For Jim Nesbitt's *The Last Second Chance*

"If Chandler's noir was a neon sign in the LA sunset, Nesbitt's noir is the Shiner Bock sign buzzing outside the last honky-tonk you'll hit before the long drive to the next one. On the way you'll pass towns with names like Crumley and Portis. Roll down the window; it's a hot night. It's a fast ride."

— James Lileks, author of *Casablanca Tango*, columnist for the *National Review* and *Star Tribune* of Minneapolis, creator of *LILEKS.com*

"Jim Nesbitt has written what might be the year's best hardboiled thriller. It's a wild yarn with flashes of Stephen King, James Ellroy and Raymond Chandler served up in a unique style that nobody but Nesbitt could deliver."

— Paul Finebaum, ESPN college football analyst, author, host of *The Paul Finebaum Show*

"In 'The Last Second Chance,' Jim Nesbitt gives readers a splendid first opportunity to meet Ed Earl Burch, as flawed a Luckies-smoking, whiskey-drinking, serial-married hero as ever walked the scarred earth of Dirty Texas. The story is familiar -- ex-cop Burch sets out to avenge the death of a friend -- but Nesbitt writes with such grit and hard-bitten humor that the well-trodden turf springs forth as brand new. In Burch, Nesbitt has created a more angst-ridden and bad-ass version of Michael Connelly's Harry Bosch and a Tex-Mex landscape much meaner than the streets of L.A. Add hate-worthy lowlifes and a diminutive dame, Carla Sue Cantrell, who cracks wiser than the guys, and you've got a book with gumption. Here's hoping Nesbitt soon gives us second chance to hang out with Ed Earl Burch."

— Bob Morris, Edgar finalist, author of *Baja Florida* and *A Deadly Silver Sea*

More Praise

"I'm a science writer. I wrote a book about hallucinogens and your brain that has underground comics in it (for those of you on drugs) and interviews with medicinal chemists and psychopharmacologists. So why am I writing this with the very highest praise for any kind of writing, and now a first novel, by Jim Nesbitt? I'll tell you -- it's because whenever I read anything he writes, in my head there's a running dialog: That's the best sentence I've ever read. Where did he get that word? That analogy could slice an onion. Who even writes like this anymore? Part of it's because, as he likes to say, for three decades he chased presidential candidates, hurricanes, earthquakes, rodeo cowboys, ranchers, neo-Nazis and nuns as a roving correspondent. That'll stock up your word supply. Also, as he once described himself: he's a storyteller, born of Scots-Irish hillbilly stock. Now he's written *The Right Wrong Number*, an Ed Earl Burch Novel. Burch – and these are all Nesbitt's descriptions, is a cashiered vice and homicide detective with bad knees and a battered soul. In the novel he plays a deadly game with a short blonde with a taste for muscle cars, crystal meth and the high-wire double-cross. See what I mean? And then the story begins. If you like to read, if you appreciate words and people who run them brilliantly through their paces, give this book a read. And his next one, and the one after that. You'll be enthralled, like I was."

– Cheryl Pellerin, author of *Trips: How Hallucinogens Work in Your Brain*

THE LAST SECOND CHANCE

An Ed Earl Burch Novel

JIM NESBITT

THE LAST SECOND CHANCE
An Ed Earl Burch Novel

ISBN 1519243065
ISBN 9781519243065

Cover photograph by Andrew Palochko.
Used with permission.

For Pam and the Panther

CHAPTER 1

It felt good. Real good. Warm and wet. Lots of suction. Her hair spread out over a grimy pillow. Her cheeks puffed. He gripped the top rail of the headboard for leverage.

Music and loud voices drifted from downstairs. There was the sound of breaking glass and a burst of profanity. The green neon of a street sign flashed through the louvers of a door that led to the catwalk outside. His man Mano stood on the other side of the hallway door. She brought him back to the room with her tongue, a thumb and two fingers. The feeling made him thrust harder. She gagged and bit him.

"Pinche puta. Ya me mordiste el pito. Si me lo haces sangrar te mato."

"No te lo quise morder. Lo que pasa es que eres mucho hombre para mi."

He smiled. Too much man. She smiled back and opened her arms and legs for him. He slapped her twice across the face. He grabbed her left nipple and twisted hard, causing her to gasp in pain and grab his wrist. He forced himself between her thighs.

"Muy hombre, eh? Muy hombre? Siente que tan."

He slapped her again. She bit his arm and raked a shoulder with her nails. He grabbed the headboard railing again and looked down at her. Sweat rolled from his chest onto her belly. There was a large red welt on her face. Her lower lip was swollen and bleeding. She stared at him, teeth bared, grunting at each of this thrusts.

"Madre santa. Puedes seguirle eternamente."

Forever. Maybe so. The old woman said he could. In anything he wanted to do. As long as he believed. As long as he walked with the power. As long as he drank blood and muttered chants at the candles and shrunken skulls and tokens she kept on her plywood altar. He could be a bird or a snake or a big cat.

But he didn't believe. He walked through the rituals. He chanted the chants while thinking of whores. He cut the throats of chickens and goats and ate the flesh of these sacrificed animals. But he didn't do it for the pleasure of some ancient spirit. He did it for the power it gave him over her sons and nephews, the muscle he needed for his runs across the border.

He didn't believe in forever or life as a crow or a cougar. He believed in a fast run and a blinding flash of pain at the end. And anything that gave him that sweet taste of power and control. Nothing more.

His thumb and forefinger twisted her other nipple. A cry took the place of a grunt. He believed in this. He owned this whore. She clawed at his arm, drawing more blood. He laughed and watched blood drip onto her swollen face.

"Drink that and live forever. The old woman says so."

The door to the catwalk splintered open.

He turned his head to see a short man in a gray suit aiming a pump shotgun at him. He saw Mano stepping through the hallway door, bringing his pistol to bear.

The shotgun boomed.

The wall behind the headboard rushed toward his face.

He saw red, then white. Flashes and pain.

Then nothing.

CHAPTER 2

Burch was tired and needed a drink, a shower and a snooze. Instead, he was in a two-room office next to the Central Expressway, looking at an expense form he didn't want to finish and a surveillance report he didn't want to start.

Traffic noise drilled through the walls. It was the hollow roar of motors and moving metal rattling off the concrete of the roadbed, the overpass for Mockingbird Lane and the cluster of buildings that formed his modest little office park. His digs were on the top floor of a two-story walkup, the backbone of a broken C of steel-spined buildings with brick veneer and a parking lot of buckled and sun-blasted concrete. It was the kind of place that featured a winning view of the access road and was easy to miss with a sneeze or a glance up at the time and temperature that flashed from the sign for the Dr. Pepper plant.

Last office on the left. Boss-secretary arrangement. No elevator. No windows. No Effie Perine to answer the phone. An air conditioner that rattled and wheezed but didn't cool. An electric lock on the corridor door that opened with a loud buzz and a dull clunk. An answering machine that was one of two concessions to modern times. A dentist used to work here. He could see the grime-rimmed circle where the chair once stood and the four holes that once held the anchor bolts. Those holes were natural magnets for the toes of careless cowboy boots. His favorites wore their mark -- Justins, bearing the skin of some South American river snake with a tongue-twisting name he could never remember.

The dentist was gone. The complex was fresh out of receivership -- testimony to the shifting fortunes of the Texas oil and real estate bust. He was here with a cut-rate lease that trickled money to some Yankee bottom-feeders who scarfed up the paper on these buildings when the original owner went belly up and the feds seized the S&L that floated the project. The bust left its own Mark of Cain. You could see it on the cars that flowed up and down Greenville or Abrams or Cedar Springs. BMWs and Mercedes, flashy and new when oil was forty dollars a barrel, now rivaling the rides of Mex and Salvadoran illegals for shabbiness and disrepair, limping along with dents, dirt and bald tires.

Behind the wheels of these fallen status symbols were folks who once made a bundle working for independent oil outfits, realtors, banks and S&Ls. Now they worried about making the rent or mortgage. No money for a bent fender. Nothing for custom detailing. Plenty for a stiff drink or something narcotic to ease the pain of a rapidly draining bank account. Black humor on the bar rail was the rule.

This line from Rita, a hard-hitting redhead who was once a high-flying realtor: "What's a few dents among bankrupt friends?" Delivered with perfect timing and a perfectly pitched laugh. But her eyes seemed glazed with dread as she gunned a shooter and signaled the `tender for another in the same motion.

Downtown buildings also bore the mark. No cloven hoof. No triple sixes. Just the ghostly outlines of logos for the busted banks of Texas, bolt holes and all, barely covered by the gleaming signs of outsiders who now controlled the state's atrophied financial muscle and the keys to its broken entrepreneurial pride. The four letters of a marauding North Carolina bank, the most obnoxious of the pinstriped carpetbaggers, gave the Texas bidnessman a new obscenity to mutter.

Scavengers did real well off the bust. He should know; his business doubled when panicky lawyers needed a real fast line on a missing partner from a soured deal and nervous S&L officers wanted

4

to reach out and touch an out-of-luck developer who never seemed to be at home anymore. Low overhead seemed to be the key. At least for him. A framed license hung on his wall. A damp, dark-blue linen jacket hung on a broken hat rack. So did the shoulder holster that housed his semi-auto, a Colt in the only caliber God meant for a man to carry -- eight fat boys in .45 ACP. Corbon 230-grain hollow-points. Flying Ashtrays. Because they hit like a runaway dump truck and did ungodly damage inside a body cavity.

He lit a Lucky with a dented nickel Zippo and glanced at the butts that choked a red tin Whitbread Ale ashtray -- a souvenir from a pub crawl through London with his first ex-wife. She was in his dreams again. Woke him up at 4 a.m. like clockwork, like the nights they first split up. Back again, sweet and haunting. He glanced at his favorite John Wayne picture, the one in the cheap gilded metal frame and the cracked glass.

It was a still from *True Grit* that showed the Duke with the reins in his teeth and his hands filled with guns, galloping across the meadow, aiming to kill Ned Pepper. He used to love the Duke -- gunsmoke and the glory of the Old West. Duty, honor and a man doing what a man had to do. But the Duke was dead and so was his taste for swagger, bravado and other forms of Hollywood horseshit. He kept the picture for luck, a reminder of how he used to be and how things used to be with her.

He made a mistake on the expense report and fumed. The white-out was buried some place under a scatter of newsprint, files, Wendy's wrappers, Coke bottles, girlie and gun magazines, crisscross directories and the phone. He moved the pile, clearing more space on the table that served as his desk, throwing trash into the gray metal wastebasket.

His eye caught the bottle of Maker's Mark. It sat near the wastebasket, tucked against the right rear leg of the table. Why not? It was well past six, though you couldn't tell that from the *Tejano* heat that was part blast furnace, part sauna and part of the D's merciless charm.

A small refrigerator sat on a filing cabinet to his right -- his second concession to modern times and creature comforts. He popped open the door and reached for a frosted juice glass and some ice. He felt a small stream of coolness walk through the hairs of his forearm and touch the damp fabric of his rolled-up sleeve.

One drink led to three. Three led him to the couch and some sleep stolen by a long stakeout and the fluttery images of his first ex. He felt puffy and clammy when he woke up. His shirt stuck to the Naugahyde skin of the couch and his mouth tasted like pennies and old socks.

It was dark and hot. His belly rumbled.

A quick phone call, a ten-block ride and a rap on the front door brought him to a small Mex joint on Ross. It was a hole in the wall, barely wider than the dented metal door that carved a fan-shaped groove on the floor every time a customer walked in.

The uneven red letters of a hand-painted sign said *Cafe Garcia*. Arturo Garcia was the owner, a weathered man with a wrestler's build and a waxed moustache the color of iron filings. His hard-drinking Anglo regulars called him *El Rey* and his place of business the *Cafe de Los Borrachos y Diablos*.

Drunks and devils had to eat up front and finish before midnight. But for the man who tracked down the pregnant, teenage daughter of Arturo Garcia, there was always an after-hours plate of *huevos con chorizo* and cold *cervezas*. The front room was hot, the air was still and laden with the smell of grease and stale cigarette smoke. A formica counter -- black flecked with white, trimmed in aluminum -- ran down the right wall. Seven bare-topped tables with bentwood chairs ran down the left, ringside seats for torn and grease-stained bullfight posters and the slick beer calendars with the big-chested models holding beaded bottles of *El Sol, Tecate* or *Carta Blanca*.

Flashing eyes, shiny manes of raven hair and all those curves spilling around stretched fabric stirred up the confused mind of the modern beer drinker. A faded notice for a long-ago bullfight didn't stand a chance.

Arturo led him back to the cramped kitchen. No *abrazo*. No small talk. Just a tight smile around a dark brown double corona, a curt nod and a short sweep of the arm toward a scarred wooden table, a plate and bottled beer poured into a pony glass.

A trail of cigar smoke and a swinging kitchen door marked Arturo's silent return to the front room. He settled behind his food, elbows on the table, head down, as the clack of an adding machine drifted through the service counter window. His mind was groggy and blank. His eyes watched his fork move a hot mess of yellow, red and brown. The sound of Arturo doing the day's receipts stopped. He heard a lock tumble open and the scrape of the front door. He took a short sip of beer and drug out a damp pack of Luckies from his shirt pocket.

He stood up.

The kitchen door swung open.

CHAPTER 3

There was a big .45 in her tiny hand. It was pointed toward him. He could see the black hole of its ugly snout and the curved spur of the cocked hammer. He could feel the sweat starting to break across the bridge of his nose and steam the lower part of his round-rimmed glasses. The Colt 1911 looked ridiculously large, its worn finish a cheap contrast to the hammered silver bracelet she wore on her wrist, its shape a clunky insult to the line of her thin, tanned arms.

His mind tossed up a line from a Michael Herr story about a mysterious Vietnamese woman who kept killing American officers on the streets of Saigon with a Colt semi-auto. Army investigators doubted the killer was really a woman; more likely a Viet Cong wearing an *ao dai*. One khakied sleuth trumped up this bit of logic: "A .45? Now that's a big, big gun for a iddy-biddy Vietnamese woman."

Acquired wisdom. Recalled just in time and under pressure. Showed that sweat wasn't soaking his brain cells. Just his shirt. She eyed him slowly, keeping the Colt's business end centered on his paunch. He pointed to the pine chair to his left. She nodded and he sat down. He glanced at the pack of Luckies on the table before him. She nodded again. When he looked at her through the curling, blue-gray smoke, she smiled.

"You Ed Earl Burch?"

"The same."

"You say that proud."

"Naw, just weary. Mind?"

He pointed the Lucky toward his glass of beer, its bubbles dying from smoke, heat and dead air. She didn't nod. He waited. His back was hot, wet and stuck to the back of the chair. His forehead was clammy. The shock of having a gun pointed at him was wearing off.

He studied the woman's face -- handsome instead of pretty; heavy makeup, a long, flinty jawline and lots of eyeliner framing the kind of blue eyes you'd see on a Siamese cat. Those eyes were what you'd first notice if she didn't have the gun -- clear and permanently startled.

He took in the rest. Short, straight, swept-from-the-forehead hair -- not quite dishwater blonde, not quite light brown. White blouse, rolled up sleeves and a brocade vest with a blue and purple paisley pattern. Tight jeans hugging muscular legs and flared hips. Wrangler, not Guess. Boots that used to be brown. Cracked leather vamps and a riding heel. And a brown leather shoulder bag big enough to hide the Colt, but small enough to match her tiny frame.

No answer to his question, but the tension had eased up. He reached for the glass. The gun came up, centered on his broad forehead. Those startled eyes got narrow and cold. Wrong again.

He parked his forearm back on the tabletop, resting both hands in front, thumbs inward, so she could see them. No tricks from me, lady, so no nervous tugs on that trigger. No calculated pulls, either, pretty please.

"My call, Big 'Un."

"You bet."

"Want to know what's up, right? Want to know why dinner's been interrupted, right? Why Arturo would let someone like me in? You'd even like to know just who in the hell you've pissed off?"

Questions that had crossed his mind, delivered at a rapid pace that sure wasn't East Dallas or Mesquite. Maybe Plano or Highland Park. Not the sound of a Yankee transplant, but not a pure Texas twang.

Some up-holler South sanded smooth and buried near the back of her mouth.

He said nothing. He took another sweet drag of Lucky. Its hot tip was burning toward the knuckles of his left hand. Wonder if she'll let me reach over and fetch the ashtray? Nah. He twisted the butt into his food, frowning at the task, drawing the silence down a little tighter.

Let's do sums. Nothing in his current catalogue of jobs. Surveillance work for a jeweler who didn't trust his partner. Some background work for a lawyer with a couple of drug-dealing clients. A flyer from a Houston firm trying to track down a fugitive scrap-metal merchant in hopes of grabbing his assets. A North Dallas divorce case he didn't want to take.

More sums. If this were a pro hit, he'd be dead by now, a close-up shot to the back of the head with a .22, Ruger or Hi-Standard, not a Colt .45.

A simple case of an extremely pissed-off client would draw a shotgun blast or a bunch of bullets from one of the Wonder Nines. Probably a drive-by, probably in the parking lot, the signature of a Jamaican posse. Which made it the style of choice for anyone who wanted to make something that wasn't look like a drug hit.

So she didn't want him dead. Not right away, anyway. Most likely, she was sent to say something or take him some place. He relaxed and kept quiet, picking up details in the dim light. Her vest had buttons of silver or pewter. The second button of her blouse was un-buttoned, giving a glimpse of deep cleavage. Above her left eye was a tiny, crescent-shaped scar that makeup didn't hide.

The silence continued. The heft of the big semi-auto didn't seem to tire her. It always tuckered him. A few rounds at the range made his left wrist throb where that car wreck from a decade ago snapped it in two. But when it came to guns, he was wearied by more than the weakness of badly-mended bones.

He had killed four times in twenty years. All four deserved it. All except one were trying to kill him. And the one exception would have, given the chance. It wasn't death brought about by his own hand that bothered him. He was square on that.

It was all those other deaths seen while knocking around the fringes of that oxymoron known as law enforcement. The baby crushed in the head-on that spared her drunk mother, an expert in the field of check kiting. The maid lying lifeless in the living room of her shotgun house, her sightless stare at the ceiling matched by the third eye her ex-lover put in the middle of her forehead with a .32 revolver. The son of a high-powered builder, garroted in his bathtub by his male lover, a crystal meth addict and sculptor who wanted the boy to lever more money from the old man and flipped when he got turned down. The stock-scam queen who looked like his first ex-wife, her throat cut by a greedy partner.

And one more he didn't want to talk about. Ever again. That's what made his wrist weary when he pulled down with his own Colt slabsides. That's what made it tough to stay sharp on the range, making a grim and gritty business out of practice that used to bring on a professional's pride.

He was getting annoyed. His beer was warm and flat, his food was cold and skewered by a dead butt, white and crumpled in the center of the refried beans.

He reached for the pack of Luckies. She put a hole in the wall near his left ear, causing the sheetrock to explode a cloud of white powder across his shoulder, the side of his face and the tabletop. He heard his own grunt, felt his heart lurch and knew the warm feeling in his crotch wasn't just sweat.

"Goddamit. Why in the fuck did you do that?"

She smiled. The echo of the Colt made his voice sound small and telescoped the distance between him and her. He could smell burnt powder and piss. He could see a wisp of smoke curl from the gun barrel, its dark eye on him again.

"Awww, your pants are wet, Big 'Un."

"Mind if I do something about that?"

"Just so long as it's slow and easy."

"How 'bout this?"

He edged his left hand off the tabletop, spreading his fingers wide as he moved his arm up and back, reaching for the bandana in his hip pocket. He pinched the square of cotton between his thumb and forefinger, drawing it from the taut confines of his jeans. He kept his other fingers flexed open as his hand came back into her view.

"Very good. You're learning, Big 'Un. Might not have to pull any more nasty surprises."

"One's plenty."

He wiped his crotch, hoping to sop up some of the piss that was making a spreading dark spot on his jeans. Fool's work. He draped the bandana across his lap. The smell of piss drifted up through the cloth.

"You finished? Squared away? Ready to hear what I have to say? Well, are you, Big 'Un?"

He kept quiet but lit another Lucky. The hand that held his Zippo shook. He looked up. Her startled eyes had narrowed again. For a second, he thought she'd send the second round right into his brainpan. He remembered what Pete Makovy, the academy's ageless rangemaster, used to say about the stopping power of a 9 mm and a .45 -- one's like getting hit by a fast-moving sedan, the other like a slow-moving freight train.

She chuckled drily and grabbed a rickety bentwood chair to sit down.

"You son of a bitch. You piss in your pants, then you try to piss me off. I'm starting to like you, Big 'Un. You're ugly, you're shaky, but you got *cojones*. Too bad you pissed on them."

Then she said a name. Teddy Roy Bonafacio.

CHAPTER 4

It was a name from his past. Not recent. But not so distant either. From a time like this one. Between wives. Alone, but on the force. Making the mindless shuttle between work and a one-bedroom on one of the M Streets off Greenville. Driving a faded red Impala then, a dented red Ford pickup now. Carrying the same Colt in the same shoulder holster.

Teddy Roy was a bad boy who wore his diapers in Del Rio but did most of his growing up in West Dallas, in a tiny pocket of barrio just north of I-30, that bumpy beeline of concrete to Fort Worth. Centered on the Gabe P. Allen Elementary School and flanked by Singleton Boulevard, the neighborhood was pure, hard-working Chicano poor, separated from the gleaming towers of downtown by the concrete sluiceway of the Trinity River, rusty railroad tracks, a belt of low-slung warehouses and lots of long green.

Some called him T-Roy. Ladies mostly. Others called him Boneface -- the bloods and homies he took on in knife fights and other turf battles as a kid. His mother was from Monohans -- part West Texas oil-field trash, part Mexican ranch hand. T-Roy got her red hair and bad temper. His father was a carpenter from Nueva Rosita, an illegal who crossed the river near Del Rio, then brought his baby son and his ill-humored American wife to Dallas. T-Roy got his high cheekbones and lean body, but none of his nose for honest work.

By his late teens, his daddy was dead and T-Roy had already done county time for a nasty bit of knife work on an older blood named Oscar Moon. During a gang all-skate, T-Roy stabbed Moon in the eye with a horn-handled hunting knife he carried in his boot.

Moon refused to press charges so the most they could get T-Roy on was some minor-league assault beefs from the free-for-all. He bided the time of T-Roy's jail term with loud boasts at the Red Dog Lounge and Social Club. Knocking back slugs of bad scotch and milk, breakfast of hookers. Moon would see the patch over his dead eye and yell to the other patrons.

Gonna get that Boneface. Cut his balls off. Stuff em down his throat. Fuck him uppppp. Cut his balls offfff.

The scotch roared through his head. The milk made him belch.

Two days after T-Roy hit the street, Moon's body was found on the Trinity riverbed, stuffed in an old refrigerator. His patch was missing. So were his pants. His severed cock was stuffed in the socket of his dead eye. His balls were carefully placed in the egg tray of the refrigerator door.

Working the riverbed with two patrol guys, Burch and his partner, Wynn Moore, found two items of interest -- a Nesbitt orange soda bottle and a used condom in exotic black and gold -- and the expected panorama of rusty box springs, abandoned cars and splintered fruit and vegetable boxes.

No weapon. No witnesses. No matter. Looked like T-Roy beat Moon to the punch. Looked like a likely reason to talk at T-Roy. That's how his partner saw it.

Wynn Moore was his mentor back then, a wiry guy with long sideburns and slicked-back black hair -- an ex-Marine who rolled his own and had a long face puckered with acne scars. In his off-hours, he made furniture and painted miniatures.

Burch was the cub detective, a year or so out of patrol, following the master. The Colt was new.

Moore didn't give much of a damn about seeing T-Roy fry for Moon's murder.

"A wetback knifing a nigger -- I could give a shit, right, sport model?"

Moon's murder did provide an opening for what Moore was interested in -- a lever on Neville Ross, a citizen of South Dallas who dabbled in hookers, narcotics, chop shops, illegals and the occasional contract hit. T-Roy was a spotter for Ross, who plugged illegals into the manpower gap of construction crews, restaurants, factories and warehouses. T-Roy also ran a small squad of teen dealers, selling grass, 'ludes and crank bearing the Neville Ross brand.

The killing marked T-Roy as enforcer material. But the finishing touches were too jarring and splashy. It showed T-Roy was a lethal comer. It also made him a liability. Ross would put him on ice for a while, then bring him back as mean muscle.

Unless Moore got to him first.

"See it this way, sport model. Our boy might be mean, but he might be scared shitless, too, first killin' an' all."

A pause to pick his stained teeth. They were eating at Sonny Bryan's. Beef brisket for Burch, ribs for Moore. Pearl for both.

"Don't know, Wynn. The little shit cut Moon's cock and balls off. Placed them just so. Don't strike me as the scared shitless type. I think he found his callin'."

"Lookit. We pick him up, dust him up, scare piss out of the boy."

"What with? A picture of Ol' Sparky and stories 'bout the way things used to be when you could fry a man for killin' somebody?"

"Cute, sport model. You ought to be on the furniture what talks -- late night."

Wynn took a pull from his bottle.

"We use what we got, son. Your ugly puss, my natural meaness. We convince the boy we're ten times worse than Neville Ross. Take him for a ride. Shove a gun barrel down his throat and dry fire a few times. Whip the shit out of him. Who knows what the boy might give us?"

Maybe something on Ross. Maybe not. Maybe a pop for Moon's murder. Or not. Maybe something on Ross and a pop for the murder, if they were real good and real lucky.

"That would make my dick as big as a beer can, sport model. But let's not get greedy, right? Just put the ball in play and see what turns up."

Simple stuff. Nothing complex. See an opening, take a shot. To Moore, this was the main maxim of detective work. Moore wanted to nail Ross but had nothing. He didn't want T-Roy but could lean on him and get something. Maybe. That was all he asked.

They scouted T-Roy's haunts. Tough work to keep a low profile for two Anglo cops in a Chicano neighborhood. Mostly, they tapped Moore's snitches, working the older cop's broken Tex-Mex and his beefy frame.

Nothing until they talked to Jaime Quinones, a part-time bartender and full-time weenie flasher. Jaime had a flattened nose from club fights as a welterweight. He also had a whiny, raspy voice that wanted to give them useless advice and no information.

"You want to watch this T-Roy fucker. He's mean. He's slick. A little puke. Skinny like a goat. You know he did that blood, don' you?"

"That a true fact? You there?"

"Nah. Nah. Just givin' you the talk, man. I don' run with no shit like him."

"Just kiddies and old ladies, right pard? Scare them clear to Christmas with a flash of your Johnson."

"I tole you I don' do that no more. *Verdad.*"

Jaime held up two fingers, Boy Scout style, then crossed himself. He was backlit by a fluorescent lamp that hung over the rack of bottles behind the bar. A single customer hunched over a beer at the far end, next to the men's room. They stood near the front door.

"Maybe it's smooth, young boys now."

Jaime glared at him, then forced his face to relax. Moore kept quiet, watching the banter, keeping a steady gaze on Jaime's puffy face. When Moore finally spoke, his voice was soft.

"Seen you down by the park, Jaime. Near the swing sets and them kiddies. Boys at vice wouldn't like that. Might have to ruin your day. Might have to ruin your parole officer's day."

"Man, I'm straight. Don' know where T-Roy's at."

"Just tell what you do know."

Two names and one address. Chita Alvarez and Consuela Martinez. The address was for Alvarez, T-Roy's ex-main squeeze. Said to be pissed. Said to hate T-Roy and the *puta* who stole him away. Said to be a looker who could pick up quarters with certain parts of her body.

She lived in a small apartment off Henderson, not far from the Baylor Medical Center. She worked the night shift as a practical nurse. She hated cops. She hated T-Roy more.

"You tell that *cabron* he's got the dick of a monkey and the breath of a dog. You tell him I hope he likes it in prison. You tell him some big black son of a bitch is gonna fuck him in the ass and make him his punk. And you tell him that daughter of a whore has the clap."

"You bet. Just tell us where he's at."

"You're cops. Sons of whores. Why should I tell you shit?"

"Cause you hate him a whole lot."

Moore was talking. His voice was soft and soothing. Burch was standing to the side, keeping an eye on the courtyard of the two-story building and the iron-and-concrete catwalk that wrapped around the inside of the second floor. Architecture by Holiday Inn.

Low-angle light from the setting sun caught the rusted ends of rebar poking through breaks in the catwalk. Cracks showed in the building's brick veneer. Work by the boys at Slap-Em-Up Construction.

She lived in a first-floor unit. When they knocked on her door, she let them do a fast check of her two empty rooms but herded them out when they were done. She stood outside the open door, clutching a white terrycloth robe around the curve of her hips and breasts. Her feet were bare, her dark hair pulled back into a loose pony tail.

She thought about Moore's last line. Her eyes flashed. She hissed out an address in South Oak Cliff, near Polk Street.

"Consuela's?"

"No. The place of a friend. The whore lives someplace else."

The anger was gone from her voice. It had the flat tone of sadness and regret. Moore caught the change, nodded at him and brushed past Chita on his way to the door. She grabbed Moore's arm and started to curse in fast-forward Spanish. Burch wrapped both arms around her from behind, hoisting her up on his right hip.

Moore pulled out a Case pocket knife, sliced Chita's phone line then put a twenty-dollar bill next to the disabled phone and walked outside. Chita spat in Moore's scarred face. She struggled against the strength of Burch's arms. Her robe gaped open. Her large brown breasts spilled out in the twilight.

"*Adios, bonita.* Money's for the phone man. And the peek."

He let her go, stepping away quickly in case she aimed a foot at his balls. She did. She missed.

"Got to move, got to move, sport model. She'll make that call from someplace."

They cut across town. Moore drove. Burch watched the view from the window change from apartment complexes to the office towers of downtown. Nieman Marcus flashed by. He could see the winged horse on the Magnolia Petroleum building, red and riding across the city skyline. As they turned onto Polk, the quality of buildings quickly downshifted to boarded-up storefronts, discount shops and dark bars.

They did a fast pass down a side street, looking for the address Chita gave them. They found it and parked a half block away, on the opposite side of the street.

It was a mustard-colored house, once a grand Victorian dame, now faded and split into two apartments -- one above, one below. A dark, muddy alley ran off to the left. A streetlamp four doors down cast weak light across the right side of the front porch but heightened the shadow of shrubbery that ran along the walkway and wrapped round the left front corner.

The top floor was their target. On the left side of the house, where the bushes ended in deep shadow, a darkened iron staircase ran from the ground to a dormer window that had been converted into a doorway. It looked like the only way out, unless an interior staircase led to the front door.

"Don't like it, Wynn."

"Don't worry, sport model."

To do what Moore wanted to do, they had to play it alone. Backup would mean questions from up top. Backup would make their business T-Roy and murder instead of a grab for a lever on Ross.

"Don't like it ay-tall, Wynn."

Moore grunted and got out of the car.

"Bring the pump."

He grabbed the 12-gauge Winchester, jacked a round of buckshot in the chamber and joined Moore. They circled the block on foot and searched for the alley. They worked their way down the muddy track, hoping a dog didn't bark.

There was a garage behind the house. Its closed door faced the alley. Ten yards of mud, grass and bushes stood between the garage and the house. The mud and grass were a guess. The bushes were smudges of black against the light color of the house.

Light streamed from a window at the left rear of the house, probably the kitchen of the bottom-floor tenant. The top floor was dark. They could hear the accordion runs and waltz-time beat of Tex-Mex music from one of the rear windows.

Moore motioned him to a shadowy spot on the far side of the alley, a position that let him cover the dormer door and the rear porch. It also gave him quick access to the front. He thumbed off the shotgun's safety. He pulled the thumb catch off the holster of the Colt, but kept the gun in leather.

Moore pulled his own gun of choice, a Smith & Wesson wheelgun in .44 Special, and slipped off his hand-tooled boots. Burch watched as his partner eased up the staircase in his socks, pausing every two or three steps to listen and catch his breath. The staircase faced the street, forcing Moore to keep his head cocked up and to the left to keep an eye on the windows and door above. The music played on.

Moore made it to a small deck that topped the first flight of stairs. The deck also marked a sharp turn for the second flight. Moore climbed the first three steps, facing the door and windows head on, arm and pistol extended.

The door slammed open. He heard the boom of a shotgun and saw its flash stab down toward Moore. Burch brought his own gun up and started to fire. The nude body of a young woman filled his sights. Her head was thrown back. Someone was holding her by the hair, using her body as a shield. A second somebody was throwing buckshot at Moore, who was sprawled on the stairs, his gun pointed toward the girl and shooter.

The girl pitched forward, pushed from behind. She tumbled down the stairs, slamming into Moore as the shooter let loose another blast. Burch fired his first shot toward the door. As he pumped the next round into the chamber, he saw a flash of white scoot out and swing over the railing.

Another flash and boom from the door. Lead shot whickered into the tree branches above his head. Burch pumped two more rounds that way and heard a wet smack, a grunt and the sound of metal clattering on iron. He looked toward the bushes below the staircase, searching for whoever had dropped over the side. He heard a car fire up with a rattling roar.

A black `63 Impala peeled away from the near curb as he lumbered toward the street. He fired two rounds, blowing out the back window and the left tail light. The car swerved, sideswiped a parked pickup and sped out of range.

He heard a loud groan from the staircase. Moore was sprawled on the deck, facing the door with gun still in hand. His sock-clad feet were on the stairs, his shoulders and head jammed against the bottom of the deck railing. The girl's body rested across Moore's stomach. A long bloody groove ran a ragged path up her back. He started to climb the stair and check out the shooter. Moore stopped him with a raspy voice.

"Sumbitch is dead."

Quick, ragged breaths.

"Saw his chest blow open, sport model."

"Easy, Wynn. Save it."

"Ahhhh, I'm gone. Always did want to die with my boots off and a young girl on top of me."

Moore's gun dropped out of his hand with a loud, solitary clank. Burch heard the first siren in the distance.

Chapter 5

The captain's breath held the stale stench of cigarettes and coffee, a smell that started out sweet, like a fresh Lucky, and ended up like a blast from an uncovered sewer.

It was a smell from his teens, the breath of a dead aunt who popped pills, drank gin straight from the bottle and babbled about blood pressure medicine and the drinking habits of her husband, the best house painter in Coppell. When sober.

She took him riding one summer Sunday near dusk, out into the prairie nothing north of Fort Worth where the light was fading on what little there was to see -- rusted barbed wire, the heads and rumps of cattle, the occasional frame house.

They were headed toward a small country church outside of Roanoke, his aunt's latest religious fancy. Something with Free Will or Holiness or Primitive in the title. As they topped a small rise she turned off the engine and let the car drift downhill.

"Hey-hah! Look at this, boy -- freewheelin' I call it. Savin' gasoline and havin' our fun at the same time!"

Her dark hair was pulled back from a puffy face and piled up on her head in a style last popular when ration cards got you gas and meat. The wind caught lose strands and blew them across her face. Her dress was dark silk with a floral print and covered a big-boned body. The wind caught the gaps between buttons and gave him a glimpse of white underneath.

The sound of the service drifted into the night as the tires of his aunt's '56 Fairlane crunched across gravel. A hymn. Call and response. She slipped her arm into his and leaned against him heavily as they headed toward the white, clapboard church. She stumbled twice.

"Damn but you're gettin' to be a man, son. Feel that arm of yours. Good thing you're my nephew or I might get ideas about you."

They sat in the back pew. She tapped the shoulder of one lady, then another, her voice rasping a greeting that was two stops past whisper and shot into the quick silence of the song's final amen. Heads turned. His aunt waved. The heads snapped back around.

She sat close. She leaned across him to reach for a hymnal or Bible, her breasts brushing his arm every time. As they shared a book for scripture or hymn, she rested her arm on the inside of his thigh. He felt the first stirrings of a hardon and tried to slide away from her. There was no room between him and a fat farmer in bib overalls to his right.

"... leaning on Jesus, leaning on Jesus ..."

His aunt's high, warbly voice. And her breath -- sweet, then the bite of something rotten. The song ended. She folded up the hymnal and aimed it toward the rack. The book dropped to the floor and his aunt leaned across his lap, her breasts pressing into his thigh.

"Better get your mind on the Lord, boy. Let his spirit chase away those bad thoughts about your old auntie."

Twenty years later, he flinched every time a blast of the captain's breath hit his nostrils and saw the face of his dead aunt, her bright red lipstick and boozy smile, playing the churchly whore with a young nephew.

The volume of the captain's voice stuck with him, but not the words. So did the bottom line -- the first and biggest black mark in a steady slide toward the street.

They both fucked up. But Moore was dead and only he was around to get the hammer -- suspension and a recommendation for dismissal. The personnel board rejected the recommendation but upheld the suspension and put a stinging rebuke in his jacket that stopped just short of blaming him for Moore's death.

⋏

T-Roy was the luckier bastard. Nothing in his jacket and new status in the Ross stable. He crossed the river and continued working both sides of the border as an enforcer and foreman of Ross' drug operation. But not before he pulled one more trick that was crazy-quick and mean.

After roaring away in the night, T-Roy dumped the Impala and its buckshot scars, switched to a new ride and drove straight to the apartment of Chita Alvarez. They found her wrapped in a bedsheet, her throat slashed, her lips pulled back across clenched teeth and a dinner candle shoved up her vagina.

"Guess she made the call," he said, fingering the double sawbuck Moore had left by the phone.

Sewer Breath nodded, watching an evidence tech snap pictures of the body.

"T-Roy's got a nice touch with the ladies. You know, you two shitheads got her killed too."

That made two girlfriends in one evening; the dead girl on top of Moore was Consuela Martinez. The dead shooter was Rene Estaban, one of T-Roy's dealers, Moore's killer in fact but not in Burch's mind.

There was a trap door under his feet. He could do one of three things -- quit now, stay on board and try to lightfoot his way to retirement as a nervous do-nothing or stomp on that trap door like he didn't care if it ever sprung open. Big feet made it an easy choice. He donned the tough guy act like a thrift store leisure suit, pretending to have balls of brass and a hide that could take on all comers.

The truth was another matter.

He was afraid to leave the department; it was the only job that made him feel worthwhile. He had to carry the scorn of fellow officers and his own sense of shame; it was the price of redemption. Any good Baptist knew that. Just ask his dead aunt.

Burch did his work and survived the early shit assignments of supervisors trying to get him to turn in his badge. He weathered graveyard shifts and a stint with vice, peeping through a vent in the men's room at the bus station while the other guys hustled hookers on Harry Hines, ignored call girls at the Adolphus and checked out pasties and G-strings at strip joints.

There was a certain freedom here. He knew the suits would boot his ass, but he didn't care and took pleasure from the job, working it the way Moore taught him, taking chances and landing another berth with homicide when the D's murder rate spiked so high that old sins were forgiven for any murder detective with a pulse.

Forgiven, but not forgotten.

He also landed another marriage and another divorce, the second of three and the one that hurt him least. She was a cocktail waitress who popped bubble-gum bubbles the size of the Goodyear blimp. It barely lasted the weekend in Ruidoso that kicked it off.

A pro on the street and a fuckup at home -- the cop's *perfecta*. All part of the steady slide. And all a reminder of better times, bad memories and the gulf between how things were now and how things used to be.

Burch tried not to think about Moore or T-Roy -- one was dead, the other out of his reach. He fought off thoughts of his first wife and tried to ignore the pain from all the severed wiring and ripped-up circuitry that the death of a long love leaves.

It didn't help much. Life kept blowing up on him, tearing the lid off stuff he was trying to bury.

He found himself walking along, thinking about the night of Moore's death, hearing the rattle of his gun on the iron deck. At night, he would dream of T-Roy, standing on the banks of the Rio Grande, laughing and pointing at him. Or a dream vision of his first ex, smiling, her breasts swaying, taking another man's cock into her mouth.

The anger and shame would rise, filling his throat with a tight ball of tension and making him feel like there was nothing but a gaping hole under his feet. He read through the small hours of morning, filling his mind with another man's words, hoping they would keep him awake and hold off the images that came with sleep.

He lashed out at partners, citizens and soon-to-be-former girlfriends. He took long plods down the back streets off Greenville, reciting the names of cross streets as he huffed along -- Monticello, McCommas, Marquita, Llano.

But Burch was too slow to outrun blame and bad dreams.

A gunfight in an apartment complex on Gaston brought him the next round with Captain Sewer Breath, now a hot rod with IAD. He was riding alone, answering a call for backup from two detectives searching for a guy using stolen credit cards.

Three crunched cars hung him up on Henderson. The two cops, Silvers and Morton, didn't wait. Their knock drew five rounds of 9 mm from a side window, killing Silvers with a slug through the neck and wounding Morton in the belly and leg.

As he wheeled around to the rear of the building, he heard the last of the dull, short pops, muffled by a cold mist that hid the downtown office towers. He ran toward the sound, edging his way up the raised squares of concrete that served as patios for each unit.

A screen window was open. He could see a Kenmore gas stove in pea green, a clock with a cracked plastic face and the archway above the counter that gave him a partial view of the front room.

The shooter edged into view, his head facing the front window, his pistol in a two-hand grip and angled the same way. His chest faced the kitchen, framed by the archway. Four Flying Ashtrays from the Colt slammed the shooter into the wall, dead from two slugs to the chest.

Burch didn't yell "Freeze!" He wasn't sorry.

A holdup artist named Johnny Zanger was the shooter, wanted for killing a liquor store clerk near Waco. Sewer Breath tried to make much of his late arrival as backup.

"Fucked up again, didn't you cowboy? Grabbin' donuts or a taco, weren't you?"

"Naw, I was eatin' a fender sandwich on Henderson."

"The hell you talkin' about?"

"Three car pile up. Jaws of life. Ambulances. Garlic with lunch today, sir?"

"What? Lissen to me, you needledick piece of shit ..."

"No, you listen, cockbite. You got a dead cop because they got careless and ran into a badass. Not because I was out slappin' my monkey."

The traffic report saved him. For a time.

⋏

Saloons -- that's where he felt at home. Bars with icy beer and headbusting whiskey, not ferns and cute happy-hour gimmicks. Joints with smoke and big drinks, not franchise outfits with a lot of brass and loud talk. Waitresses jaded and sharp-tongued. Tenders with a dead-eyed look for strangers and troublemakers, a tight smile and a fast pour for a regular.

He hit Joe Miller's on Tuesdays, Thursdays and sometimes Fridays, bumming Luckies off Louie Canelakes, the best Chicago bartender ever born to a mother from Forth Worth. On Wednesday nights he would have *huevos con chorizo* at *El Rey's*. When he had that itch he'd call Darlene or Ginny or Carol Ann, a nurse, a secretary and a court clerk who had a taste for him and Friday night steaks at the Hofbrau.

Carol Ann was a chunky clerk with clear blue eyes, hair the color of Silver Queen corn and one of the best pickup lines a drunk woman ever put on him.

"I got one rule, just one rule ..."

She held up one finger, steadied herself against the bar with her other hand and tried to focus on his face.

"One rule."

"Tha's right. Quit interuptin'. One rule. If there's two pairs of jeans slung over my bedpost at night, mine gotta have the smallest waistband."

"Helluva rule."

"Damn straight."

"Rule like that might make me a candidate."

She hooked a thumb under his belt, took a pull from her beer and pressed her breasts into his forearm.

"Just might."

In winter, he would drink Maker's Mark shots. When big heat hit the D, he would order a glass of ice water and a glass of Coke on the side to slake his thirst after a run or workout. The whiskey would be in a shot glass. The water and Coke in juice glasses. The tenders called it the Ed Earl Burch Summer Drinking System.

When Louie opened his bar on Henderson, he never had to explain the system. A nod and a smile would do. Then he could talk to Whitey, Deb or Louie. On Tuesdays, Thursdays and sometimes Fridays.

Burch was sitting in Louie's, knocking back shots and bitching about the Rangers to Whitey, when Lew Stuart told him T-Roy got killed in a Reynosa whorehouse.

It was a contract job after crossing Ross. It closed a circle and left him with work and the well-grooved routines of a man trying to fill up the empty time left by another busted marriage -- his third and last, he swore.

That one liked sculpting, nine ball and bass fishing. She hung on for almost three years. She loved Hemingway and learned to hate him when she finally figured out he wasn't Papa and would never take her to Cuba.

For reasons Burch never understood -- other than the huge slice of his salary that flowed toward Louie's bottom line -- he seemed to be a favorite. Louie ignored other regulars with barely concealed disdain, a scowl screwed on just beneath bushy, iron-and-black hair, an ever-present cigarette hanging off his lip, its ember almost touching the wiry hairs of his beard. But the wedding picture from Burch's third marriage was still stuck in the frame of Louie's liquor license and the man always broke away from talking and pouring for other customers to favor him with a grave and formalized greeting.

"Mr. Burch."

"Mr. Louie."

Louie would shake his hand and blast him with cigarette smoke.

"Always a pleasure."

"What's the line tonight?"

"Raiders and seven. I got the under and it's sweet."

Louie's over-unders were never sour. One time he came in and asked about the presidential debates.

"I don't know shit about politics, but I got the over on Udall and it's sweet."

Most nights, Burch talked to no one. He read the sports page or nursed a Dominican cigar in silence, surrounded by the soothing noises of a real bar.

It was sound to get lost in. On Tuesdays, Thursdays and sometimes Fridays. It was a place where he could forget Moore, the first ex and the varied shapes of the sphincters who wanted him to do his job someplace else.

But mostly there was work and long, lonely hours in a ratty apartment. It was all he had. Guys like Sewer Breath were always hanging around, waiting for a working stiff's miscue. Burch tried not to oblige but too often did. When the meth freak muscle boy sculptor garroted the son of the skyscraper king, Burch got steamed at the father for making him wait at the security desk downstairs, downing two coffees, while the man finished a business meeting in a top-floor office with a chopper's eye view of the city.

The father wore horn-rimmed glasses, had rheumy blue eyes and a smile that could freeze a fire hydrant in mid-summer. He had an eye for art and stakehorsed a small Deep Ellum gallery. He also had a taste for

Oreo cookies, the kind where he was the creamy white center and two black hustlers, any two, were the well-muscled wafers.

"I understand you want to talk to me about Alan and the whereabouts of his killer."

Burch nodded and got the cold smile.

"I have given my attorney a statement that details everything I know about my son and that man. I don't have anything else to add and can't think of a solitary thing that I have left out. As for the whereabouts of this killer, I should think that is your job to track him down."

The smile again, meant as an icy dustoff. Burch lit a Lucky. The man frowned at the smell of smoke.

"Do you mind ..."

"Yeah, I do. I mind waiting downstairs with the hired help because you're too damn busy to talk to me about your son's death. And I mind one huge helluva lot getting a bunch of uppity bullshit about statements given to attorneys. I got a couple of questions and if you want to make your next meeting, you'll answer them."

No smile, just frost. They stared at each other. Burch blew smoke toward the father's face, causing him to blink.

"Gotcha. You don't seem too upset by your son's death."

"I'm afraid I don't show emotion very well."

"A rock would do a better job."

Burch concentrated on taking a drag from his Lucky. He felt the father's eyes on him, then heard the quick sound of a tongue being popped against the back of the teeth.

"My son and I were never close. In my mind, he was a mistake -- a breach of contract between my wife and I."

"Did he hate you?"

"Hate was too strong an emotion for our relationship. Oh, how to put it -- casual indifference? Yes, that would be the phrase."

"Did you introduce Alan to Sam?"

A cough, then an annoyed tone.

"They met at a reception I threw for a visiting artist."

"Who introduced them?"

"I hardly know. It seemed to be a case of boy meets boy."

"How did you feel about that?"

"Feel? How was I supposed to feel -- my son was a homosexual. That didn't make me particularly proud, but we had reached an accommodation."

Burch stared a hole into the frost. The father's eyes broke toward paper on his desk.

"You knew Sam already, right?"

"He was a sculptor of some talent, good enough to win regional recognition."

"But you knew him from someplace other than your art circles, right?"

"Just what are you saying, detective?"

"Just this -- rump rangering seems to run in the family. You and Sam were suck buddies long before he started dragging his thing through your son's back door. And I bet Sam let you watch. Now, I don't give a popcorn fart about what two or three adults do behind closed doors -- they can fuck zebras for all I care. But I do care about somebody pimpin' their son out just to keep some meth-head artist on the reservation. Helluva way to keep your gallery afloat. Or was it true love between you and Sam?"

The father turned heel and left the room. A bodyguard stepped up.

"Not today, son. I have no desire to kick your young ass across this pretty office."

"Oh, we don't have to muscle a shithead like you. Fact is, I have to leave you spotless so the man can make the one phone call that will flush your career."

Sewer Breath was waiting when he got back to the office. Another suspension with recommendation for dismissal. Another ruling by the board that gave him some time off, but left him on the force. And he tracked down Sam during his hiatus, running him to ground in Toronto, living with an older art professor, working in a gallery just off Yonge Street.

Two RCMP plainclothesmen walked through the front door. Burch came through the back. When they called Sam's name in clipped, cold tones, he started to run. Burch caught him in the throat with a clothesline forearm Lee Roy Jordan would have loved.

Sprawled on the floor, gagging for breath, Sam drew the same cool, appraising look from the Mounties that patrons used for the welded triangles of hammered steel and the garage door-sized swath of canvas with the three, broad zigzags of black and yellow paint he tried to sell for five or six figures. There was the quick up-and-down -- all that was missing was a click of the program against the teeth, a slight intake of breath and a move to the next *object d'art*.

Cuffs from the Mounties. Burch leaned down, pinning Sam's arms back, listening to him wheeze, talking low like a parent to a child.

"Now this gaggin -- nothin' like your old boyfriend felt when you wrapped that wire around his neck. No sir. That wire bit deep ..."

Handcuffs ratcheted tight against the wrist.

"... and that boy, he turned red, then blue and started swallowing his tongue, right? And pissin' and shittin' right there in the bathtub, right? A bad way to die. I wouldn't want to go that way if I had a choice. But you know, you might get lucky. Death Row's gettin' overpopulated, so they're bringing in the Big Needle. Just a shot and you're gone. It's a good way to go out, don't you think?"

Sam stopped wheezing.

"What the hell are you talkin' about, you cracker dumbass?"

Burch jerked Sam's head back with a handful of well-moussed hair and leaned in close.

"Just this -- I'll be watchin' you die. I'll wave you bye-bye and enjoy it. You think about that when they wheel you in that room."

♠

Burch never called his city Big D. Just the D. No adjectives. No modifiers. Like death and divorce, none were necessary. Just a cold

THE LAST SECOND CHANCE

letter for a city that could cut your heart out, eat it, then smile. If a profit could be turned.

There are blue and bitter winter mornings when Dallas seems particularly icy and soulless. In the brittle sunlight, its glass towers are glittering but mirthless. Its streets have no warmth and offer no shelter from the piercing wind.

On a morning like this, a retired Braniff Airlines mechanic opened the lid on his first coffee and unchained a parking lot near the West End for the rush hour crunch. He found a hooker named Candy Slice, bound and gagged with strips of her own pantyhose, between an abandoned Subaru and a dented Eldorado.

Her pimp, Ronnie Bedoin, a skinny Cajun with hair that looked like it had been rinsed in brown axle grease, tried to brush off Burch's questions with bottom-line logic that would have won over Ivan Boesky.

"Man, why get your head heated up? I don't. Whores get killed. Part of the business. Least she wasn't the top filly in my stable."

Burch took it personal. He bounced Bedoin into the cinderblock wall of the bar they were in and started banging his head against the concrete. In front of his partner, a public defender who liked seedy nightlife and an off-duty cop pulling a security shift for the bar.

That earned him his final suspension. Sewer Breath took his badge and his old service revolver, the one he never carried once he got the Colt.

"Of all the dumbass ways I thought you'd finally fuck up, I would have never picked playing wallball with the pimp of a dead hooker in broad daylight with his own partner, a lawyer and another cop lookin' on. Must have been true love."

Close.

Three weeks after his first wife left him for a Jew-boy salesman who pumped iron and wore gold neck chains, Candy Slice found him in a bar on Harry Hines, deep in a whiskey fog. He knew her from her prime days with Ross' stable; he had busted her twice. Prime had been some years ago. For both of them.

Her real name was Ruby Sweat. She was from Nacogdoches. When he was with vice, he treated her with the rough respect he gave all the hookers he came across. No freebies. No hand jobs in the squad car. No blow jobs in the restroom of the Tastee Freeze. Sometimes a cup of coffee on nights when a blue norther hit town.

They talked. She took him home. No fee.

There was a small, red heart tattooed just above the mousy brown pelt of her sex -- a color that didn't match her auburn hair. He ran his finger along the long scar that ran the length of her belly, the mark of a C-section. She grabbed a flap of his fat, the part that flopped from his narrow hips toward his crotch, and gave it a shake.

"Battle scars, baby. We both got `em."

She fucked him slow, grinding him between ample hips, riding high at first, then pitching forward so she could better match him thrust for thrust. When they finished, she said: "Don't worry much about losing her, baby. You ain't a grown up till you got at least one divorce under your belt."

He said nothing.

"And don't worry about the size of your dick none `cause she left you for another man. You got a real active tongue. That's an asset that makes up for a lot."

He grunted: "Some compensation."

"Now don't pout, sugar. It's what it's all about. Compensation and adaptation."

This was after she told him his seed tasted like boiled okra.

CHAPTER 6

"Thought T-Roy was dead."

"Wrong thought, Big 'Un."

"Thought he crossed ol' Neville and wound up in an unfortunate accident."

"You heard wrong."

He felt his jaw tighten. She was still pointing the Colt at his paunch.

"Heard he got greedy. Wanted to be *El Jefe*. Heard they splattered his young ass while he was layin' pipe. Down Reynosa way."

"You got the greed part right. And the pipe. And they did do some splattering. But that mean little fucker is still alive."

"What's that to me?"

"Don't make me laugh, Big 'Un, I know you're not that stupid. T-Roy did your partner, right? And he's still alive, right?"

"That was a long time ago, lady. And I never did like the Maltese Falcon. Besides, T-Roy didn't pull that trigger. Boy named Estaban did. And I killed him already."

"Ah, Big 'Un. Don't job me like this. You know you'd love to see T-Roy dead."

"Maybe so. But I'm a lazy sumbitch. I'd shoot T-Roy dead if I saw him walking on the same side of the street I was, but I'll be goddammed if I'll traipse clear down to Mexico to kill his skinny little butt."

"Get up. We're going to see somebody."

She draped his coat over her left arm, covering the big Colt. She flicked her head, motioning toward the door.

"Leave the bandana. You'll smell up my car."

"I'll stain your seats."

"No, just your jacket."

They walked out of the cafe and into the stale night heat. He looked back at her. She flicked her head again, toward a midnight blue '67 Cutlass with a white rag top and vanity plates that said: LATER. Detroit muscle. Made before the Arabs and their oil embargo.

She flipped him the keys and watched as he unlocked the door. She whistled, then pitched his jacket, hitting him in the face. By the time he clawed the fabric away and draped the jacket across the rolled leather bucket of the driver's seat, she was opening the passenger door with her own set of keys, her eyes on him, the gun leveled through the open door.

The car fired up with the rattle of glass packs. He kept the four-speed Muncie in neutral and punched the accelerator twice, rapping the pipes, drinking in the rich noise of a big V-8, a 330-cubic-inch Jetfire Rocket with a four-barrel carb. It was a sound that echoed the boom times, from the heady days of jerkoffs at cocktail parties pushing the notion that Texas was the nation's Third Coast. It was a sound that bellowed, 'Fuck You, Yankee! Freeze In The Goddam Dark!'

"My, my. This is a ride."

"Knock yourself out, Big 'Un. Head up Central."

He pulled out slowly in first to clear the other parked cars, then stepped on it hard after shifting into second, enjoying the powerful pull of classic American Iron as he banged the shifter into third and fourth.

"Easy now, Big 'Un. You won't like what happens if a cop pulls us over."

"Thought you tole me to knock myself out."

When they reached Central, the best 1930s parkway ever built in the 1950s, the traffic was typically stop and go for no particular reason. In a few months, it would get worse when the state started a ten-year project to widen the road all the way up to the LBJ. That took the shine off of driving an endangered species of auto. It gave him some long, silent minutes to think about things he had forgotten.

The girl and her gun didn't count. They weren't even there. His mind was on Moore, T-Roy and the anger he had to eat in his last six years on the force. He saw Moore and Consuela, dead on the deck. He heard Sewer Breath and the slights of every other asshole who used Moore's death as a lever on him.

"Quit pounding the wheel!"

"What?"

"You heard me. Quit poundin' the damn wheel. Traffic will clear in a minute. No big deal, right?"

He looked at her with an arched eyebrow.

"Right. No big deal."

His jaw was clenched and sore. Blood touched his tongue from the hole he had chewed in the side of his mouth.

Central opened up as they went under the LBJ and past the new construction around Richardson. Past Plano, he spurred the big eight, watching the tach jump and the speedometer climb well past eighty. They crossed the Grayson County line and took a farm-to-market east toward Tom Bean.

The Colt stayed leveled at his paunch.

The land had an uneven roll to it -- grassy hills and scrubby pastures frosted by moonlight, broken by trees that only bordered creek banks and bottom land. A ribbon of gravel and dirt ran to their left, away from the road and around the base of a hill. She pointed. He turned.

They drove for more than a mile, passing cattle, horses and peacocks that screamed at the dark of early morning. Next up -- a brick wall with razor wire on top and an arched stone gateway with surveillance cameras. The road started to rise up the side of another large hill, bare of trees, pointing toward a low-slung ranch house, bathed in floodlights, with a wrap-around porch, rocking chairs flanking the front door and, at the center of a thicket of antennae, a satellite dish on the roof.

There was a widow's walk on the brow of the roof. Two men with binoculars and scoped assault rifles watched them drive up. One scanned the inside of the car with a Star Scope. He looked back down the road as they got out of the car.

The view was a security man's dream -- an eight-mile horizon from the highest point of land in this section of the county, a tree line that was more than a half mile away, clear ground between the house and the wall except for some dogwoods, some chinaberry trees, a springhouse and a small barn.

"Ross's place, right?"

She said nothing.

"Modest home for a modest man. Didn't think he was the ranching type, though. Thought pimps, dealers and chop shops were his style."

"Get with it, Big 'Un. He's retired. A gentleman rancher. A little oil. A few head of cattle. Some horses."

"And some muscle boys with Star Scopes and guns that go brrrrrrup, brrrrrrup, brrrrrrup. Yeah, the good life."

Burch laughed, but it came out sharp, dry and without a speck of humor. She watched him. The Colt was gone, inside her purse, he guessed. He laughed again -- the bark of a dog.

"So the boys have me covered and you can put that popgun away, right lady? I'm covered, right?"

He spun around, holding his hands up in mock surrender, kicking up dust with his boots.

"Cover me, boys. I'm a fairly dangerous man who's pissed in his pants and let a iddy, biddy girl drag him the hell out of his own favorite cafe."

He shuffled his feet in the dust. He laughed his dog laugh.

"Look out. Look out."

"Get a grip, Big 'Un."

"Grip this, sweetcheeks. Only watch out, ol' John Henry might piss on you."

She said nothing. He kept shuffling to the beat of anger that was pumping up from deep inside.

"You know, I fuckin' love this. You've got me thinking about a dead man who used to be my friend. You tell me a scumbag I thought was dead is alive and kickin'. And you bring me up here to see how life has been good to a piece of shit I used to chase when I wore a badge I can't wear no more."

He could feel the blood flushing his face and feel the muscles of his neck and jaw cord up.

"This is so fuckin' lovely I can't stand it. I drew a line a long time ago. You hear me? I drew a line. And now you and your cute damn Colt and Neville-fuckin'-Ross want me to erase that line. Right? Well, you listen. I ate a lot of shit from assholes who are no better than your buddy, Mr. Ross. They wore badges, but they weren't a damn bit different.

"Now I got a life doin' what I know how to do. It ain't much, but I sleep at night, I don't work for no assholes and I don't have to eat shit no more. There ain't no room for T-Roy or the ghosts of dead partners."

"An elegant speech, Mr. Burch. Perhaps you would care to give it to me instead of the girl."

Ross stood on the top step of the porch, looking every inch the *patrón*. His dark hair was white now, thick and slicked back from his temples and a high forehead. His face was fat, sleek and tanned. He wore a red silk shirt. The rest of his outfit was Johnny Cash black -- a leather vest, twill trousers and hand-tooled boots with underslung riding heels.

He also wore a smile.

"Why 'shore, Neville. She's bored with me anyhow. We'll talk over whiskey. But none of that cheap shit you used to give your whores. Make it the good stuff."

CHAPTER 7

They sat around the head of a long table with high-backed, leather-covered chairs. Four of them now -- Ross, the woman, himself and and a short, squatty guy wearing a too-tight black suit in shiny polyester and a lump on his right hip.

The walls were stucco. The ceiling had exposed beams. The lamp above the table was made of crude black iron -- one hoop inside another inside a third big enough to band a wagon wheel. The High Chaparral, he thought, glancing around for Blue, Manolito and Buck.

Ross called the short one Bolo and circled his finger once. Bolo nodded.

"*Jefe*," he said, in a whisper of reverence.

Bolo slid a full shot glass in front of Burch and two juice glasses on the side, one filled with ice water, the other with Coke. Near his left hand, Bolo placed a pack of Luckies -- unwrapped, with three cigarettes tapped part way out.

"Maker's Mark, Mr. Burch. Like you would get down at Louie's. On Tuesdays and Thursdays. With two backs. Ice water and Coca-Cola. Correct?"

"Correct. And sometimes Fridays."

"Sometimes Fridays. Forgive me. I also regret we do not have a Zippo in the house."

"Brought my own."

"Of course."

Burch knocked back the Maker's, cutting the burn in his throat by sucking some air through his teeth. He ignored the Coke and ice water. He fished a battered pack of Luckies out of his shirt pocket, tapped out one with a serious kink near the brand and lit it, blowing smoke through his nostrils and closing the Zippo with a sharp snap.

"Silence is the way to make a stunt like this work. Have ol' Bolo set down my favorite drink and my brand of smokes and not say a damn word. Let me get the shakes about someone tailing me in my favorite bar. Folks don't get shook up if you point it out. Just pissed."

"A subtlety I will have to master."

"And tell your boy if he wants to fuck with my mind while I'm drinking, then buy me a damn drink. Anonymously. Helps heighten the tension."

"An excellent suggestion."

"Jes' tryin' to be friendly, Neville. Don't mean nothin' by it."

He stared at Ross, who was leaning forward in his chair, his arms on the table. A shot of tequila, a salt shaker and five slices of lime sat on a small wood square, flanked by two sleeves of silk.

Ross tossed down the shot, ignored the salt and lime, ignored Burch's stare and signaled Bolo by circling his finger again. Only then did he look at Burch, grinning slightly just before gunning the second shot, laughing loudly after he finished and waited for his guest to down his whiskey.

"Drink then talk, eh? I trust this bourbon is to your liking."

"It ain't pimp juice."

"These references, Mr. Burch. I left those activities a long time ago. I am a rancher now. The fillies I take care of these days have four legs and don't talk back."

"Bet you miss the tryouts. Used to do your recruiting from the back of a van, as I recall. Fifteen-year-old runaways and such. Round or two of mattress polo to see if they had the go. Yessir, I bet you miss being a pimp, Neville. All that young wool. Maybe you give them horses a tryout now, huh?"

He never saw Bolo's left fist, only white light from the pain of hard knuckles smacking into his jaw. His head slammed into the sharp angles of the solid chairback. He tasted blood on his tongue. He gripped both armrests and started to rise, stopping at the sight of a Charter Arms Bulldog, in .44 magnum, pointed at his nose.

Ross nodded. Bolo holstered the revolver, then draped a small towel over his arm, like a waiter, offering it to him and his bloody mouth.

"Next time, bubba."

"*Chinga su madre.*"

Bolo bowed, then stepped aside. He looked at Ross.

"Happy hour's over, right?"

"Alcohol and blood don't mix, do they Mr. Burch? Unless you like the pain. Do you like pain, Mr. Burch? We can fix you right up if you do. Bolo would like that."

"So would I. Bolo might not do so well if I see him coming."

"That's the point, isn't it? A man like yourself never sees it coming. You just plow along and get sidestepped by people far smarter than you. Sometimes you get blindsided. Every so often, you screw up just right and put the arm on somebody within reach. But usually it's the wrong somebody."

"My life as a detective, Neville."

"Call me Mr. Ross. A sign of respect."

"Your whiskey's not that good, Neville. And Bolo doesn't hit that hard."

The woman chuckled and shook her head. Ross frowned. He could feel Bolo tense up and glare at the back of his head. A huge knot was beginning to push up at the line where his hair ended and his bald pate began. His jaw felt hot and stiff.

CHAPTER 8

"We have a mutual friend. How is it you bubba types would say it? Ah, yes -- this fella needs killin'."

"T-Roy, right?"

Neville made a clucking sound.

"So, the lovely Carla Sue told you. I was hoping to make it a surprise. A gift to such a worthy and wholly unsuccessful adversary, a chance for a real trophy for all those fruitless years of police work."

"Kinda a consolation prize for not catchin' you, right? Well, I don't need no more trophies -- won a few bowlin', got a bass or two on the wall at the house, got my state cham-peen-ship football plaque. Why would I want T-Roy stuffed and mounted?"

"Revenge? The sport of it? The money I'll pay you? The chance to keep the company of this lovely woman? The chance to redeem yourself? Take your pick, Mr. Burch. Or take it all."

"So, I'd get to work for you."

"Consider it a business arrangement that would be to our mutual benefit."

"I thought you blew his ass away in Reynosa, but your guys messed up, huh? What kept you from trying again?"

"A sense that I acted too hastily and without proper consideration of the delicate balance between myself and certain of my associates. Let us just say that they found conflict between myself and a man I once regarded as my son more than a bit distressing. They saw it as bad for business. Fortunately for me, they also saw the advantage in maintaining the fiction that I was successful in my attempt to kill my son."

"Kept any avenging cops from Dallas out of T-Roy's hair."

"And kept you away from any further connection between him and myself."

"And all that's changed?"

"Correct, Mr. Burch. The balance has shifted. Our friend has angered my associates as well as me. Powerful people on both sides of the border. He has gotten too greedy -- too big for his britches, I think you'd say."

"Can the goddam high hat, Neville. You're South Oak Cliff white trash, remember?"

Ross glared, then forced himself to relax, the tension flowing out of his face, the heat ducking back from his face and eyes. When he spoke, it was in that forced voice of culture and politeness that scraped across Burch's nerves like a rusty knife blade.

"Our friend has become very powerful down there on the border. He's got his own little army of former freedom fighters, as our president calls them. He is also allied with a family that has long been in the smuggling business, headed by a woman who styles herself as a *bruja*."

"A what?"

"A witch. As I was saying, our friend has got muscle, but he also has some powerful pressures being brought to bear on him. Some gentlemen I know of the Columbian persuasion want him out of our affairs."

"So, let the boys from Cali take him out."

"It is not that simple, Mr. Burch. They want me to pay for my earlier transgression by taking care of this matter. They were mad at me for trying to destroy a valuable asset, but they still consider him a creature of my creation."

Ross paused to light a panatela with a green wrapper. He took his time, rolling the cigar through the flame of a wooden match for an even draw.

"When a peccary is in a patch of briar and you want him out in the open ..."

Ross blew smoke across the table.

"... sometimes smoke is the only way ..."

Ross pointed the cigar at Burch.

"... and you, my friend, are my smoke."

"No, no, no -- goddamit! Just why in hell would I carry your water? And don't talk to me about Wynn-damn-Moore because I've drawn a line on all that. You want T-Roy dead, kill him your own damn self."

"I want T-Roy dead. You will kill him. You will have no choice."

"A man always has choices, Neville."

"Not one like you, Mr. Burch. You still don't get it, do you? You are already in a box, one of my creation. You can kiss your shabby little office, your peeper's license and your precious gin mill good-bye."

Ross' mouth started to shift into a smile. It never made it. There was a loud roar and the whooshing rush of flame, smoke and debris flying down the hallway and into the room.

The flames wrapped around Ross, setting his hair on fire and drawing a wail from a sleek face now lined with pain. Burch felt something thump heavily into his right shoulder, knocking him out of his chair. It was Bolo, his hands to his neck, great gouts of blood pumping between palms and fingers that couldn't dam the flood.

His shirt was wet and sticky. Just Bolo's blood, he hoped. His knee slipped in the wetness that was quickly spreading across the floor, pitching him forward on top of Bolo's twitching body. He groped for the Bulldog, grabbing its rubbery Pachmayr grip. He fished through Bolo's jacket pockets, landing two speed loaders laden with circles of hollow-point.

His vision was wobbly, like he was looking through seven layers of glass at someone else's hand gripping the pistol. Something was wrong with his head.

Automatic weapon fire echoed outside the room -- short, quick pops followed by the long, ripping sound of someone emptying a full clip.

It sounded like a chain falling on a concrete floor. And it was moving closer. He shifted into a crouch and saw Ross stumbling around, his face and scalp blackened where a poolside tan and razor-cut hair used to be. His shirt was ripped and smouldering.

A steady cry came from Ross' burned lips, low-pitched and in a minor key, like an Apache warrior mourning his dead. The woman moved into sight, the big Colt in her hand. Her eyes were still startled, but cold. The crescent-shaped scar was white and ghostly against her darkened face.

She fired eight shots into Neville Ross, the full clip, her slugs ripping his chest and blowing chunks of bone and flesh from his head. The top half of his body snapped up and back from the impact and his well-tooled boots kicked out in the opposite direction, dumping him onto the earth-colored tiles.

Burch tried to raise his pistol, but couldn't move. She calmly changed clips, thumbing the button that dropped the spent magazine onto the floor, slapping home a fresh packet of slugs and tripping the slide forward in crisp and practiced movements.

She turned toward Burch. He felt a cold, prickling sensation move across his scalp. Her blouse was splattered with blood.

"C'mon Big 'Un. Let's get your sorry ass out of here."

CHAPTER 9

He could barely walk. It felt like the tendons and muscles in his right leg were severed; he had to drag it along. Pain shot from his heel into the roof of his mouth when he did.

She scooted under his right shoulder, wrapping one thin arm around his waist, keeping the Colt free for action with the other. He kept the Bulldog level in his left hand as they clumped down a staircase into a narrow passageway cut through rock and soil, braced by timbers.

They came up through a cut in the stone foundation of the springhouse, stepping past stone ledges where fruits and meats used to be kept when the Kiowas and Comanches swept down from Kansas to kill the *Tejanos* and steal their horses and cattle.

From the doorway, they could see the Cutlass, etched in the flood-lights and the flicker of flame that licked the front door of the big house and portions of the porch. The bright flash of assault rifles stabbed from the barn and the darkness surrounding the house. It was answered by equally bright flashes from the roof and windows of the house.

A tail of fire leapt from the front of the barn, arcing toward the strongpoint on top of the roof, taking it out with a roar and a starburst. A dark group of bodies ran toward the porch, spraying lead into the windows and the fire-framed door.

Two men in ninja black crouched behind a bush not more than 20 yards in front of the springhouse door, their attention and covering fire focused on the big house. Burch and the woman eased forward like teammates in a sack race, as fast as a turtle and as silent as a cricket on a hot summer night.

When the two men turned, Burch and the woman took them down -- she firing the Colt at the man on the right, he firing the Bulldog at the man on the left. Four shots each. Clean kills. She ran toward the Cutlass. He hobbled to the bodies, picking up a Heckler & Koch MP-5 with two clips, taped butt to butt.

As she opened the driver's side door, three men moved from the shadows toward the Cutlass. Burch spun on his bad leg, tasting bile in his throat as he leveled the submachine gun and let loose a long burst, chopping them down with a stab of white flame.

The V-8 rumbled to life as she kicked the Cutlass into reverse, throwing a spray of dust that spread into the glare of the floodlights, fishtailing her way to where he stood. A burst from near the porch shattered the right headlight. He heard the bullets zip past his head. As he grabbed the rooftop to swing into the car, he fired another long burst toward the shooter.

"Close that damn door, Big 'Un. They don't want to let us live any much longer."

He flipped clips on the MP-5 and rolled down the window. She punched the accelerator, throwing him back into the bucket seat. He heard bullets smack into the side of the car, each sounding like a sharp-nosed can opener cracking a beer. He saw the source of the fire and answered back with short bursts of 9 mm.

They tore toward the gate. He looked at her. She was grinning.

"You think this is fun?"

No answer. She kept her left hand on the wheel. With her right hand, she dropped a spent clip out of the Colt.

"Reach in the glove and get me another clip, Big 'Un."

"Just who in the hell are you?"

Chapter 10

Carla Sue Cantrell talked fast and flat, skidding her words like a car hitting a patch of black ice.

If you were listening, you always wanted to grab the wheel and make her slow down. But Carla Sue always kept a tight grip and never let anybody steer what she had to say.

She loved vodka on the rocks, the sharp rush of high-quality crank and vintage Detroit iron. She liked big guns and the shock it put on a man's face when someone her size pulled down with one. Like this big, dumb pee-eye with the bald head and boots.

So cool with the Luckies, the low voice and the slow answers. Trying to eye the angles. Pushing her the slightest bit. Using what he had -- age and size. Edging right up to her limit, then backing up. Relaxing when he thought he knew the game.

That's when she squeezed off a round. Not so cool then. Not so in control. Hard to be when the Levis are full of piss and the face is powdered with sheetrock dust.

Not so cool now. His face was drawn with pain, the lines shadowed by the faint light of the dashboard as he fed bullets into the revolver. His shirt was torn and bloody. But he pulled his weight back at the Ross spread. Not too swift, but stubborn and steady. Not shy about shooting somebody, either.

He'd need to be.

Her aunt -- now just what would Big Lucy say? Probably blow a blue-white jet of True menthol past perfectly painted red lips and talk about sorry Tennessee trash always knowing how to show its ass.

Thirty years ago, Big Lucy was a black-haired, full-bodied woman with wide, green eyes and long legs. She came west as a dancer, swinging tassels on the Jacksboro Highway and nabbing a fast-rising Texas Instruments executive while she still headed the marquee and didn't have to grant too many private audiences for paying customers.

Big Lucy and Uncle Lane lived the North Dallas life now -- registered Republican, golf on Saturday, church on Sunday, money every other day of the week. And how 'bout them Cowboys! It was the life they served up to her like sliced brisket on wax paper -- private school, a Camaro, a Nieman-Marcus card and a little pin money on the side.

She learned to rein in her drawl in school and flatten her up-holler vowels, keeping just enough Southern sugar to snap a young man's head around. But she was bored with the car, the cards and the boys who wore Duck Head slacks and Gant shirts and got sick in the grass outside the dance on Sloe Gin and Bud tall boys.

And she wasn't a Native Texan. Something they spelled in capital letters. Something they let you know about in big and little ways. Why that mattered, she never knew because it seemed like everybody's family was from someplace else, Southerners mostly, looking for one last shot after losing it all in the Civil War. It was a state full of the offspring of losers who moved here for the last second chance.

She was born in the mountains of East Tennessee. She came to Dallas when daddy and mama got whacked by the semi. The coroner whispered something about daddy's blood alcohol. The sheriff shook his head about the car being on the wrong side of the suicide lane -- a fatal move on mountain blacktop. Good people. Damn shame.

Her Uncle Harlan, daddy's brother, didn't whisper or shake his head.

"That sumbitch never could slow down in no goddam aw-toe. And when he started dippin' that corn, he thought he was Lee Petty his own goddam 'sef. If the sorry bastard wasn't dead, I'd shoot him right now."

They were standing at the edge of a small patch of corn, back behind the Cantrell homeplace, back where the holler ran quickly to the spine of the ridge. It was summer and the locusts were whirring in the heat. She was home and old enough to ask the questions Lucy and Lane didn't want to answer.

Harlan had a .45 in his left hand. He racked the slide with a sudden snap of the wrist. Paint cans and milk jugs stood on a rock ledge at the back of the holler. He raised the semi-auto and fired a full clip. Geysers of water shot up from the shattered jugs and cans.

He was a small, wiry man with sandy hair and the sharp jawline, nose and mouth of a mountain grit. He killed gooks in Korea. He once shot a man in Georgia while running 'shine to Atlanta. Seems there was a slight dispute about sales territory. The man died. Harlan was caught on a later run and did time up in Chillicothe, Ohio, same as Junior Johnson. For the shine. Not the killing.

He ran a poultry farm now. And a piece of a crystal meth lab that floated between here and Cocke County, Tennessee, home of the East Tennessee Gun Syndrome, a certified psycho-social phenomenon, documented by experts who found that the mountain folk of that county would just as soon shoot a man as argue with him.

The boom of the big Colt relaxed him. It cooled the fire that flared in his eyes when he talked about Carla Sue's dead mama and daddy. Those eyes were the same startled blue as Carla Sue's. He picked up another clip and handed the pistol and the column of bullets to his niece.

"Bust the rest of 'em, girl. Go on. That Colt ain't got more kick than you do."

She eyed him with a cold look, slapped the clip home and tripped the slide release that racked in the first round. Geysers of water shot up from the rock ledge again. Cans and jugs got scattered, full of jagged holes.

Harlan Cantrell laughed, walked up and hugged his niece.

"This is the boss gun. None better. You got it and you got them. Cold. And ain't no one knowin' a slip of a girl like you can handle it. Till you prove 'em wrong."

The Colt wasn't the only thing she learned to handle during summers at the Cantrell homeplace. A cousin, Eldon Cantrell, taught her how to rip through mountain curves in his Olds 442, giving her a taste for vintage GM iron and a touch of the icy speed that Uncle Harlan's friends cooked up in various hideaways in North Carolina and Tennessee.

Eldon took her on a run to Knoxville on a July night when the thunderheads refused to give up their rain, refused to die and flashed their dry lightning against the tired peaks that crowded the road to town. US 11 E, Bloody 11, killer blacktop for truckers and drunks and people not mindful of its curves and its third lane of speedy passing and occasional suicide.

"Now girl, you're gonna walk on in that bus station and buy a ticket just like you was takin' the Greydog someplace."

"Where?"

"Don't matter. Here's a fifty. Just walk up to the window and buy a seat to Nashville. Yeah, that'll be good. Nashville. There's one leavin' at 11. Gives us plenty of time."

"Why buy a ticket? You just want me to put this suitcase in a locker, right? Why not just do that?"

"These boys are shitsuckers and are likely to have the station covered. They'll be lookin' for me. And they'll be lookin' for somebody to just walk in and drop somethin' in a locker. They don't know you, got no idea who you are. You look like one of those damn UT girls goin' home to mama. If they got somebody watchin', he'll check you out for your looks but won't think you're carryin' anythin' he'd be interested in."

Eldon paused to spit tobacco juice into a Dixie cup crammed with a piece of paper towel. He glared at her, his shaggy hair and his heavy-lidded eyes highlighted by the dash lamp. She could feel her pulse quicken, but she liked the small current of fear flowing up from her stomach to her throat. It made her feel sharp and alive, like she was plugged into every circuit offered by the dark world whipping past the window of her cousin's Olds.

"You unnerstan' what I'm tellin' you, girl?"

"It ain't hard."

Eldon laughed.

"Naw, it ain't hard. But you runnin' a risk. So am I. If ol' Unc' found out I was using you for this run, he'd kill me first and cuss me later."

"But you did it anyway. How come?"

Eldon laughed again.

"Cause I know you like the thrill, girl. Even if you don't know that yet. And I like to watch you get your blood up."

She could see his grin, a vee of uneven, stained teeth, washed green by the dashboard light. She cut him off with one of her cold looks.

"I get the ticket. I dump the suitcase in a locker. Then what?"

"You got time to kill. You need to get a paper or get something to eat. You do a doublecheck with a baggage guy or somebody. Say somethin' like, 'Do I got enough time to grab a bite to eat before the next Nashville bus leaves?' They say yes. And you walk out of the station. You come out the front door. Take a left. Take another left at the corner and come down two blocks."

"Left. Left. Two blocks. Then what?"

"We see a couple boys in a honky-tonk and trade money for that locker key you'll have in your little hand."

She nodded and felt the current of fear crank up a few amps. She put her hand on her purse and felt the thick lump of the Colt inside, hammer back, safety on, a round in the chamber -- the only item carried in a stained pouch of leather.

The bus station was on a side street between Henley and Gay. Eldon dropped her off six blocks away, where Cumberland, the main drag through the UT campus, climbed out of the Second Creek valley to the concrete-covered ridgetop of downtown.

The station was spare and grimy -- worn gray linoleum, braces of plastic seats connected by aluminum bars, a single ticket counter and the battered, swinging doors that led to the buses and diesel fumes out back.

A clump of people stood around two vending machines, mulling over their choices of cold sodas, rubbery candy bars and stale crackers. Another clump stood in the middle of a station, a family seeing off their buzz-topped son, looking like a freshly shorn sheep in dull Army fatigues.

An old black woman snored loudly in one row of seats. A thin young man in a brown cowboy hat, faded jean jacket with a fake sheepskin collar and cracked tan boots sat in another row, flipping through a deck of cards, whistling "Dead Flowers." An older man, paunchy and wearing a greasy L&N Railroad gimme cap, leaned against the wall near the lockers, smoking and reading a newspaper.

"Ticket to Nashville, please."

"One way or round trip?"

"One way. Got friends bringin' me back."

"Hate to lose business from a pretty woman like you."

She smiled into the smiling face of the ticket clerk, a pudgy man with thick glasses framed in black plastic and a wiry swath of gray hair that swept up from just above his right ear across a shiny bald head.

"Thank you. When does that bus leave?"

"Eleven sharp."

"Do I have enough time to grab some supper?"

"Sure do. There's a cafe down on Gay. Around the corner and up three blocks."

"Now, you're sure I've got enough time?"

"Sugar, I wouldn't let that bus leave without you."

"You're sweet."

She gave him another smile and walked over to the lockers, punching two quarters in the slot, turning the key and hoisting the suitcase inside. Turning toward the front door, she gave the ticket clerk a wave and walked out.

"You took your sweet time, girl."

"Didn't think I was supposed to look like I was in a hurry."

Eldon fired up the Olds. In 10 minutes, they were at a small, cinderblock bar on Chapman Highway. Dull black paint. A gravel

THE LAST SECOND CHANCE

parking lot with a scattering of pickups and Harleys. No name out front. Just a small, neon Pabst Blue Ribbon sign in the window, barely visible to the traffic zipping past.

She followed him inside. Three men rode the bar rail -- jeans, windbreakers, gimme caps and bulk marked them as part of the swing shift at the big chemical plant that semi-regularly spilled acetate into the Tennessee River, making the town smell like a freshly shellacked coffee table.

Two bikers played pool in the back, ducking in and out of the shaded light above the table to make their shots. Behind the stick, a huge blond-bearded man in a black shirt that barely covered his belly dipped glasses into a tub of sudsy water, his thick forearms twined with the tattoos of purple and green snakes.

The 'tender caught Eldon's eye and jerked his head toward a door behind and to the right of the pool table. Eldon nodded, turned and pointed to a stool at the short end of the bar, a nook with a good view of the front door and the rest of the bar.

"Sit there. Wait for me."

Her cousin slapped a ten on the bar and flashed his crooked V grin at the 'tender.

"Bud longneck, Bear. Coffee for the girl. Keep an eye on her for me, son. Them Romeos back there don't know she'll bite. Don't know if they've had their shots this year."

Bear palmed the ten with one hand and pulled and popped the cap off a Budweiser with the other, handing the beaded bottle to Eldon. He waddled down the duckboards to the coffee machine, poured a cup into a thick, white mug and waddled it down to her.

"Anythin' with this? Cookie, maybe? Milk?"

Bear's voice was a rumble through layers of phlegm and cigarette tar. He punctuated his question with a hack and a ball of mucous spat sideways into a bar rag.

"Vodka. Rocks. Whatever's in the well, provided you ain't pissed in there."

Eldon laughed.

"Tole you she bit. Now mind your manners Bear, and mind her while I do some bidness."

"Sounds like a goddam Texan, El. Where'd you get her, anyway? Girl's got an edge on her. You like to see that."

"Convent. She's my personal nun."

A chuckle rumbled up from underneath Bear's beard, but got cut off by another hack and another pause to spit into the bar rag. He dropped three ice cubes into a juice glass, poured in a shot of Popov and put it next to her coffee. The ring and pinkie finger on the hand holding the bottle were missing.

Eldon was gone. She heard the door to the back room click shut. She drank a sip of vodka, washing it down with dark, sour coffee. The minutes clicked by. The three chemical workers drained their last drafts, paid up and trailed out the door.

The bikers stayed, racking up another game. Bear started to close up, stacking chairs on tables, dumping ash trays, wiping the bar with the same rag he used for a spitoon. Bear pulled and popped caps off of two longnecks and brought them back to the bikers.

More minutes clicked by. The back door opened on Eldon and a short, stocky man wearing glasses and a black leather jacket with tarnished brass studs, his long greasy black hair pulled back in a ponytail. They walked up to her. The bikers stopped their game to watch.

"Go with this boy and take him to where that little thing we've got to trade is."

She cocked her eyebrow at him.

"Should I ride with him?"

"No, lead him to the spot, give him the item, come on back and finish your coffee."

Eldon looked at the other man.

"You got twenty minutes from the time she hits the door to check the goods and call your boss with the okay. You don't want to be late. Your boss don't want you to be late. We don't want you to be late."

Eldon tossed her the key to the Olds. She fired it up and pulled slowly toward the front of the lot, watching Ponytail climb into a gray '62 Chevy Apache pickup, bullnosed and decked out with mags and chrome sidepipes. She had no idea what to do, no idea what Eldon had in mind. She rapped the glass pacs twice, chewing the inside of her mouth, wondering what her next move should be. And then she relaxed.

Take him on a wild goose chase, girl. Drive him someplace where he'll have to cut it close to call on time, then head back to the bar. Simple stuff.

She led Ponytail through the north side of town, out toward the Clinton Highway, letting the Olds unwind for a fast five minute run before ducking onto a deserted sideroad and taking the first fork she could find. Only the pickup's lights made the same turns.

Her headlights picked up a swath of gravel and a dumpster. She slammed the car into a bootlegger's turnabout that left her facing the pickup as it whipped past and started a screeching halt in the middle of the road. By the time Ponytail stopped his rig and backed up, she was back on the blacktop, facing the highway, waiting for him to ease alongside, door to door.

Ponytail rolled down his window. Carla Sue pitched the locker key at his face.

"Bus station, bud."

"Gawdamn bitch, you had this key all the while."

"You catch on quick. You got twenty minutes. Don't keep my cousin waitin'."

She burned rubber and was back in the bar's gravel lot inside of eight minutes, two minutes sooner than Ponytail could get to the bus station. Eldon was sitting at the bar. The two bikers were still playing pool. Bear was standing across from her cousin, his forearms folded across his bulging belly.

She nodded and Eldon headed back to the rear room. Bear handed her a lukewarm cup of coffee. She pushed it back and ordered another round of Popov on ice. The vodka burned the back of her throat but didn't cut the pure current of nature's own speedy chemicals that made her sharp and edgy.

The clack and scatter of pool balls set her teeth on edge. The minutes no longer clicked, they crawled. She pictured Eldon sitting in the back room, across from some greasy biker, grinning his vee grin, talking grit to the man in loud, friendly tones, hand resting near the butt of the Smith & Wesson .357 stuffed down the front of his pants.

A ringing phone made her jump. Bear picked up, listened, grunted a response and hung up. He nodded to one of the bikers. The biker walked to the rear door and rapped twice. Eldon opened the door, carrying a small canvas gym bag and grinning his grin.

An older man, tall, rail thin and with a gray pompadour that made him look like Porter Wagoner's daddy, stood in the door. A nod from him. A biker moved toward Eldon with a pool cue in hand, butt first.

She stood up and started to yell, but her cousin saw her move before she could speak, spun on his heel while pulling his pistol and jammed the barrel into the biker's gut. She heard the sharp click of a pulled back hammer.

"You 'bout dead real fast if you don't back off."

Bear pulled a sawed-off pump shotgun from under the bar, swinging it up, jacking a round home and leveling it toward Eldon's head in a smooth, fast arc.

The Colt was in her hand. She was screaming Eldon's name as she blew chunks out of Bear's back and head, screaming to hear her own voice over the roar of the semi-auto, screaming to bleed off some of the current that threatened to spike through the top of her head.

Her screams shot into the sudden silence of an emptied clip. She saw smoke rolling out of the open breech of her gun. She smelled burnt powder. She saw Bear's body jammed against the duckboards and the back of the bar. Eldon stood in the middle of the bar, his pistol leveled at Porter's daddy.

"You fuckers picked the wrong folks to diddle with. Here's how things are gonna go. Little sister here is gonna get my car. She's gonna pull it to the door. She's gonna honk twice. If she don't honk, I'm gonna empty this damn pistol in your face. You got all this?"

Porter's daddy, his face spotted with blood and brains, nodded.

"Girl, pick up your spent brass, reload and get the car."

She pocketed eight empty shells and straightened up to change clips. She slipped the catch off the slide, heard it snap forward and centered the sights on the forehead of Porter's daddy.

"Mister, you tried to kill my cousin. I can't allow that."

One shot gave Porter's daddy a third eye and knocked his body into the rear room.

"Goddamit, why'd you waste him?"

She cut him off with a look. Eldon cussed under his breath. He was facing the bikers.

"You boys got enough juice to deal with this?"

"Naw, man. We're just hired muscle."

"Bullshit. Tell you what you better do if you don't want my folks comin' down here to kill your sorry asses. You boys better torch this joint and get gone."

The two bikers looked at each other.

"This ain't no game, boys. I'm pullin' the plug wires on your bikes. When I see flames comin' out of this joint, you'll see those wires again."

From the window of the Olds, Carla Sue watched the flames rise up behind the neon Pabst sign. She watched Eldon pitch the plug wires and felt herself pushed into her seat as he quickly pulled away.

"You done fine, girl. Saved your cousin's ass, that's for sure. Now we got to go deal with Unc'."

"He'll know about this."

"Kinda hard to hide it -- you just blew away the boss of one of his prime retail outlets. That old man was a shit to deal with and would cut you in a minute, but he *did* move some product."

"That man tried to kill you."

"Wrong. Bear did that. And you got Bear. If it'd a stopped there, all we'd have to deal with is Unc' being cross-eyed about me dragging you along to a killin'. But you killed Mac Bodine, a prime shitbird for sure, but someone ol' Unc' was fond of."

"*Fond of? Fond of?*"

Carla Sue couldn't stand it. She thought her head was about to explode again. Bad enough she could still hear the gunfire and feel the phantom buck of the Colt in her hand. Now she had to put up with this macho horseshit about two old brigands who loved each other so much they had to try to kill each other regularly to prove it.

"How the fuck could Uncle Harlan be fond of someone who'd have his nephew killed?"

She was screeching now. Eldon was scrunching his shoulders, grimacing at the sound of her voice. He held his hand up, palm toward her.

"I know, it's twisted, true enough. But Mac and Unc' have been foxin' with each other for damn near thirty years. They hate each other, they've ripped each other off, but they been dancin' this dance so long, I'm not sure Unc' will know what to do with Mac gone and nobody to go up against. I think Unc' actually likes the ol' boy."

"Too damn late for that. He'll be pissed, right?"

"Yeah, but he'll take it out on me. You're his shinin' pride and can't do no wrong. Just keep your mouth shut and let me tell it this way -- Mac pulled a double-cross, I smelled it coming and Mac got killed in the crossfire. You weren't even in the bar. You weren't part of the deal. You were sitting in the car, listenin' to the radio, keepin' the engine runnin', gettin' us gone when things went crazy."

They rode on in silence. The thunderheads were gone. So was the lightning. The worn mountain peaks were out there in the darkness, black bulks felt rather than seen.

She shivered, her mind replaying the images of slugs from her gun slamming into Bear's back and skull and the third eye popping into the forehead of Mac Bodine, centered just below the crest of his gray pompadour.

She didn't try to lock these visions out of her mind; she forced herself to watch them roll across like some grainy Super Eight snuff loop. No tits or cocks. None of her screams, either. Just two men dying at her hand. And just one thought rolling along with the images.

This is what it's like. This is killing. I did it. I'd do it again to anybody who tried to kill me and mine.

It made her feel sharp and cold, like an ice pick left in the snow.

When they finally ground through the last of the rutted gravel switchbacks in the half-mile road to Uncle Harlan's house, it was four in the morning and he was standing on the porch, a pump shotgun cradled in his arms and a Colt stuffed down his trousers. About a dozen other men, carrying shotguns and Ruger Mini-14s, the famous long-gun of the Ku Klux Klan, milled about in the front yard, smoking and talking in low voices.

"Where you two been?"

Eldon told it the way he said he would. Harlan said nothing and looked down at the worn slats of the porch, worrying splits in the wood with the toe of his left boot. He looked up.

"They was here. About ten of 'em. Dogs got wind of 'em comin' up the holler. Had to bust up my poker game. Joe Pride got killed but we got seven of theirs. Sorry bastards."

She could see the front windows had been blown out and the big wooden door kicked in. She walked over to feel the bright yellow splinters that marked where the hinges had popped free of the door frame. Harlan walked over and stared into her eyes.

"You done the killin', didn't you, girl?"

She was afraid to answer. He kept staring.

"You killed Mac."

"Yessir. He tried to kill Eldon."

Her voice was filled with dread and pride.

"Good. He tried to kill me. Glad you did it. Saves me the trouble."

Harlan leaned his shotgun against the porch railing. He walked over to Eldon and knocked him down the steps with one punch.

"You know what that's for."

Her uncle turned and walked into his dark, slug-scarred house.

⅄

Eldon had expectations. Once, they were vague. Now, with blood on her hands, they were concrete and certain. Carla Sue had other ideas.

A cherry-red Cutlass caught her eye one night while she and Eldon were cruising through Mousy's, a drive-in that served up death dogs, fat cheeseburgers and pit barbecue. So did the car's owner, Buddy Deal, a 28-year-old garage mechanic with curly blond hair and a chipped front tooth, a layabout who lived to run hard and trade paint and dented sheet metal on short track Saturday nights.

"That thing drive as good as it looks, or is it like you, all show and no go?"

Buddy's friends hooted.

"Better check yourself for a suckin' chest wound, Buddy-row, that sassy thing done sent a round clean through you."

Buddy walked up to the side of Eldon's car.

"Only one way to find out, little sister."

He tossed her the keys. She fishtailed out of Mousy's lot and headed out a wicked road with a two-mile straightaway and a sudden hairpin turn, followed by a slalom run up the side of Flat Top Mountain. Buddy draped himself into the corner of the passenger side bucket, lazily smoking a Camel as she banged through the gears and slammed the Cutlass hard through the curves.

They pulled onto an overlook at the top of the mountain. She sat on the warm hood of the Cutlass, legs dangling over the grille. He stood in front of her, leaning close, resting a hand on either side of her hips.

"I got one question, little sister -- do you fuck as good as you drive?"

She didn't answer. She unbuckled his belt, unzipped his fly and wrapped her hand around his cock.

"Only one way to find out."

His hard hands cupped her ass. The belt buckle felt cold as it whisked along the side of her bare thigh. She could feel the heat of the engine through the back of her open blouse.

⅄

Eldon felt cheated. He broke into her room one night, his words rushed by the meth and roughened by the whiskey. He started to climb into her bed but was stopped by a cocked Colt jammed into his right nostril.

"You're about to be deader than hell if you don't put your ass in reverse."

"Aw, you wouldn't shoot your cousin. Now, put that thing away."

"You got three options and only one of them leaves you alive -- I scream and Uncle Harlan comes in here and kills you, I pull this trigger and splatter what few brains you got, or you get gone."

She backed him out of her bed and right out the open window he climbed in through. But not before he made a promise she never thought he'd have the guts to keep.

Her next summer at Harlan's was her last. Two bikers boomed up the holler. Low-slung Harleys with bright chrome and Fat Bob gas tanks in deeply lacquered black. The lead rider was tall, with ropy muscles, a handlebar moustache, swept-back hair that fell to his shoulders like a black mane and eyebrows that slashed across his face like a single stroke of grease pencil.

His second was short and fat, with a belly that rolled out between the flaps of his leather vest, kinky brown hair topped by a bandana tied Aunt Jemima style and piggish eyes that hid behind sweaty flesh that looked like it had been dipped in bacon fat.

They weren't part of Mac Bodine's old outfit. They were from an East Coast gang that bought crystal meth from Harlan's lab, two outsiders who drifted through mountain towns in summer and down to Florida when it got cold. June could find them in Blowing Rock; December in Daytona Beach.

"Can we talk to you, Mr. Cantrell? Got some business to discuss."

"You talkin' to me now."

"Some place private."

"Boys, ain't nothin' more private than these hills. Don't mind the girl. She's quiet as a tomb."

They were standing on the porch. The two bikers were at the bottom of four framed railroad ties that served as steps. Harlan was cupping a hand-rolled cigarette in his left hand. Carla Sue stood to her uncle's left and slightly behind him, the Colt in her right hand, cocked and unlocked, hidden by his back.

The bikers had a proposition; a cut of the profits on heroin and coke shipped wholesale from a Texas outfit in return for the use of his many mountain safehavens.

The Texans would move the stuff north to the hideaways. The bikers would pick it up.

"It's a stretch for me, boys. Lemme think on it. Give you an answer in the mornin.' Stayin' at the same place as always?"

Pig Eyes stepped up on the second railroad tie.

"What the fuck is there to think about? It's a no-brainer. You'll be gettin' a shitload of jack just for lettin' us use your hideouts. C'mon, man. Roll with it."

"Can it, Dirt. We're strangers here and this is Mister Cantrell's house."

"The fuck you talkin' 'bout? We're offerin' a sweet deal if this country puke can see it. You gone soft, or what?"

The tall biker grabbed Pig Eyes by the hair and threw him into the dirt. When the fat biker tried to get up, he got a boot to the belly, then a gloved fist to the jaw.

"Mr. Cantrell, I apologize. Dirt here's a shithead and I'm sorry he had to open his yap. I hope you won't let him sour you on the deal. It's a good one and you know we're good people to do business with. 'Ceptin' Dirt."

"Don't know that, don't know much 'bout you at all. Like what I see even less. Now get that sorry sack of puss off my land. You come back here tomorrow for coffee. Alone. We'll hash it out then."

She waited until the Harleys faded from earshot. She eased down the hammer on the Colt and looked her uncle in the eye.

"I say fuck 'em. Bad enough you're already dealing with these sorry needledicks. What happens when you bring in these jokers from Texas? They'll gang up on you sure as shit. Start runnin' you out of your own hideouts. Take that lab of yours too."

"Enough, girl."

"Might kill you along the way. You know they might. Get in here, learn what's what. Try to take you down."

"Might do that anyway, girl. Gettin' a mouth on you, know that? Been hangin' round that Eldon too much. Or is it Buddy Deal? Didn't think I knowed about that, did you?"

"Don't shift gears, Unc'. You know I'm right. And Eldon's too gutless to teach me to cuss."

Harlan cut the deal. With one proviso. He set the schedule. He arranged for his drivers to meet the Texans east of Knoxville and drive the loads to the hideaways. His boys would drive the loads to the bikers.

The Texans squawked. So did the bikers. They wanted more volume. And more control. But they did business.

Carla Sue was wrong about Eldon. On the morning after the tenth run from Texas, Harlan sat over his morning coffee. Eldon walked in with a Remington pump and scattered her uncle's brains across the kitchen table.

"Old man doin' things the old way. Thought you was still runnin' shine, didn't you? Dotin' on that girl and treatin' me like a sorry old mule. Wouldn't listen to a thing I had to say. Let's see what that cunt has to say about this."

The Colt was upstairs. She was in the living room. Eldon was between her and the stairs. She could hear him slipping fresh shells into the shotgun as he walked through the dining room. She flattened herself next to the doorway nearest to him, gripping an iron shovel from the fireplace set.

As he stepped through the doorway, she smacked him in the face, breaking his nose with the flat blade of the shovel, feeling the hit vibrate through her forearms, hearing the metal strike bone like a muffled gong.

He went down like a deer taking a slug. She grabbed the shotgun and made sure the safety was off.

"You gonna tell me who set you to this, cuz."

"Go to hell, bitch."

"You gonna die right now, Eldon. But you gonna tell."

His nose was bloody and flat. He was sprawled on his back, his feet in the living room, his head and torso in the dining room. She stood near his feet and aimed at his left knee.

The boom and his scream filled the room. She smelled the burnt powder. He vomited a thin ribbon of white gruel on a shirt of red and green plaid.

"You gonna tell me what I want to know. Which of them bikers?"

She was wrong about that, too. Eldon gave her two names. And a reason to head back to Texas. Maybe Mexico. She let him bleed to death on the floor.

CHAPTER 11

Cider Jones stared into the eyes of a woman who would see no more. He did this with all his murder cases. He would sit on his heels, leaning over their faces, ignoring the bustle of the evidence techs, ignoring the gore of a knife or bullet wound, ignoring the stench of days-old death, carrying on a silent conversation with the dead.

They never answered. It didn't matter. With this quiet act of communion, his eyes drank in the soul of the victim and gave him answers to questions he had yet to ask. When the time was right, they would rise to the surface, dark and fast, like fish from the bottom of a deep pool.

His grandmother, the daughter of a Comanche medicine man, taught him this. The redneck in him, from a father who was an Odessa roustabout, lounged in the back of his mind with a thick wad of Redman bulging his cheek, spitting dark jets of juice at such mysticism.

Cider Jones did it anyway.

Her eyes were green, flecked with bronze. Her hair was full and frizzy, tinted a reddish blond. Her nose was wide and flat, her lips fleshy and flared, her brown skin deeply tanned. Cruise-ship, yacht or island dark. Not Houston poolside.

Someone got close enough to pump four heavy-caliber bullets into her chest. Close enough for powder burns to blacken a wheat-colored sun dress. Close enough to make her back look like somebody had gouged out the flesh with an ice cream scoop.

The shoot took place in the living room. Two, maybe three days ago. The shooter was in a hurry, taking only enough time to drag her into the dining room, away from prying eyes and the chance parting of heavy drapes drawn across the front window, but rippled by a stream of cold from the air conditioning vents.

No signs of a struggle. No signs that the place had been stripped. That made it a hit. By a killer she knew. Maybe.

They were in a town house off San Felipe, near Post Oak. Upscale Anglo turf. Young bankers, brokers and oil traders on the come. Not a tall Hispanic looker with muscular legs, hair colored by somebody far cheaper than Lady Clairol, a rose tattooed along her ankle and skin that looked like charred mahogany.

The kept talent in this neighborhood had a silken finish and styles so carefully colored the hair never looked like it got touched by a bottle. This one took her tequila straight and raw. Other things, too.

On her left wrist, there was a bracelet of coiled copper. At the break, two sculpted heads with screaming mouths, glaring eyes and flowing hair faced each other. Medusas, maybe.

He eased out of his crouch, hearing the cartilage chips in his left knee pop and crack. His sacrifice to the god-a-mighty of Texas, that high altar, high school football. One last look at her eyes as he rubbed the gimpy joint, his fingers feeling the zipper scars through light poplin pants and the chips that floated like pebbles just under the rubbery skin that covered his kneecap.

The bedroom didn't tell him much. Just that she didn't live here. The closet held three blouses, two pairs of slacks and the loud print of an off-the-shoulder number his girlfriend called a ya-ya dress. Two pairs of sandals were on the floor.

In the dresser were bras, panties and two pairs of well-worn jeans. Some jewelry scattered on top.

The living room told him more. Dried and blackened blood on the carpet. Her pocketbook, twenty-five hundred dollars in cash, a Smith & Wesson Model 459 in matte chrome, a passport and an international driver's license. Astrid Quinones. From Matamoros.

One of those high-dollar metal briefcases in gunmetal gray sat beside a couch covered in sea-green print. Triple scales were on the coffee table. A scratch pad sat beside scales. A 214 telephone number and the letters EEB were scrawled in pencil on the top sheet.

By their threesome, on a small table next to an overstuffed chair covered in the same print as the couch, sat an empty shot glass and two juice glasses -- one half-filled with water, the other with two fingers of Coke and melted ice.

Just like you might see at Louie's. On a Tuesday or Thursday night. And sometimes Fridays.

Chapter 12

T-Roy backhanded the man across the face, starting the blow from his knees, driving the man toward the wall, following with a forearm chop to the windpipe, screaming as the man slid to the floor coughing and gagging.

"¡Cono! ¡Eres mierda!"

A boot to the man's face.

"I give you a job, all the money and weapons in the world and you still fuck it up!"

A boot to his ribs.

"I wanted Ross here! Not there. Not dead. He's no fuckin' good to me dead. Not right now."

A boot to his crotch.

"You had an in! I got you through his front fuckin' door! An easy fuckin' snatch, you said. *No problema*, you said. Well my friend, you've got a big problem now. Me!"

He was bending over the man, yelling into his pain-creased face, spittle flying across the few inches that separated them. He straightened up, running the fingers of his left hand through his coarse red hair.

With his right hand, he pulled a chrome-plated .357 Colt Python from his waistband, jammed the barrel in the man's mouth and pulled the trigger six times.

"Get that worm meat off my damn floor! Get a bucket and mop! And get me another fuckin' shirt!"

Mano and El Gordo moved in and grabbed the body. T-Roy looked down at the toes of his caramel-colored, lizard-skin boots. A stain of blood and brains spread across the tops. His jeans were also splattered.

"Boots and jeans, goddamit!"

He stripped off his shirt, a bone-white rancher with real pearl snaps, letting it drop at his feet. He kicked off his boots, scaling them across the room, causing the two men to duck. He whipped the tooled belt with the silver bullrider's buckle through the loops and shucked his jeans.

Standing next to his desk in navy silk bikini briefs, T-Roy flipped open the Colt, pushed the ejector rod and shook spent brass onto the floor with a brassy clatter and threaded fresh hollow points into the cylinder, snapping it back in place. He paced the floor, slapping his bare leg with the belt, raising small red welts on freckled flesh with every stroke.

The welts were the same color as the puckered scars that ran between his shoulder blades and the flesh that covered the spot where one of his kidneys used to be -- reminders of Reynosa.

The Ross snatch should have worked. He had two insiders -- the woman and the security chief for the *rancho*. She was supposed to hold Ross until his boys broke through. With Ross in hand, he could take it all -- the chop shops, the illegals, the drugs -- and have a machine that ran from Mexico to the Oklahoma line.

With Ross in hand, he could cut a deal with the younger honchos, guys who would do business with him, guys he would have been in business with four or five years ago if the oldster hadn't held him back, then sniffed out his scheme and tried to kill him.

After cutting a deal with the young *machos*, he could have killed Ross slow, cut him up piece by piece. Or let the old woman's followers have the pimp buzzard for those special rites. No college drifter this time.

A *patrón*. A man of power. Strong, strong stuff. And hand-delivered by him, T-Roy. Another tie between a man who didn't believe and those who believed too much in something too twisted even for him.

But the blonde woman was gone and Ross was dead. So was the security chief, chopped down in the crossfire. He thought about the woman, Carla Sue. Tiny, but bold, she came to Ross with her dead uncle's ice lab and his mountain hideaways tied up in a neat package, cutting a quick cash deal and cozying up to the old pimp in a way that had him pawing the ground like a young bull.

This was just before he and Ross had their little disagreement. They had planned the uncle's death. T-Roy made the offer to the girl's cousin himself. After the split, she contacted T-Roy and kept him advised of Ross's moves. For a hefty fee. Delivered to an account in Belize. Her role in the strike cost extra. Lots of extra.

Her Cutlass was spotted as it blew out of the ranch. The boys said a big, bald-headed dude was at her side. Maybe holding a gun to her head. Maybe not. Hard to tell. New player. No one knew about him.

Without Ross in hand, there was no chance for a quick coup and a cover-up of the carnage at the ranch. His boys had to beat feet, leaving more than a few of their own behind, but also leaving a smoking hulk of a house and a gaping hole in the once-muscular Ross organization.

Big damn deal. All he had done was stir up a hornet's nest. Ross's boys would want revenge. They didn't burn with hatred for him like Ross did -- nothing matched a father's rage at a son's betrayal. But his strike had given them plenty of reason to come gunning for him, those who were left. Damn few, but dangerous.

And the firefight brought the FBI, DEA and ATF into the mix. Big headlines, too. DRUG WAR IN GRAYSON COUNTY! BRAZEN ATTACK -- ROCKETS AND MACHINE GUNS! IS NO ONE SAFE? He didn't even want to think how those headlines would play down Cali way. Those boys were pissed at him already.

He could hear the one he called *El Lagarto*, a thin, bald, hawk-beaked man with glittery eyes, a rasping voice and the slow, but jerky moves of a lizard in the sun.

"Señor Bonafacio, we value your friendship and your continued participation in our business ventures. But we must maintain the security of our pipeline to *El Norte* and must make sure all of our partners are happy and a part of the program. We cannot afford someone pursuing their own agenda. It endangers us, it endangers the others. Surely you see the wisdom in this?"

He could see *El Lagarto* tapping the ash off a thin puro with a russet-colored wrapper, his tongue flicking out rapidly to meet it as he brought it to his mouth, his eyes closing quickly as he puffed. This was the only time that one relaxed. And T-Roy was sure the man was anything but relaxed right now.

At least he'd had the sense not to use boys from his inner circle or the old woman's. Some ex-contra toughs made up most of the strike team, leavened by some of his lower-level muscle. Choppers leased through three front organizations and returned intact. A pickup in two King Airs pulled off without a hitch.

The dead man was a contra honcho, skilled but very unpopular. No loss to his men -- they liked T-Roy's supply of money, drugs, pussy and action. More of it. More reliable than Uncle Sam, too.

Mano walked through the door, his homey since Dallas, the man who kept that shotgun jockey from finishing him off in Reynosa. He whispered in T-Roy's ear, draping a veiny, muscular arm across skinny shoulders.

"It's Astrid. Somebody iced her at the safe house."

"Who?"

"Workin' on it, man. Our guy says the cops found her with four slugs in the chest. Close range. A .45. Dead two, maybe three days. Tops. I'll have the who in a couple hours."

T-Roy felt like someone had driven an ice pick between his eyes. The room wobbled. He held onto Mano as the bigger man eased him into a chair. A bottle of mescal floated in front of his face. He grabbed it, tilting the bottle back until the kerosine-flavored liquor burned the back of his throat, choking the liquid down until he needed to take a breath.

He sent Astrid to Houston on a rush job -- resupply for some Houston dealers who'd just knocked off a brace of Jamaican competitors and were enjoying a sudden spike in demand.

Ten keys. Brought in by four Guatamalan mules. Astrid was the collector. Spread the cash across four bank accounts, three front companies and two lawyers. Then go shopping and catch some sun. See you in a week.

Wild Astrid. She'd walked up to him in a Matamoros *cantina*, planted one leg on the chair next to his, hiked her skirt up to her hip, grabbed his hand and guided it to his pistol. With the gun out of his waistband and still in his hand, she placed the barrel between the lips of her pussy.

"How do you know I won't pull the trigger?"

She laughed, then leaned forward, her hot breath brushing his ear.

"Because you want to put your cock there, *vato*. The best you've ever had. And feel this tongue?"

It snaked into his ear.

"Think of how it will feel on *la gloria*."

She was right -- bar none. She liked it fast and rough. Threesomes and foursomes. Whips on her flesh. And his. She also had an eye for business angles and was fast enough with a pistol to handle cash runs across the border. He let her work her way from his bed into his operation.

The boys didn't like it. Mano in particular. She made Mano a part of their next four-way, first wearing out T-Roy and a young whore named Gabrielle, then fucking Mano to a frazzle, bruising his rib cage along the way.

A storm of sex. And set on being his right hand in business. She was on her way when he sent her to Houston. Now she was gone.

"Get hold of those Houston pukes. Somebody got to them and I want to know who."

"Already linin' that up."

"And get the Badhair. I want him on this."

"You sure?"

"Just what in the fuck do you think, Mano? Get it done. Get a name. Give it to the Badhair. I want him to make somebody very, very dead. And I want that somebody's head sittin' right fuckin' here on this desk."

"We got other problems."

T-Roy's face twisted in pain and rage. He cocked the Python and fired a round into the ceiling.

"There's nothin' else. Got me? Nothin'."

The room was silent except for the swishing sound of El Gordo's mop.

CHAPTER 13

"Pull in there."

"Where?"

"Right the hell where I'm pointin', slick."

"You don't have to use that tone."

"What are you, the ghost of ex-wives past?"

Carla Sue ignored the shot.

"That house?"

Her voice was pissy and sharp.

"Yellow one. Panel truck out front. Concrete deer in the yard."

Burch's voice was low and raspy, down an octave from the sharpness of a few seconds ago.

"Where you goin'?"

"See a slow man about a fast dog. You got somethin' for all this hardware?"

She pulled a black duffle bag from the backseat.

"Load it up. And gather up any other gear you need. You got any money?"

"How much?"

"Old boy in there is kinda partial to Ben Franklin's portrait. Eight K will do. Ten'd be better -- buy us some silence."

She fished a dozen packets of hundred-dollar bills from the duffle and slapped them into his chest. Each packet held a grand and had the smell of new money.

"Wait here. Any trouble, get gone."

He eased out of the car, favoring the bad leg. She saw him wince and make a clicking sound with his tongue. He tucked the Bulldog down the front of his pants, butt toward his left hip. He flipped his jacket over the gun and limped toward the front door.

It took forever and was painful to watch. A dog started barking from the backyard. A floodlight flipped on before he reached the small concrete slab that served as a front porch.

"Kill that damn light, Hooter, it's makin' me blind."

"'Sposed to. Who the hell are you?"

"If you can't see who it is, you dumb country cocksucker, then what good's that light?"

"Worth it to piss off a sorry-ass cop."

"Ex-cop. You gonna let me in or not?"

"Only thing keepin' you out is that limp. One of them wives whack you on the knee? Late on that alimony again, I expect."

Burch hobbled to the screen door. Hooter Goodson held it open with his left hand. He knew Hooter held a double-barreled sawed-off in his right, hidden by shadow.

"Need a car, son. Fast, but not flashy. Cash deal. And you get that Cutlass out front. Was a cherry till some ol' boys used it for target practice tonight. Chop it. Ditch it. And fast. Somebody will be lookin' for it."

"Won't be nice folk, will it?"

"Naw, son. Not like me ay-tall. You got you somethin' a man would call a drink?"

Hooter walked back toward the kitchen. Burch sat in the dark at the dining room table, stretching his bum leg in front of him, leaning back in the chair. Hooter plunked down a bottle of Evan Williams and handed him two empty highball glasses.

"Pour."

Hooter was a second cousin on his daddy's side, a Friar Tuck beard fringing a moon face, balding and blessed with big forearms and a beer belly. Twenty-three years ago, they played ball together in Coppell, the right side of the line for the '65 Rattlers, AAA regional champs, winners of the state championship. By a touchdown. Texas gridiron immortals.

Burch became a cop after two years in Germany as a tank mechanic. Hooter stole cars, ran a chop shop and did light time in Huntsville for grand theft auto. Hooter also introduced him to his third ex-wife, Juanita, the bass-fishing queen and Hemingway freak. Burch liked him anyway.

His cousin lived on the bad side of Weatherford these days, on a broken block of asbestos-sided bungalows decorated with rusty awnings, cheesy lawn ornaments and battered automobiles. A mean dog in every back yard. A shotgun next to every bed. At every kitchen window, a wife in curlers and Daisy Dukes or sweats, squinting through cigarette smoke.

"You in bad trouble, cuz?"

"Could be. You don't want to know."

"Think I got what you need. An old Monaco. Looks like a rust bucket, but it's got a worked 383, new trans, good retreads, AM-FM, air ..."

"Can the sales pitch. This is me you're talkin' to. Price?"

"For the car and losin' the Cutlass? Ten."

"C'mon, Hooter, you'll make that much choppin' the Cutlass. Six."

"Cuz, you ain't in no position to dicker. Eight."

"Seven if you gin up a .45. Lost mine."

"C'mon cuz, throw in that extra stack of Franklins."

Burch fanned five more bills in his hand. His cousin nodded and said one word: "Done." They smiled at each other, took dainty sips of whiskey and listened to night sounds -- a dog barking, the whine of tires up on the main highway, the whirring of locusts. Hooter spoke first, pushing up from the table.

"You'll need a holster. Don't got no shoulder rigs. Bianchi or Leatherman?"

"Bianchi will do. Left handed."

"Silvertips or jacketed? Got Corbon Flyin' Ashtrays. Got hardball, too."

"Damn, son. You speakin' the language of my tribe. Four boxes of Flyin' Ashtrays and four of hardball. Better make that six of each. And a mess of 9 mm, full jacket."

"You declared war?"

"Peace through firepower, son."

A dry chuckle. The cousins knocked back their bourbons. Burch flicked his thumb across seventy-five Franklins, pocketing the two remaining bundles and the five bills of the broken packet. They shook hands.

"Oh, yeah. Need some clothes -- jeans, shirt, some skivvies. These are kinda tattered."

"Kinda smell like piss."

"That too."

CHAPTER 14

There was a simple reason they called him Cider. At a Halloween party when he was a rookie, he drank a punch made of cider, vodka and cinnamon schnapps until he puked in the backseat of his partner's yellow Nova.

It was also the reason he only drank beer now and rarely had more than two. His real name was Willis Quanah Jones. Nobody seemed to remember. Not even his girlfriend.

"Hey, Medicine Man -- line two. Somebody wants a rainmaker."

"Bite my ass, beaner."

"Serve it up with some verde sauce and a Carta Blanca."

"Comer mierda, cabron!"

Jones punched up the call, raising the middle finger of his right hand toward the ceiling as he did so, drawing a cackle and a cough.

"Jones."

"Yah-ta-hey."

Woman's laughter, long and rich. Sarah Lasterman, assistant ME, big and black, hair in cornrows, thick glasses and a More cigarillo stitched to her lower lip. He could see the gurneys and stiffs, smell the formaldehyde.

"Cut the redman shit -- Cortez put you up to this, Sarah?"

"Since when do I need some stupid Mex to tell me how to yank your breed chain, baby?"

"Whatchugot?"

"What-I-got is one dead as hell *bonita puta* Mexican national that you'll never get in the sack. Dead about forty-eight hours before she was found, not much more. Four slugs from a .45 -- four jacketed hollow points. Heavy slugs, close up. Ohh, wee, somebody wanted her very dead."

"What else?"

"Type O. Traces of cocaine and alcohol."

"Bourbon?"

"You know we can't tell that. Barely get these lame fuckers to give us what they do. Don't go askin' what brand of liquor she drank before she got dead. Who is she, baby?"

"Astrid Quinones."

"Fits the look -- stunnin' but cheap, baby. Copy on the way. Later."

Her blood type matched what was found on the carpet. The scrap of paper with the scrawled initials and Dallas phone number matched the handwriting in her checkbook, one of five found in her purse, bearing the account numbers and names of four different companies that could be traced to three low-rent local lawyers and not much further.

Papers on the townhouse ran to one of the lawyers and one of the companies. The metal briefcase was empty and had her prints all over it. The scales spelled a coke deal. But no coke. And no money, either. What was she -- solo flyer or subordinate? A fax to DEA and the *federales* in Mexico City might give him some answers. He wouldn't hold his breath.

Jones shuffled through another set of papers. The phone number was for the office of a Dallas pee-eye, an ex-homicider named Burch, Edward Earl, DOB 12/05/48, Height: 6'1", Weight: 240 pounds. Hair: dark brown and thinning. Eyes: brown and not too bright. Prints and jacket to follow. And a copy of his pistol permit -- a Colt 1911 in .45 ACP.

Another bingo from the airlines -- Southwest sold a ticket to an E. Burch the day before Quinones was snuffed. Cash. No return. He stared at the faxed photo of Burch. My, my, it's gettin' warm in here, Jones thought. Bet we get a match on those prints from the juice glasses too.

A call to DPD gave him a brief sketch: homicide, vice then homicide -- an odd bounce. Partner killed chasing a scumbag named Bonafacio. Loner who drank heavy and wasn't a team player. Solid arrest record with some high-profile cases. Three suspensions for getting crosswise with the brass. Beefs about excessive force, most of them bullshit. And one that wasn't. Forced resignation for beating the shit out of a pimp. Four kills, all clean.

Cider popped open a desk drawer and fished out a napkin, a styrofoam coffee cup and a pouch of Levi Garrett chaw. He stuffed the napkin in the cup and placed a big, stringy ball of tobacco in his mouth. Most cops dipped Cope or Skoal. Walt Garrison said just a pinch between cheek and gum. But hell, Walt was just a football player and a cowpuncher, not a cop and an Indian mystic.

Chawin' and chewin'. Working the tobacco in his jaw while working out the rough math of the facts on his desk.

Wouldn't be the first time an ex-cop took to the other side of the street. Particularly if he got screwed over by the force -- heavy undertone of that from the Dallas cop who gave him the backgrounder. Said Burch did some work for the white-powder bar in Dallas and Houston and seemed to be an ace in a growing Texas niche market -- finding wayward S&L clients with non-performing loans.

"Cider, ID on one."

"Jones."

"Got those prints from Dallas. They're a match."

"You sure?"

"Clean overlay. Thumb and three fingers, right hand, on one juice glass. Thumb and forefinger on the shot. How much more do you want?"

"This guy was a cop, man. I want to be sure before I put his name on the wire."

"Well, you can be sure 'cause I'm sure."

Jones punched up another line and put out the tag on Burch. Murder. Armed and dangerous. One of their own turned bad. Cortez floated in, slurping his coffee and waving a fax.

"*Federales* came through for once. Your Astrid was *culo caliente* for a dude named Teddy Roy Bonafacio. A bad boy, that one. Big timer round Matamoros -- smack, meth, blow, illegals, you name it. State boys had him for dead about six years back, killed in a whorehouse in Reynosa. But the feds say that was bullshit. They think he was behind those North Texas fireworks where that old Dallas *patron* got snuffed. Roth or Ross."

"That Green Beret thing that's got ATF all batshit?"

"You the man," said Cortez, pointing at him with the forefinger and pinkie of his left hand, dipping the digits like a divining rod.

"No, *you* the man," he said, flashing his hand the same way.

Old ritual. It meant something once. It was reflex now.

Cider Jones checked his notes as he sluiced some tobacco juice into the cup. There it was -- Bonafacio, the guy Burch was chasing when his partner got killed. But that was a long time ago -- twelve years. A long wait for revenge.

His intercom buzzed, the lieutenant on the line.

"You and Cortez need to *vamanos* to a little shindig they got off of Westheimer. Three bodies -- Anglo lawyer and two clients, a blood and an Anglo. Both dealers. Got stuff that ties into your shoot."

"How'd it go down?"

"Lead. Heavy caliber."

"How long?"

"Five, six hours -- tops. What's come up on your San Felipe shoot?"

"Just put out something on a Dallas PI named Ed Earl Burch. Ex-cop. Murder want. Prints match. Victim was iced with a .45. Burch carries one."

"You boys scoot on over to this other thing. I'll holler up Dallas and get them to check on this ol' boy."

He hung up, fished the chaw out of his cheek, dumped it in the cup, took one last spit.

"C'mon, beaner, think we got us a vigilante out on a mercy shoot."

In his office, the lieutenant placed a long-distance call. But not to Dallas. Mano answered on the third ring.

CHAPTER 15

She reached across the table and slid his coffee cup closer to the pot in her other hand, pouring fast, sliding the full cup back and plopping down two fresh containers of non-dairy creamer in a quick motion.

He didn't notice. He was facing the front window of the Dixie House, his thick left arm draped along the back of the booth, the biceps dark and bulging through the short sleeve of a thin, white polyester dress shirt some years gone from the Men's Store at Sears.

Folds of fat rolled from his neck, spilling over a frayed and open collar. His huge right hand balanced on the table's edge, pinkie down, thumb up and rubbing the second knuckle of a bent forefinger, right where the flesh started to lighten from walnut to salmon.

A small, black plastic box that looked like a cassette player or radio sat inside the curve of this hand. A wire ran from the box to the plug in his right ear.

"Anythin' else?"

He didn't answer. His head didn't move. His eyes stayed centered on the window. She leaned across the table.

"I said -- will there be anythin' else? Pie, ice cream, cake? We got carrot cake today. And some peach cobbler that's pretty good. Sound good to you?"

"No. Go 'way."

He turned his head and peeled off his mirrored shades. His eyes were black coals, burning slow, surrounded by jaundiced ivory shot with thin lines of red. His nose was humped and buckled like cheap asphalt, bottomed by a close-cropped Fu Manchu moustache that rode over and around pulpy, scarred lips.

His cheeks and jowls were rubbery and cratered -- hot wax dribbled across latex. The furrows of his forehead rolled up and under the line of the worst toupee she had ever seen. It looked like a black poodle with Astroturf® curls, crouching over his broad brow, skewed toward his left ear.

She couldn't break her startled stare. His ugliness, his fierce eyes, held her there, frozen, with the coffee pot wavering in her hand.

"What'chu lookin' at, lady?"

His voice was pinched and high-pitched, like a boy just before he hits puberty. She bit her lower lip, fighting back a nervous laugh.

"Maybe you don't hear good. Hear 'dis -- check and keep the coffee comin'. No pie. No cake. And no starin'. I 'member people what stare."

"Yessir."

Something moved on his head. Her eyes shifted to his toupee. It was pitching down the slope of his forehead, sliding on a sheen of sweat like a hound hitting a slick kitchen floor.

"What'chu starin' at?"

A laugh bubbled up and choked her. She walked away quickly, coughing and shaking her head. Willie 'Badhair' Stonecipher ripped the toupee from his head, staring at the liner, dragging a paper napkin over his sweaty dome.

"Damn glue."

Badhair jammed the toupee on his bald dome, holding the shades in front of his face, staring at his tiny reflection, hoping to get the fit right. Now it looked like a poodle resting its haunches on the back of his head.

He slapped on the sunglasses, then resumed his watch. Across the street, cops were standing next to the roped-off entrance to a small office complex -- three stories of weathered brick veneer, golden-colored glass marred by huge strips of peeled tinting.

Before the waitress bothered him, Badhair had been watching two plainclothes drive up in an LTD with blackwall tires. A blocky dude, barely six foot, with reddish-brown skin, an unruly shock of coal-black hair and a slight limp was in the lead, pulling on a blue polyester blazer, smoothing it over a big revolver in a shoulder rig. He was followed by a plump, bald-headed Mex wearing Ray-Ban® aviator shades, sipping from a styrofoam cup and pulling at the tail of a khaki suitcoat that was too tight across his rump.

Badhair glanced at the small, black plastic box in his hand. He adjusted the squelch and volume, listening to transmissions from a bug slipped into the spine of one of the law volumes that lined one wall of the office where the two detectives were plying their trade.

"... *kee-ryst, lookit this one's hand ... snapped back out of the socket ...*"

"... *to talk with a gag in your mouth ...*"

"... *this one talked, most definitely ... through the fuckin' gag. Didn't help ...*"

"... *I make three entry wounds, big gun ...*"

"... *our boy, but a little bloody for his tastes ...*"

"... *cop gone crazy? Not bloody enough, maybe. But what's this got to do with a dead partner?*"

"... *knows? But the fucker's phone number is right in this shyster's day book, bigger than your dick. Right there -- Ed Earl Burch ...*"

"... *bag of money, why's it still here?*"

"... *revenge, not money ... if these slugs are .45, it's Burch ...*"

"... *for ballistics ...*"

"*Fuck ballistics, man ... as shit to switch barrels on a Colt ... a cop, man ... just to fuck with us ...*"

Badhair shook his head and laughed. Cops got this Burch pegged for this hit and Astrid, stupid fuckers. Well, he did use a .45 to nail these three, slipping right through the outer door of the lawyer's office as Skinny and Ice Ray walked in. A slug to the back of each head. Sad to kill a brother, but the job's the job.

A wall clock read 4:32 a.m. when Badhair pulled the trigger. He had been following the boys since spotting them in a bar near Pasadena around midnight. They were the fuckers who said they needed more product after icing some Jamaican competition. They were the reason Astrid came to Houston. They led him to the office of Henderson "Hank" Crutcher, West Texas State, UT Law School and white-powder lawyer.

Crutcher was about to shake hands with his clients when Badhair killed them. The lawyer ran into his office, reached for a hammerless Colt .38 and screamed when a beefy paw slammed the drawer on his hand.

Mister lawyer-man was surely torn by his immediate fear of Badhair and his more distant fear of whoever was paying him. Wouldn't say shit if he had a mouthful, at first. So gag him with a silk rag from his fancy blazer and start snappin' back fingers.

Had him tryin' to scream through the gag, crying and shaking like a wet dog in a cold rain. Still nothin'. Another finger. Lawyer-man passed out. Dash his face with water from a thermos. Lawyer-man gave him the name he already had -- Burch. Said Burch was the man who set it all up, had Skinny and Ice Ray make the meet, say to expect their man Ed Earl.

Bullshit. The gag and another finger. Lawyer-man passed out again. More water, slaps to the face. Badhair's bad eyes and bad toupee up close in lawyer-man's face. Who the man, motherfucker? Who the man send Burch? Who? Badhair gripping that last finger, the pinkie. Lawyer-man shakin' that dog shake, his eyes rollin' back.

Lawyer-man noddin' his head now. Gag out. One name -- Neville Ross. Paid them each fifty thou to set it up for Burch. Rogue cop. Got it bad in for T-Roy. Never saw the man. Just the money and plane tickets to Belize for a long vacation. Please, please don't kill me, say the lawyer-man.

Badhair laughed his high laugh, broke lawyer-man's pinkie and cut off his scream with three rounds from the .45. Flying Ashtrays. 'Cause they gouge up a man's innards oh so sweet. And he did switch barrels on the Colt. That much those cops did get right.

Sipping coffee seven hours later, Badhair could still hear the scream. He played it in his mind a few times, savoring the tone and the way the roar of his pistol cut it off. He continued eavesdropping on the cops across the street.

Heard one cop tease the other about starin' into eyes of dead people. Caused him to frown and shake his head -- hoodoo stuff. Heard Dallas cops came up empty at Burch's apartment and office, but found stuff that showed the pee-eye was doing work for Crutcher and an attorney up there. Cops figured Burch whacked Astrid then tied up loose ends by nailing Crutcher and the two dealers. Stupid shits.

Badhair scribbled the Dallas attorney's name, Doug Bartell. Meant nothing to him. Heard one other juicy bit of info -- feds thought Burch might have been at the Ross ranch during the raid. One of Ross' muscle guys gave them a line on a guy answering his description and a woman leaving the scene in a vintage Cutlass, partial Texas plates. A snitch spotted a car like that in a body shop up Weatherford way, owned by Burch's cousin, an ex-con.

He pushed the table back and waddled toward the rest rooms and the phone booths, hitching his blousy surplus fatigues with the six bulging side pockets and the personal black dye job. His running shoes squeaked on the waxed floor. It was a tight fit inside the booth. Caused him to sweat. Caused the toupee to slide.

Badhair gripped the handset, screwed off the mouthpiece and snapped two alligator clips on the small, metal contact tabs inside. Wires ran to a pocket scrambler/descrambler he fished from one of the bellowed side pockets. He called the number Mano gave him. T-Roy answered.

"Your ol' fren set this up. Paid off Skinny, Ice and lawyer man. Sent Burch down here. Kill off your ol' lady."

"You sure 'bout that, Bad? We know for sure it's this Burch motherfucker?"

"Got it from lawyer-man his own self. He in no position to lie."

"Don't want to know."

"It's cool, T. Cops think Burch ice these fuckers to cover his tracks. Colt kill your ol' lady. Colt kill these guys. Two plus two for them stupid fucks."

"Cops know where Burch is at?"

"Got a line on him. Think he at the Ross place durin' the raid. Left there with some bitch in a Cutlass. Think they ditch that car in Weatherford. Mean anythin' to you?"

"Sure does, Bad. Sure does. Done good, my man. Done real fine. Stick with them cops for awhile. They got two good reasons to go after our Mr. Burch now. And Bad? I want you to fuck Burch up bad before you ice him -- cut his fuckin' head off, bring it to me. And kill the bitch with him. You hear that? Kill the bitch. Ten grand more and all the pussy you can lick if you do. And if you don't, don't come back."

"I heard that, T. Mr. Badhair will meet Mr. Burch. And Mr. Burch won't live to tell nobody 'bout it. That's a promise from the Badhair to you, T. Keep that cash col' an' that pussy warm."

CHAPTER 16

They crossed the Brazos in the dark and the Colorado just after dawn, leaving the Comanche Plateau and cutting down through the Hill Country, watching the ridgelines turn from black to slate gray to gray-green in the rising light.

It was a deceptive land -- scenic from afar, scrubby and scraggly up close, a green and rolling panorama built on dusty disappointment.

Burch remembered a map he saved from a tattered textbook because its title caught his fancy -- 'Physiography'. In black and white, it showed the weathered face of Texas, craggy whorls and cuts he used to trace as a schoolboy -- the Caprock and the Llano Estacado of the Panhandle, the Lampasas Cut Plains west of Waco, the Edwards Plateau that stretched south and east of San Angelo, the Balcones Escarpment, the wall of limestone that divided the rich, black prairie of the east from the scrubby brush of the west, the rocky lower lip of the land they were now riding through.

Through the night, they stayed on back roads, sticking to the thin, farm-to-market strips of blacktop that arched and dipped across hogbacks and sharply cut ridges. They ghosted through deeply shadowed towns like Chalk Mountain, Priddy and Goldthwaite.

Burch fooled with the radio as he drove through the dark, tuning in an old Ray Price song, its back-slap, shuffle beat, fiddle and high harmony drifting up low from the speakers, keeping him company. Carla Sue curled up in back, snoring softly.

Why did you turn up again?
I was doin' fine ...
I thought that I'd forgotten you,
But I know it isn't true ...

Damn fine question and a damn fool thought. Care to comment T-Roy? What about it, Neville, old son? And while you're down there, hopefully rotting in one of hell's lower chambers, shoot a call up to Wynn Moore. Hell, call his ex-wives. Get them all in on this. Big conference hookup -- the dead, the divorced, the damned and the runnin' scared.

When they left Hooter's, she filled him in on the frame. Ol' Neville was right -- boxed in tighter than a dead man's lips. Double whammy -- cops pegging him for murder, T-Roy gunning for revenge. A choice that was no choice at all, just the only option open to him.

Nice touch with the juice glasses and the shot. He flashed on the shyster who asked him to do some legwork on those Houston druggies -- Bartell. Fat, fish-eyed bastard. Always bragging about his turbo-charged Mooney and his mile-high Don Juan act. *Yessir, get them girlies to fly Air Bartell. Take her up to fifteen thou, set ol' Iron George, the auto-pilot. Slip Mr. Fun into some gum-poppin' honey. Nothin' like it, son.*

They met at Louie's. He had his usual. They dickered through a couple of rounds, maybe three or four. Who keeps count? Then he went to take a piss. When he came back, fresh drinks were on the table. Dead soldiers swept into the briefcase. Who would notice?

Not him, sure as hell. Behind the whiskey curve and eyeing a big redhead in jeans and a tight top. Never know when you'll meet a next ex-wife. Old joke from an ex-cop. Bartell drained his glass and laughed. Now Burch knew why.

He also knew Carla Sue meant to kill T-Roy. A grit girl's blood grudge that wouldn't be denied. If she didn't get killed first. And if he didn't beat her to the punch. Hell no, he didn't want to cut and run.

THE LAST SECOND CHANCE

His blood was up, he wanted to hug the chaos and havoc, rub up hard against it and get him some.

And that surprised him, given his recent years of backpedaling, peeling his life down to the barest of essentials and avoiding the dictates of others. This sure wasn't his call, but he was tired of backing up and backing down just for the sake of being left alone. These shits weren't going to leave him be. They'd want him dead and wouldn't quit until he was.

So, why not dodge on down to Mexico and hook 'em up with T-Roy? No choice but to, and that made him feel free and lively, off the hook and no longer looking for the back door.

He tapped the wheel with his high school ring, keeping time with the music. Buck Owens.

Lips, put a smile on my face,
Eyes, don't let her see you shed a tear ...
Don't let her know, don't let her know, the way I feel ...

By all means, don't ever let any woman who's kicked you in the ribcage know a damn thing. Sing it, Okie. Damn, he felt good and loved listening to this music.

White lines whipped into the arc of his headlights. A mule deer scrambled from a brush-filled ditch and swerved toward the brightness. Burch saw wild, white-rimmed eyes in the glare. He cut the wheel hard to the left, heard the crunch of gravel as he skidded onto the shoulder, then the squeal of rubber as the tires again found their grip on the blacktop.

"You sure know how to give a girl a wake-up call. You fallin' asleep over there?"

"Deer. Sumbitch tried to kiss headlights."

"They do that. Buck or doe?"

"Buck. Big sumbitch. Eight points, at least."

"Venison stew."

His belly rumbled, sour from whiskey and coffee. They rolled into Llano and pulled into the first hash house they could find. His leg almost buckled as he got out of the car. It was stiff and sore.

She looked at him once, then walked toward the cafe door.

"Suck it up, Big `Un."

"Thanks for the sympathy."

"I'm too damn hungry to nursemaid an ol' cripple who keeps tryin' to run over deer."

She turned on her heel, stopping him with a hand to the chest and a harsh whisper.

"We got to get some food. We also got to switch rides and ditch that Dodge. Cops'll find your cousin, sure as shit."

"Your turn to find the ride. They'll remember me for all the wrong reasons. They'll remember you, too, but as something they'd like to chase 'round a double wide."

"Jesus, Big 'Un. Sweet talk."

She rolled her eyes skyward. Above her head hung a rusty sign, its letters outlined in neon tubes that had burned out about the time LBJ started showing his surgery scars out in the Rose Garden and pulling beagles up by their ears.

J&S Cafe.

The initials of his third ex-wife. He knew where to take it from here.

Chapter 17

The voices were squeaky and shrill -- wet fingers drawn across glass -- scratching through the loud, white hiss of a television set jammed between channels, volume up, the electronic blanket of noise he needed to drown out his dreams and let sleep come to him.

T-Roy squirmed and made a small noise, deep in his throat, like a dog bothered by nightmares and starting to whimper. It is a cry that is always louder in a person's mind than it is in reality. Until the nightmare rises up through the layers of sleep, pushing the scream along, filling the throat until it fills the room of real life, the ears of the real person sleeping in the same bed or the hallways where the silent men who take the money to guard a life sit and pass the small hours, padding their way to the last door on the left with quick, quiet feet, guns drawn and held high, to see if something is really wrong or if it is just another nightly visitation for *El Rojo Loco*.

He wasn't to the stage of screams and the sudden, snapping arrival of sweaty consciousness. He wasn't even where you think you're screaming and screaming and wonder why no one can hear you.

He was someplace else, somewhere down below the white noise and the ceiling fan stirring the humid air of his room, down where dreams and other things hold you, never letting you rise fast enough to run from them, always making you stay and stay, stuck there in the quick-sand of visions and fear.

He buried his face in a sweat-stained pillow.

In the vision of sleep, he was hiding from the voices, digging into soft dirt, then dragging a boulder behind him, sealing himself in darkness. The smell of the earth was strong and wet; he held the taste of pennies, clay and water in his mouth. The stone was cold and made his hands turn blue.

He listened for the voices. He thought they were gone.

A roar filled his darkness and he was hurtling through earth and stone, rushing through the soft clay and running up against hardness, feeling it open and wrap around him before bursting out on the other side and into more dirt, more granite. They were after him. He heard their voices again, not Spanish, not Anglo, not any language he could think of. Something ancient and lost, something once heard in the land but now gone.

In a shower of dirt and clay and rock, he broke through the earth's surface and saw himself at the side of a broad causeway. In the distance, he could see a large city, dominated by flat-topped temples with steep, stepped sides. The city sat in the middle of a lake with this causeway and six others leading to its center.

Mountains rimmed the valley where the lake city stood. Their peaks were familiar to him, but he couldn't place them. He spun to the sound of shouts and the steely clash of battle. A troop of men, some on horseback, most on foot, were being forced his way by a larger mass of barefooted men, wielding studded clubs and shields.

The troop fired wheellock pistols and harquebuses, raking the larger mass of enemy with shot. Crossbow bolts also took their toll, skewering men clad in animal skins and bright plumes of feathers. But the weight of their numbers was telling, pushing the troop back toward a man in the leggings, body-armor and curve-brimmed helmet of a conquistador. The man sat on a large, white horse, its head bowed, its flanks scored with long cuts and flecked with blood.

"Christians! Rally to me! Christians! Rally to me!"

A barefoot man wearing the skin and head of a jaguar broke through the troop, sprinting toward the man on horseback, leaping and swinging his obsidian-edged warclub in a glittering arc that ended in a dull, pulpy thud that caved in the Christian's skull, knocking the helmet to his feet, where it spun in the dust of the causeway.

A sword was in his hand. He could not move. He looked at his feet. A hand rose from the earth and gripped his left ankle. He chopped at the hand with his sword and cut it through at the wrist. It still gripped his ankle, but he could move now and meet the Jaguar Knight, holding the pulsing heart of the conquistador in one hand and his club in the other.

The Jaguar Knight tore a hunk of the heart with his teeth, tipping his head back to let the blood run down his cheeks as he chewed and swallowed, his eyes shadowed by the cat head that covered his skull.

T-Roy ran toward the Jaguar Knight, swinging the blade back and forth in short, whooshing cuts that brought him closer to the smiling face, the skin-clad body and the blood-streaked cheeks.

The blade chopped into the neck of the Jaguar Knight, neatly severing the head from the body. The head bounced into the air and sprouted another skin-clad body. The other body sprouted another head, capped by a cat skull. Both heads laughed at him.

He swung his blade at the neck of the new Jaguar Knight. Again, the head was neatly severed. Again, it bounced once and instantly sprouted a new body. Three heads laughed at him. He swung a fourth time. Four heads laughed.

The laughing heads closed in, speaking their squeaky, shrill talk, laughing at him, spinning him around until all he saw were flashing teeth, cat skulls, spotted skins and one quivering heart, ragged where it had been torn.

The spinning stopped. He was naked, stooped and climbing a steep set of stone stairs. The lake city was below, the six causeways spreading from the center like a starburst. Jaguar Knights lined the sides of the steps he was climbing. He felt a lash rip his back. The knights pointed at him and laughed.

A shout from above. Cheers from the Jaguar Knights. A figure at the top of the stairs held a pulsing heart in his hands, raising it to the skies, singing out in that squeaky, shrill voice and ancient tongue.

Another yell from above.

The body of a conquistador tumbled down the stone steps, rolling and gaining speed, knocking his feet out, sending him on the same long tumble down the same stone steps. Down to the bottom, where the Jaguar Knights and men in priestly robes tore strips of flesh from the bodies of conquistadors, dipping the strips in chilemole sauce and sucking them down with a loud smack of the lips.

Hands grabbed him. The Jaguar Knights passed his rigid body up their line of spotted skins, up the side of the stone temple, up toward the flat top and the priests above. He sailed up on their palms, gliding smoothly to where a man stood next to a stone table, his shoulders covered with a mantle of black feathers, his head topped by a parrot mask and a plume of purple and yellow feathers.

T-Roy was flat on his back, staring at the sky, his cut shoulders rubbed by the rough stone table. Parrot Head flashed an obsidian knife, shiny at the point and cutting edges, dull in the middle of the blade, and spoke the squeaky, ancient tongue.

The blade disappeared from his sight. He felt a sharp pain below his rib cage and heard the sound of stone striking gristle, a sound he could feel in his skull and teeth. He tried to cry out and couldn't.

Parrot Head screamed and held a fistful of bloody pulp where he could see it. His heart, beating and pumping gouts of blood down the wrists of the man who held it.

Parrot Head held his heart high, toward the sky, toward a shadow that blotted the sun and cried out with a raucous squawk and hiss as it moved closer and grew larger, its features growing clearer, its size dwarfing Parrot Head.

The hissing grew louder, radiating from the head of a snake with glittering bronze eyes and a shiny, brown skin, flecked with gold. Its neck was ringed with white and brown feathers. Two broad, scale-covered wings spread from its body. It moved closer until it was all that he could see, its tongue, broad and thick, not thin and split, flicked toward his heart.

He tried to scream and could not.

Parrot Head bowed before the winged snake, holding his heart in one hand above him. But it wasn't Parrot Head anymore. The mask was off. The feathered mantle was gone. It was Mano, offering his heart to the winged snake and its wide, yellow tongue. The tongue scooped up the heart, rolling it back into the mouth. The snake swallowed, closing its eyes. It hovered over him, its head swinging from side to side, its mouth unhinging, its tongue curling out to touch his face.

The scream started from the hole in his side, moved up to where his heart used to be and filled his throat. The hiss and squawk filled his ears. He tried to drown it out with his own voice, a sound he couldn't hear, a sound he knew would save him.

His mouth was wide open, the cords of his neck strained. No sound. He couldn't get it out of his throat. It stayed there, denying him, wedging itself tight. He needed his screams. He needed to fling them at the mouth and tongue and unblinking eyes that floated so close he could count the scales around the flat, blunt snout.

He felt the tongue enter the hole in his side. He felt it press below his rib cage. The scream finally broke free, a flood of sound that drowned the hissing and smothered the feeling of something foreign in his body. He couldn't open his mouth wide enough to get it out. His jaw popped and sent a sharp pain shooting into his skull. The scream rolled on, causing his body to shake and the muscles of his legs, belly and arms to tighten.

Shaking and screams. More shaking. More screams. Shaking that he couldn't control and didn't start. Shaking and Mano's voice. Screams to drown out that voice and blot out the face of the snake. Mano's voice breaking through. The snake pulling back, growing smaller in the sky.

T-Roy felt himself rising through layers of water and oil, slow then fast, bubbling toward the hands that shook his body. His eyes snapped open and Mano's face floated above him.

"*Jefe, jefe. Jefe, jefe.*"

It took a moment for Mano to realize his boss was awake.

"Another bad dream, *jefe?*"

He nodded and stared at his oldest and only friend.

"The snake that flies again, *jefe?*"

He nodded.

"That and other things."

"What other things?"

He said nothing. Mano handed him a bottle of mescal. He propped himself on his side and drank until the liquor burned the back of his throat. He looked at Mano.

"I know you better, my friend. I know who you really are."

CHAPTER 18

Cider Jones watched Cortez ladle *ranchero* sauce over his fried eggs, then slice through the yokes with a knife, turning his plate into a palate of nauseating yellow-brown fluid, flecked with chunks of white.

Cortez dipped a rolled corn tortilla into the mess and bit off the end, following it with a forkful of *chorizo*. A fat droplet of gruel ran from the corner of his mouth. His cheeks were puffed with food. He tried to talk, but gagged.

"Chew your damn food, beaner. If you choke to death before you tell me what those Weatherford cops had to say, I will be pissed."

"Fuck your -- ackkk, annngh ..."

Coughing choked off the insult. Cider drained his coffee cup, stuffed a napkin in it and fished the Levi Garrett pouch from his jacket pocket. Cortez gulped some water and wiped his mouth with the back of his hand.

"Disgustin' damn habit, breed. And usin' their fine china as a spitcan. Didn't mama teach you better than that?"

Cider said nothing and worked the tobacco into his lower lip. Cortez mopped up more gruel with a tortilla. It was always this way after working a stiff -- he couldn't eat and Cortez had to stuff his face with *huevos con chorizo* and corn tortillas.

Cortez had Burch pegged for both shoots -- Quinones and the triple at Crutcher's office. Crutcher -- a real dirtbag whoredog. Bad enough to represent these damn dealers, he fronted for them on real-estate deals and aircraft leases and rumor had him dipping in as a not-so-silent partner on the black end of the business.

Timing screwed up Cortez's line. Hard for Burch to nip up to North Texas for that Ross shindig, then bop back down to Houston to pop Crutcher and the boys. You could make things fit if Burch leased a Lear.

Something else screwed it up as well -- the look in Crutcher's dead eyes. They didn't tell him about a bald-headed ex-cop, they spoke of something far more frightening, of somebody who truly enjoyed snapping back each and every finger. Like a swizzle stick in a happy-hour highball.

The redneck lounging in the back of Cider's mind snorted and sluiced a stream of Redman into the dust. *Awright, damn it. Look at it this way, you literal-minded popdick -- it's hard to image this dog-ass pee-eye in a private jet. Harder still to peg him as somebody's idea of ideal contract talent.*

True, maybe that was somebody's bright bulb -- use an *hombre* who don't look the part. Kind of like the old slip-by cars moonshiners used to use -- creep past the revenuers in something everyday and ordinary instead of smoking past them in something souped up.

But those eyes say something different. The redneck shook his head. *Awright, awright. Either way, the killings are related and Burch was the common denominator. Got to find the boy. Got to get at him before Bonafacio does. Or the feds. Or the Rangers.* They were hot for Burch, figured him as some key player in the Ross shootout.

Got to get Cortez to stop feeding his face long enough to get what those Weatherford cops had to say.

"What they tell you?"

"Not a whole helluva lot more. Snitch spotted the Cutlass. Wanted to snag it for himself. Mentioned it to a cop who remembered a want on a Cutlass. Bingo. Found the thing being chopped up by some ex-con up there."

Plates matched those seen leaving the Ross *rancho*; hard to miss a vanity job with a single word like LATER on it. They traced it to the Tejano Leather Company, once the name of an S&M escort service owned by Ross, lately just a place to park registrations on boats and cars found scattered about the dearly departed's spread.

"Who?"

"Some Bubba, *chingado* motherfucker. Hooter somethin-or-other."

Cortez slid a fax sheet across the table. Cider scanned the paper, noting the Weatherford P.D. logo.

"Did a trey at Huntsville. Been clean since then. But Weatherford cops peg him as a chop-shop operator who supplies clean, but expensive rides to a certain clientele."

"Didn't talk much, did he?"

"Wouldn't say *mierda*. Holdin' him as an accessory. They did find paper on a bunch of cars scattered around this guy's lot. Three cars missing. Wants out on those three. All MoPar -- a Duster, a Monaco and a Fury."

"He's ditched it by now. What about the woman?"

"Cantrell. Carla June or Jean or Sue."

Cortez glanced at his notebook.

"Carla Sue. Ross's squeeze and errand girl. What's with these damn redneck Anglos, got to have two first names. Can't go around like normal people and be called Ed or Earl. It's gotta be Ed Earl or some shit like that. *Pendejos.*"

"Get off the soapbox."

"Piss off, breed. "

"How's this ex-con tie into Burch?"

"They don't know."

"We need to."

Cider slid his chair back, grimacing as he heard a stuck cartilage chip pop out of his knee joint. Cortez frowned.

"You ought to get that damn hinge worked on, breed. You limp around like an old man."

Cider carried his coffee cup toward the front door. A pay phone hung on a thin post that divided the door and the cafe's plate-glass window. He called Dallas and got the cop who gave him the Burch backgrounder.

"Goodson, Wendell Jackson, a/k/a 'Hooter.' DOB 2/13/47. Con. How's he hook up to Burch?"

"Shit, son. That's his cousin."

"Burch got a lot of family?"

"His mama and daddy are dead. So's an older brother. Got some cousins scattered around, mostly up here. And his ex-wives. Two or three of them. One's a real-estate agent in North Dallas. That's the first one, the one what broke his heart. Ran off with some Jew-boy weightlifter. Burch hates her a whole lot."

"What about the others?"

"Only one I can remember is the last one. Juanita. Can't place her last name. A real hellraiser. Played pool, liked to fish. Artsy type, though. Sculpture or something like it. Left him for some guitar player down Austin way."

"Can you get me a last name and a place? And anything on the others, if there are any?"

"You bet. Gimme a half hour."

Cider walked back to the table. Cortez was frowning at the check, trying to figure out a tip.

"Have another cup of coffee, beaner. We're gonna wait."

"Good thing. I gotta take a shit."

"That'll take just about the right amount of time."

Cider added more golden leaf to the juicy chaw he was already working. Words wormed around his brain -- loner, semi-loser, dogged, grim. An ex-cop on the run. A killer.

Where do you go for help?

So far, family. The only family Burch has left -- cousins. Are ex-wives family? Cider's gut told him ex-wives might be a good bet. There was a certain low-level caginess to it -- what cop would look for another cop at the home of an ex-wife? Almost all of them had one or three and there would be a certain unconscious bias against looking that way.

The redneck in the back of his mind nodded, working up another stream of Redman. *Now you talkin'.* A thick dollop of brown hit the dust. *Forget that medicine man stuff.*

Guess again, Daddy Popdick. Guess where this idea came from? Where?

Staring at the eyes of Ed Earl Burch's personnel jacket photo.
Shit, boy -- you sorry and beyond all hope.

Cider chuckled to himself and looked around the cafe. Behind the counter, just above the zinc-topped portal where the short-order cook slapped up plates of eggs, *chorizo* and tortillas, hung the heads of four, well-racked bucks.

One buck had sunglasses. Another had a bandana around its neck and a Rangers' cap perched above its horns. A fifth trophy sat in the middle of the horns and mangy fur -- a doe's hindquarters, tail pointing toward the ceiling and a red, cardboard arrow pointing toward the anus. A white sign was taped below the arrow -- File All Complaints Here.

Ten more minutes passed. Then it was fifteen. Cortez came back to the table, mopping his face with a folded paper towel. He waved at the waitress, pointing one finger at his coffee cup. Cider spat out some tobacco juice as she walked up with the pot.

"Tell him how disgustin' that is."

"Hon, I don't tell customers their bidness, no matter how bad it makes them look."

"See, I told you."

"Besides, you two are still here and haven't left a tip yet."

She was past forty, but could still turn a man's head, with flaming red hair that gave unavoidable testimony to the horrible wonders of chemistry and a chest that caused the top four buttons of her blouse to strain. Her eyes were green and full of carnal fun. Her legs and thighs were well-muscled and filled the cowboy cut Wranglers she wore over scuffed boots with cracked leather. Cortez eyed her.

"You best take care of your other customers. This one's gettin' set to ask you out."

She shot Cortez a cool look and placed a hand on Cider's shoulder.

"He'd be kinda cute -- if he had your hair."

She flicked a fingernail, long and blood red, at the lank, black locks that fell over his collar.

"Now, if you was to ask, a girl could like that."

From the counter came a gruff voice.

"Maxene -- move your ass and stop hustlin'."

"Kiss it, slick. I'm tryin' to get a date."

"You got orders up."

"They ain't goin' nowhere."

Cider laughed and arched an eyebrow.

"How's Saturday? If I'm back in town by then."

She whipped a pen out of her apron and wrote a number on a napkin, leaning close, giving Cider a good glance at her cleavage and a good whiff of perfume with the strong hint of sandalwood.

"Maxene!"

"Movin' it, boss. Call me Saturday, sugar."

"You don't even know my name."

"Don't need to now. You'll tell me later."

Cider laughed again and shook his head as Maxene gave him a languid, walkaway show that featured swinging hips and a muscular ass. Body of a horsewoman was Cider's guess. Cortez glared at him. Cider ignored him and walked up to the pay phone.

"Two more exes and one long-time squeeze. One of the exes lives up here, same as the first one I told you about. Cross them off your list. Now, the squeeze and the third ex are possibles -- both live down your way. I remember the squeeze now -- hot little Chicana that used to tend bar up here. Just about as bad an attitude as the first ex, more than a little semi-wild. Both of 'em used to lead our boy around by the cock, then dumped him flat."

"What about the third ex?"

"The one I told you about. Juanita Schmidt."

"Smith?"

"No, Schmidt. Hill Country German. Lives down there now. Place called Mason."

"S-C-H-M-I-D-T, Juanita? Mason, Texas?"

"You got it -- five-six, 130, DOB 2/5/51. And get this, she makes earrings and shit from the bones of dead animals. Road kill. It's the wildest damn thing I ever did hear. Can you feature it -- some snooty

New York woman payin' big bucks to have armadillo bones hanging from her ears?"

"Everybody's gotta have a gimmick. Girlfriend?"

"Lessee -- lives in Uvalde. Aguirre, Ana Patrice. Five-three, 110, DOB 3/20/62."

"They both dumped him, huh? So I guess he don't feel too charitable toward either one."

"No sir. Way I see it, it's pick 'em -- our boy probably hates 'em both and no tellin' if either one would let him in out of the rain."

He spelled back both names, hung up. Cortez stepped up, mopping sweat off his brow with a paper napkin, leaving small curls of paper on his forehead.

"What's the deal?"

"A squeeze and an ex. One in the Hill Country, the other in Uvalde. Both dumped Burch. Which would you go see?"

"The one I'm payin' alimony to. She owes me."

"Not this ex -- she's married to somebody else."

"Then I'd pick the squeeze."

"Uvalde it is, then. Let's see if the boss man will spring for a quick flight to San Antonio."

"Hell, it's only a four-hour hump. We'd be there before supper."

"Still got to call the man."

Cider picked up the phone again and glanced across the street where a large black man in a white shirt sat in a parking lot, looking like he was waiting for someone to come out of the grocery store.

Cider couldn't see the plug in the black man's ear. And he couldn't see the pinpoint of laser light that hit the plate glass of the cafe and picked up every word uttered within five feet of the pay phone.

By the time he hung up, the black man was blocks away, winding a burgundy '78 Eldorado flat out toward Hobby Airport, a satellite phone pulled from the side pocket of those black fatigues and the speed dial ripping through the numbers of a Mexican exchange.

A chopper to Uvalde. A visit from the Badhair.

CHAPTER 19

Her leg hit the nightstand, sending the lamp flying and shooting long, jerking shadows onto the opposite wall. Her heels spurred his kidneys. Her nails raked his back. Her fingers held the shaggy curls near his neck in a death grip, pulling his face to hers. She bit his tongue.

"Dammit, you drew blood!"

"Shut up and give it to me."

He started slamming her harder. She pitched her head back and gripped his ass cheeks with both hands, nails and fingers digging and kneading. Each thrust brought them closer to the edge of the bed. He tried to drag them both back to the center of the mattress. She kept pulling him forward.

Sweat kept them stuck belly to belly as they crashed onto the floor. He felt sharp pain stab through both knees and shoot down to the heel of his bad leg. She braced herself on one elbow and pushed him back. He slipped out of her with a loud, sloppy plop and fell to one side, sweeping boots, jeans, panties, spurs, a lariat, a bridle and a saddle blanket out of the way with a forearm.

He drug a throw rug and a saddle toward him, sliding the rug under his ass and leaning his back into the curving side of the saddle. She grabbed the back of his hair again, crushing his lips with a killing kiss, stabbing his mouth with her tongue as she gripped his cock and hoisted herself up, over and down on his hardness.

She rode him rough, hands pushing down on his chest, hauling her hips and ass into the air, holding there for one second, two seconds, three, then slamming down with a loud grunt, filling the small, dark room with the sound and smell of sex and two sweaty bodies.

He could see the wet gleam that ran from her face, down and over her upturned breasts. His hands gripped her wide hips, feeling the muscles of long hours on horseback, helping her movements, guiding her lightly as she lost herself in the rhythm, watching as she started to grin.

"What's funny?"

"Not a damn thing, so shut up."

She sprung up, breaking his grip and grabbing the pommel, yanking the saddle out from under him. He saw a white flash when his head smacked the bedpost.

"Dammit, you always got to make sex a contact sport."

"You gonna get your old ass up off the floor and fuck me or do I have to call the hired help in here?"

He looked up at the bed. She was in the middle of the tangled sheets, on her knees, sprawled across the saddle, her ass high in the air, her face turned back over her shoulder, waiting for him.

"You talk too damn much."

"Give it to me, old man."

"Where's your husband, Juanita?"

"Well he sure ain't here, is he?"

CHAPTER 20

S he could hear them banging and grunting in the back bedroom. In the dark, the high ceilings and solid walls guided the sound to the parlor and her place on an old-timey, overstuffed couch, where she was wide awake under a scratchy Indian blanket, listening to the sex sounds of relative strangers, smoking in the dark, watching the stars wink above the Hill Country ridgeline that cut through the moonlight above the rooftops and steeples of downtown Mason.

Which was an overstatement. Mason was one of those dying market towns that used to draw its life from the ranches and farms trying to make a go of it in the scrubby, rock-strewn land between the Llano and San Saba rivers. From her perch in the pepperbox parlor, she could see more of the Hill Country's deception -- the modest skyline that rose from the narrow valley looked like a postcard of some little town in Germany or Switzerland.

From a distance, it was easy to see why those land-hungry Germans settled in country like this at the dawn of the 1800s. From a distance, it must have looked like home. Up close, as always, it was a different story -- heat from the hand of an angry god who looked to be keeping his promise to never again wash away the sins of man with a flood, death from savages who gave no quarter, expected none and took anything they pleased.

But there was a flintiness that bolstered the distant beauty of this country, one that struck a chord with Carla Sue's mountain ancestry.

It was land she could live in, if living was in the cards. She took a deep drag on one of Burch's Luckies, taking the smoke way down, listening to crickets, watching the star-pocked sky for nothing in particular.

The couch ran across the open end of the hexagonal pepperbox, each wall dominated by a high window that ran almost from floor to ceiling, making the parlor a breezy place in the night heat, the coolest spot in this old house with the wrap-around porch and the graying, gingerbread trim.

A slow-turning ceiling fan stirred the air. She tried to imagine living here in the 1860s, with no air conditioning and the Kiowas or Comanches a threat to sweep down from the Brady Mountains, a Sharps carbine and a blackpowder Colt Dragoon at her side instead of the blue semi-automatic with the Pachmayr grips.

Close to the house, peeking around a porch post, was the dark, grinning grillwork of a `65 Chevy pickup, dog-turd brown, powered by a 350 cubic-inch engine with a four-bolt main, a four-barreled Holley carb and a four-speed transmission with a Hurst shifter. The rusted-out bed had been replaced by diamond-patterned steel plate, the kind used for the decking of a boiler room. The front window had a long crack running from the passenger side to the middle of the glass.

Carla Sue picked it up on the outskirts of Ballinger, at Bucky Roy's King of the Road used car lot. You Like It, You Buy It -- And I Tote the Note! Bucky Roy himself hustled her, cutting a chunk of Bull Of The Woods plug and working up a thick stream of juice to torment the dust of his lot while he made his pitch. She could tell because he wore a stained Resistol straw that had `Bucky Roy' branded on the crown.

"Lemme tell ya little lady, this ol' pick-em-up will flat pick-em-up. Ol' boy who owned it put ever'thang in her -- tach, four-barrel, Impala drivetrain and chassis. Ever'thang `cept a wet bar `an a bed."

Spuh-lattt! She backed up. The juice looked like it was headed for her boots.

"Course it mighta saved ol' Chester some trouble if he had put a bar in the damn thing. Might notta got killed in that knife fight down Junction way. His mama asked me to sell it for her -- Miss Kate."

Spuh-latt! She stood her ground, flinching only slightly.

"Strong woman. Has to be to see her only boy killed like he was an' her husband, Mr. Sam, dead and gone. She don't want much for it, see -- just a grand and a half. It'll help cover Chester's funeral costs."

Spuh-lattt! She shot him a cold look.

"Now, I tol' her she could get more than a deuce for somethin' this fine, but Miss Kate put her foot down. Not a penny more than a grand and a half -- don't want people thinkin' she'd try to make a dime off her boy's death."

"Will it haul a stock trailer?"

"Why, shore."

Spuh-latt! She ignored the jet of juice.

"Got a hitch an' ever'thang. You wouldn't be haulin' more than one or two mounts, right?"

Spuh-latt!

"You rodeo doncha? Barrel-racer, I bet. Seen you over at Fort Stockton. Knew I had. Back in May. You was ridin' that deep-chested buckskin. Fine damn piece of horseflesh, you don't mind me sayin'."

She smiled.

Spuh-latt!

"This'd be nigh perfect. Couldn't ask for a better rig. An' Chester and Miss Kate'd be proud to know it's goin' to a rodeo gal."

"Crank it."

The engine sounded rich and smooth, like the Cutlass, its power coursing through dual exhausts, well-muffled. She ran the RPMs up, then double-clutched it out of the lot for a quick spin around the block, listening for rattles, pings and other telltales of a dud engine. On a sidestreet, she slammed on the brakes with her hands off the wheel -- no pull.

She wheeled back into the lot, stopping next to Bucky Roy, climbing out of the cab.

"Eight."

"Little lady, this thing rides better than your horse. I couldn't let it go for less than what Miss Kate is askin'. I couldn't look that woman in the eye on the street. Engine's worth that much alone."

"Yeah, but that engine needs a tuneup for sure -- timin's off. And look at that damn windshield -- that's three, easy. Unless I don't care about drivin' down the road one day and gettin' a lapful of safety glass at eighty miles an hour."

"It looks bad, but that crack will hold. Nothin' that will keep you from usin' that truck right away. Shoot, you'll get that fixed out of your next winnin's and have a rig that'll be the envy of ever' ranch hand between here and Fort Stockton."

"There's still the tuneup. The steerin's loose and the front end's got some shimmy. That's another couple of hundred."

Spuh-latt!

"Naw, now. That engine's tighter'n a tick, little lady. And the rest -- well, this is a truck, not a see-dan. You know that. Shore you do. You're just tryin' to pull ol' Bucky Roy's leg, ain'tcha?"

"I don't want to pull your leg, mister. I'd kinda like to buy me a truck. This one, if I can get the price right. Another, if I can't. Nine."

Spuh-latt!

"Now, you're talkin' much better, but not good enough. I c'ain't come down lower than a grand and three. I gotta live in this town and folks wouldn't take it too kindly if I didn't look out for Miss Kate. She taught second grade to just about ever'body in this town. Great God in the mornin', you understand that, don'tcha?"

"Mister, I understand I'm done dickerin' with you."

Carla Sue peeled off ten hundred-dollar bills.

"Do the deal. Do up the papers. I'll be back after I gas her up."

She handed him a sheet of paper with a name, a Social Security number and a rural route scrawled on it. For Fort Stockton. Sometimes you get lucky.

"You got insurance? Them state boys will want me to have a policy number. If you don't, no nevermind, I can sell you a liability policy. Cost you two Franklins. Best damn deal in Runnels County. None better."

Spuh-latt!

She peeled off two more hundreds.

"That'd be fine. Write me up."

"Yew bet."

Smoking in the dark, she laughed at the memory of ol' Bucky Roy, tobacco chewer, dust tormentor, truck-hustlin' fool. He enjoyed the dickering. So did she, except for those dark, brown streams of punctuation that seemed to land closer to her boots than his. Every time.

She met Big 'Un at a roadside park just north of Sonora and I-10, the type of place that had two, count 'em, two picnic tables with molded concrete legs and a stone slab top, a raked pebble yard and trash cans chained to solitary concrete posts. He had dumped the Monaco behind a boarded-up service station and had swiped a license tag from god-knows-where.

They made it to Juanita's just after dark.

The back bedroom grew quiet -- low voices, a laugh or two, then silence. Two hours had been enough. At least, for one of them. Big 'Un, probably. His face had been pale with pain and lack of sleep since they left the Ross ranch. Getting thrown down two or three times by an ex-wife probably didn't help the ol' boy, no matter how wet it got his wick.

The ex didn't like her looks worth a damn, that much was certain. When they walked through the door, she lamped Carla Sue with sharp, angry eyes, deep-green lasers, framed by an unruly sweep of long, jet-black curls, set in a windburned face with high cheekbones and creases and lines that pointed to the onset of middle age.

There was a hardness settling along her jawline, turning rough beauty that once reveled in wildness and laughter into something edgy and cutting, ready to make someone pay for the fact she was now only passing handsome and didn't like her life very much. Most likely, the man unlucky enough to get close.

Poor Big 'Un. Overmatched from the get-go with that one. Good sex the only tradeoff. But only at her beck and call. A smart man would have seen that. Smarts weren't Big 'Un's long suit. And he got a sudden case of vapor lock on his smartass when the ex started in with the claws.

"Glad you decided to drop on by, Double E. Been a long time. But I don't know if we've got enough room for you two to shack up."

"Look, Juanita, it ain't that way..."

"Course it isn't. Never is until it is, is it? I think she's cute. A definite improvement on all your other girlfriends and exes. Maybe a little young, though. But you always did like to check the talent in the schoolyard. Didn't know you liked them this petite."

"Now cut the shit, J.S. I'm in a jam."

"Aw, let her puff and blow, Big 'Un. I'll just duck behind your coattails, stay out of the wind and wonder why it took you so long to file for divorce."

"Well, it speaks. Where's the pull string, Double E? Does Mattel give up-holler accents to all its talkin' dolls, now? Or just the wet-and-change models?"

"It speaks, it walks, it talks and it's been out of diapers a long time. The only thing it doesn't know how to do is keep the roots from showin' through the Clairol. You'll have to teach me some time."

"Oh, I like her, Eee Eee. Got a bite on her. And me takin' her for a piece of blonde fluff. You know how I feel about blondes, now matter how cuddly they look."

"Look, can we cut this fandango? I need your help and I need to know if you'll give it. If not, we've gotta get gone. Where's fast fingers?"

"Road gig. Gone two weeks."

Carla Sue heard a slight tightness hit the other woman's voice. Big 'Un did too and stepped over, cupping his ex-wife's elbow in one hand, gently leading her into the kitchen to talk. She heard him start to lay out their deal and turned to look at the artwork scattered around the parlor and dining room.

Kerosine lamps gave off flickering, yellow light, tagging an oily tang on the breeze stepping through the open windows. Her eye was drawn to the nearest wall, to a box about the size of a large birdhouse, hanging about head level with an open front and a peaked roof of tongue depressors painted black and white.

The walls of this little box were also made from tongue depressors, also painted an alternating white and black. Inside, was a diorama, of sorts -- the claws and legs of birds forming the base for figurines made from tiny, crossed bones. They stood around an altar formed from the ribcage of a squirrel or rat.

Behind them, a figurine sat at the keyboard of a tiny organ, its pipes the fine bones of birds. The organ player had the body of a robin and the head of a rattler. A cross of bone stretched across the back wall of the box, bleached white on flat black.

Scattered across a nearby table was the jewelry that made Juanita Schmidt faddishly famous, worth a blurb in Esquire and a short feature in People. She picked up a pair of earrings made from rattler and armadillo vertebrae. The bleached armadillo bones reminded her of that worn X-wing fighter Luke Skywalker flew in *Star Wars*.

She held the earrings up to the lobes of her ears as she looked at herself in a small wall mirror. She twirled them and let them dangle. Oh, yea-yus. Stylish. Then she looked at a price tag that reminded her why she was glad to be born a Southerner -- two hundred bucks.

Another child o' Dixie exercising the birthright of carney barkers, chicken thieves, dude ranch owners and television evangelists. It had something to do with the war -- the Yankees may have won it, but we'uns hammered out the right to rip them off. In perpetuity.

It was a tradeoff, written in blood. Payback for Shiloh, Sherman's March and all those goddam carpetbaggers. And George Steinbrenner. She couldn't stand that paunchy blowhard, his cigars or his Bronx Bombers. Gave baseball a bad name. Not that she gave much of a damn about baseball, but when Carla Sue's eye was caught by something that stuck in her craw, lack of knowledge or interest in the field never stopped her from working up a full-blown, bile-speckled opinion.

And in her opinion, George Steinbrenner deserved the stern weight of Islamic law -- public castration. Without ether. Followed by an inning on the mound against the Texas Rangers.

She heard Juanita's loud voice in the kitchen -- "Well, Eee Eee, are you playin' hide the hot dog with her?" There were tears, anger and pain in that voice. She heard Big 'Un's mumbling reply. Then the bedroom door slammed and she started her lonely vigil on the couch.

Carla Sue couldn't sleep, but it wasn't the sound of sex keeping her awake. It was her own memory -- the roar of Eldon's shotgun, the sight of her uncle, splattered across his eggs and coffee like pulp from a grapefruit, the look on Neville Ross's face, his hair smoking and his shirt on fire, as she pumped out those rounds that slammed him onto the tile.

She had waited four years for this, sleeping with Ross, running errands for him and the dicey double-cross for her. His chest hair was white and ghostly against the tan of his skin. He was old, but the ways of a pimp were still alive. He knew how to seduce a woman and make her feel like a goddess in bed. And he still had staying power, enough for two or three rounds in the night.

Afterwards, he would stroke her pussy and pubic hair and murmur, "*Mi gringa querida.*" She got to where she could even fake liking that.

She could have killed Ross many times in those four years but wanted to wait until she had a sizeable nest egg built up and a chance to nail both Ross and T-Roy. The Burch ploy looked promising -- stay close, look for an opening and play it.

But the raid on the *rancho* scotched that plan. She was afraid one of T-Roy's Rambos would ice Ross, cheating her of the chance to do it herself. She also had no faith in T-Roy; he'd whack her just for being Ross's lover and a double-crosser. So she took the shot and watched Ross die.

Carla Sue lit another Lucky and heard the bedroom door open and bare feet slap down the hallway. It was Juanita, wildhaired and wrapped in a thin kimono, black Japanese letters on white cotton.

She took the Lucky from Carla Sue's hand and took a deep drag before grabbing a bentwood chair and straddling it backwards.

"He's asleep. Listen at him snore. Like a hog snortin'."

"He needs it. It's been hard the last two days."

"You two in a lot of trouble?"

"You don't want to know."

"Yeah, I do. He meant something to me once. Still does. I don't think you ever lose that for someone, even when things go bad. You just bury it someplace and move on."

"Is that what happened, things went bad?"

"Yeah. He lost his fire for life. When I first met Ed Earl Burch, I thought he was the funniest, most hard-bitten man I'd ever seen. He was battered and knocked around, but he still cared about friends and good whiskey and having a good time and not letting those bastards squeeze him into a box.

"He seemed bigger than life and wiser than God. At least, I wanted him to be. But the closer I got, the more I realized he was just going through the motions. He was hollow inside. It was like he knew he ought to care about his friends and not let life eat him up, but it already had. He was such a good storyteller and went through the motions so well that I didn't catch on until after we got hitched."

"Sounds like what little I know about him. Seems like a guy who wants to be left alone but wants to do the right thing."

"Yeah, that's the shitty part. Wanting to do right ain't enough. And when I figured out he wanted to do right by me but was just going through the motions, I left. For ol' fast fingers."

"Who? Oh, the guitar player. He's long gone, ain't he?"

"Sure is. One of life's bitter little boomerangs. He finally figured out I was just goin' through the motions with him."

"How long?"

"About three months. Just long enough to get so horny that an ex-husband looks like Tom Selleck, even if he is bald, walks with a limp and drags some blonde cutie along with him to your front door."

Carla Sue laughed, then coughed up some smoke from the Lucky. Juanita grinned, stood up and stretched.

"I need a drink. Bourbon do you?"

"Be fine."

Juanita ambled into the kitchen and came back with a bottle of Wild Turkey and two juice glasses. She put three fingers of brown liquor in each. They tilted their drinks and Juanita eyed Carla Sue with an arched eyebrow.

"Are you sleepin' with ol' handsome in there?"

"No."

"Well, somethin's put the fire back in him. I couldn't hardly keep up and he's got this look in his eye that I haven't seen in a hellish long time."

"I think he wants to kill somebody."

"Who?"

"The same somebody I do."

CHAPTER 21

Drowsy with sleep, Ana Patrice Aguirre traced the muscular back of her boyfriend of the moment, her fingers lingering on a jagged knife scar just above his left kidney. It puckered as he leaned forward to pull on his boots.

Her ears still rang from a night tending bar at The Silver Concho, a cowboy club with cheap beer, thick smoke and loud, loud live music from Curry Slick and the New Delhi El Dorados. She was vaguely horny and reached toward his belt buckle, tugging with one hand as she rose up on her knees to press her breasts into his back.

"C'mon back here, lover. It's early. You don't have to go nowhere yet."

She nibbled on his neck, nosing her way underneath long shanks of straight black hair.

"It's afternoon. I gotta open and work happy hour."

His tone was hard and flat. She tried to change his mood by dragging her fingernails along his crotch, scratching lightly on the surface of the denim. She arched her back, brushing her nipples against his shoulder blades.

"C'mon, Luis. That bar'll still be there when we're through."

He shrugged her off with a sudden roll of his shoulders, knocking her off balance and sprawling across the sheets.

"*Pendejo!* I'm trying to give you a little action before you go trudging off to work and you knock me over. What the fuck is that?"

"I told you I have to go."

"And I told you I want you back in bed, doin' your duty."

He was putting on his shirt -- shiny grey with silvery mock-pearl speed snaps. She was on her knees in the middle of the bed, left hand on hip, right hand wagging a finger at him. He stepped to the side of the bed and swept her to him with one arm, kissing her hard then breaking away with a slap on her ass.

"Gotta beat feet, lover."

"Yeah, yeah -- just like a man. Get what you want then get gone."

He winked at her and picked up his straw Resistol with the quarterhorse crease and the rattlesnake band, smoothing his hair with one hand and settling the hat on his head with the other.

"*Adios, tragona.*"

"You call me a glutton, *cabron?*"

"*Sí,* baby. My kind of glutton. A glutton for sex. You're voracious."

She threw a pillow at him as he ducked through the door. The front door slammed and she heard his pickup crank, the engine exhaust snorting through the twin glass packs as he accelerated down the street.

Her ears were still ringing as she padded across the floor, pulling on a black San Antonio Gunslingers jersey, heading for the small bathroom that sat just outside the door -- a pee and a dose of headache powder on her mind.

Gunning the mix of powder and tap water like one of last night's shooters, she checked herself in the full length mirror that hung on the back of the door. Not bad -- jet black hair that was as straight as a Chinese girl's, thin lips with a haughty curl to them, a nose that was slightly too wide and flat, muscular dancer's legs that flashed underneath the tail of the jersey.

Still got the goods, girl, she thought.

Wandering back into the bedroom, she glanced at the clock radio and saw she had three hours to go before work. She climbed back in bed and started leafing through an old copy of *People,* the one that featured randy Prince Andy and his fling with Koo Stark, the soft-porn starlet.

Sleep drifted over her, pulling her into a gauzy dream of the prince and the porn star making love in her bed and drawing her into a slow-moving threesome. She saw the prince poised above her, smiling and rolling a condom onto the royal cock. Then Koo, offering a breast to her mouth. Then Luis, popping his pearl snaps and shucking his boots, getting ready to take his turn.

Something hard slipped inside her and she moved her hips in sleep. In her dreams, it was Andy, still smiling, but wearing a white airman's helmet. Andy became Luis, still wearing his hat, grinning and leaning down to talk dirty in her ear.

"Wake up, *chiquita*. Wake on up. You dead if you don' wake up."

That wasn't the voice of Luis. In her dreams, Luis was still inside her. But that voice belonged to somebody else. In her dreams, Luis was reaching for her breasts, tweaking her nipples the way she liked.

A huge hand clamped around her throat. Her eyes flew open to the face of a large, ugly black man, sweat popping from his jowls and forehead, eyes bulging and angry. And a high voice trying to whisper, sounding like a steam pipe popping pressure.

"Don' move, don' say nothin'. You dead if you do."

She bucked and lashed out with a free arm but found it had all the impact of smacking a sedan with a piece of bamboo. The hand on her throat got tighter. And the hardness inside her wasn't a dream, it was the fingers of his other hand, stretching her painfully.

"You liked that while you was sleepin'. Dreamin' 'bout that cock that just lef'? Well, he gone now and Mr. Badhair is here. Let's see what you got."

The hand left her throat and ripped the jersey with one pull. She coughed and tried to gulp in air. He smiled as he looked at her breasts, brown against the ripped black fabric.

"Hmmm, yeah. Nice. So very nice."

She was breathing now. She was angry.

"Go ahead, motherfucker, do what you're gonna do."

She tried to claw his face. The hand clamped back on her throat, the fingers burrowed deeper inside, causing her to cry out. He leaned into her face. She could smell sour sweat and breath that stank of coffee and stale cigarettes.

"Oh no, baby. Mr. Badhair ain't here to rape your *puta* ass. I ain't got time for that. I'm here to get some information out of you. I'm here to find out if you seen your ol' boyfrien' lately. You know -- Ed Earl Burch. Your squeeze up in Dallas."

She couldn't speak. She shook her head back and forth.

"I cain't hear you."

The fingers rammed her again. She gasped through the pain.

"Ain't seen him in four years."

A raspy breath.

"Don't know where he is."

"He call you?"

She shook her head.

"Any of his friends call you?"

She shook her head.

"I want to believe you, baby. I truly do. But I gotta be sure."

He grabbed her right hand, wrapping his fingers around her pinky.

"This gonna hurt. One more time -- you seen Burch?"

Her eyes shifted from his face to her finger and back to his face. She shook her head then stared at him because she couldn't watch what he was about to do. She clenched her jaw and felt him start to bend her finger back. She stared.

His head snapped to one side. He bellowed like a freshly castrated steer. Something black and furry slapped her in the face. She clawed it away from her eyes -- a toupee, she hadn't noticed that. She heard the dull thwack of wood on flesh and bone, and felt him fall away from her. She was yanked from the bed.

"Get the hell out of here."

Luis pushed her toward the bedroom door. She stumbled and glanced over her shoulder. The black man was crouched on the floor, but rising with a gun in his hand. Luis was stepping forward, swinging a baseball bat. He chopped at the gun hand, knocking a Colt semi-auto to the floor.

She backed into the hallway and saw the black man body slam Luis into the bedroom wall. Luis bounced off and lunged forward, slamming shoulder into midsection. The black man slapped Luis aside with a huge forearm, sending him sprawling into the hall. He grabbed Luis and pulled him up like a sack of dog food, running him head first into the bathroom.

He grabbed Luis by the hair and slammed his head into the hard, white porcelain of the toilet bowl. She could hear his skull smack the hard stone -- one, two, three, four times. The fifth time broke the bowl and sent water gushing onto the tile.

She ran for the door and didn't stop until she was at her uncle's house, ten blocks away. By that time, Badhair was headed for the outskirts of town, pointed west-northwest toward the Hill Country, stomping on the accelerator of a borrowed, black Olds 88, 70s vintage.

Four hours later, Cortez and Cider pulled up next to five cop cars and a meat wagon. Ana Patrice Aguirre was in a bathrobe on the front porch, curled up in her uncle's arms, rocking back and forth.

"Better call ahead for some law, rainmaker. I wouldn't give two shits for anybody who used to sleep with this *pendejo*."

"You're still so damn sure it's Burch."

"Who else? And it really don't matter 'cause whoever it is, he's riding the same trail we are. Only he's ahead of us."

"Make the goddam call. Get the sheriff there to hold the ex till we hit town. Tell him we'll be rollin' his way real soon."

Cider stepped up on the porch. He leaned down and looked into the young woman's eyes.

"Was Burch here?"

No answer. Her eyes were blank.

All she saw was angry eyes and a grimacing black face. All she heard was the sound of a lover's skull hitting the rim of a toilet bowl. Again and again.

CHAPTER 22

They left before dawn, running along the edge of town, keeping on the back roads until the lights of Mason, few and weak, were out of sight, then picking up a farm-to-market that headed north and west, toward Hext.

As he drove, he could see Juanita standing on her porch in the dark, wrapped in that thin kimono. He gave her the Bulldog and the only speed loader he had left, urging her to buy a box of .44s and stay with friends. She shook her head.

"Guns are your thing, Eee Eee. Not mine. And this place is all I have left in the world. This and what's left of daddy's ranch. Y'all head out there. All that's left is that double wide. Had some college boys out there, studyin' the bat cave not too long back, so it should have some canned stuff still. All you need is some milk, eggs and bread."

She wrapped her arms around her ex-husband's neck, pulling him to her so hard that he staggered. She hugged him fiercely, burying her face into his neck, then whispering into his ear.

"You take good care of yourself, fat boy, and come back and see me. Last night was a downpayment. I'll lie to the law dogs and whoever else comes knockin' on the door."

"Likely, it'll be law. But I want you down the road in case it ain't. These boys won't be playin' footsie and won't care about hurtin' you to get to me. I don't want to have to worry about that."

"I'll think about it."

"Don't think. For once in your damn life, do somethin' someone tells you to and quit lookin' it in the mouth for false teeth. Goddam, you're like a mule from hell."

"Yeah, but you had fun ridin' this mule, didn't you?"

"You know I did. But will you do me just one more favor that has nothin' to do with bumpin' uglies? Will you get the hell over to a friend's house for a few days? At least until we get set up and gone? You can't tell me you don't have an ex-boyfriend stashed around here someplace."

She leaned back in his arms and arched an eyebrow.

"Not funny, Eee Eee. Not even from you. Now get the hell gone. I'll do the same. I've got a girlfriend or two stashed around here someplace."

She stuck her tongue in his ear and stroked the front of his jeans until she could grip some hardness.

"You take care of ol' John Henry here. And that girl. I kinda like her now."

"Her? She takes care of herself and me. That's our deal. Now, cut it out or I'll have to drape you across that saddle again."

He grinned at the memory and scratched a place on his neck where Juanita had gnawed up a hickie. Carla Sue caught the grin and deadpanned disgust.

"Shit, Big 'Un, we'll have to get you a rabies shot, now. And somethin' to wipe off the grin -- you'll catch a mouthful of flies if you don't close her up."

"Uh-huh."

"Jee-zus. We're gonna have to get your ashes hauled more often. Makes you real agreeable. What's the plan -- shoot on down to the border from here? We could make Del Rio in about four hours."

"Nah, we can't cowboy it. They'll be lookin' for us at all the crossings, even with this new rig. We need to set it up, and to do that we need to lay low for a day or so."

"What you got in mind?"

"Old boy I know runs a crop dustin' service down near Mercedes. Dabbles in some contraband now and again. He could get us across."

"How do you know him?"

"Did some divorce work for him a few years back. Took some snaps that saved some of his money from the stovette he was dumping."

"*Flagrante delicto*, I take it."

"You bet. A lawyer up my way, a deputy sheriff down her way, a few others in between. Bonus for your boy here."

"Glad to see you love your job. Why don't we just blow on down to Mercedes? That's where they make those boots, isn't it?"

"What are you, some damn snowbird *tourista?* Hell, yes they make a boot down there -- damn good one, too. But that'll have to keep until your next kill-a-scumbag tour."

"Glad to see you got your smartass back. Thought Juanita might've snipped it off at the roots. Look, slick, I gotta tell you I don't like sittin' round someplace so you can drag some other somebody I don't know in on our deal. Bad enough we got one of your ex-wives in on it."

"I got her to get gone."

"You don't get it, do you? We got a real small window to hit gettin' across the border before some law grabs us or one of T-Roy's special friends decides we'd look better with a shitload of lead in our hides. Now, why don't we just get the hell down that way and over the river?"

"I get it fine. You want over the river real quiet like so T-Roy's watchers won't be alerted, you get a pro to slip you across. You don't sashay down there and boom across the International Bridge. Might as well send the sumbitch a postcard."

"Well, who the fuck is this Mercedes guy besides a pilot? Would he fly us across?"

"Maybe. Whatever's best."

"That still don't tell me who he is."

"Fella named Lefty. Old enough to be your grandad. Flew bombers in the big war, the one you read about in all them history books up in North Dallas. Flies crop dusters on this side of the river, some under-the-radar runs from the other side. Ain't been caught yet. Doubt he ever will be."

"You speak highly of him, but hero worship don't cut much with me when my ass is on the line. Just why in god's name should I trust this flyboy? He lives down on the border. He flies dope. What keeps him from sellin' our asses to T-Roy himself?"

"One thing."

"What?"

Burch tapped a Lucky out of a fresh pack, fired it with his Zippo and closed the lid with a sharp, short snap.

"What, dammit?"

"Wynn Moore -- Lefty's his brother."

"Who's Wynn Moore?"

"Pretty dumb question from a white girl who pulled a Colt on me one time."

CHAPTER 23

The doublewide was set on the lee side of a hill, rusty and dented, with the limbs of cottonwoods tangled around all sides but the front, where a dusty yard opened on one side of the dirt and gravel road that struggled up a steep grade after crossing a broad, rocky wash.

From a small, screened-in deck off the front door, you could see the wash -- a thin sheet now, a muddy torrent in spring -- and where the road climbed out of the water, across and over the next hill, back down the long and winding twenty miles to the nearest crossroads that had gall enough to call itself a town.

Twenty yards above the trailer, the gravel ran out and the road became a narrow trail with high cut banks, thigh-deep gullies and shifting soil. It was slow going, but the only way to get to the low-slung opening of a cave with thousands of whirring winged bodies and the strong and constant smell of urine.

Burch first came here with Juanita, just before her daddy died and lost most of the ranch, except for the hundred acres where the trailer sat, about a quarter mile away from the sixth-largest bat cave in the world. In spring, when the bat pups were just learning to fly, it was a wild place to visit.

The young bats were perfecting their flying skills and just learning how to use their sonar. They weren't very graceful and their avoidance system just wasn't up to the level of their parents, even in daylight. As often as not, they would slam into a visitor and tumble to the floor, stunned but quick to recover.

Above your head was a brown and pulsing mass of bats, the adults clinging to the pocked rock roof, the pups clinging to the parents. If you got real close, mom or pop would lean toward you and open their mouths in a silent scream, their eyes red and malevolent. You heard no sound, but their sonar was giving them the azimuth and range of your intrusion.

To walk into the cave you had to wear Wellingtons and a respirator, the kind painters use when spraying coats of candy-apple lacquer on a car. Tons of guano spilled across the floor of the cave in huge and shifting dunes that looked like brown sugar and smelled like the lining of every urinal between here and Grand Central Station.

Saying the smell was vile was missing two-thirds of the point of these mounds of bat shit. Crunchy underfoot, the guano dunes made a respirator a complete necessity because the urine fumes were concentrated enough to instantly sear the lungs of anyone who didn't wear one.

And if that didn't get the bare-lunged visitor, the rich amount of airborne fungi that thrived in the cave would. Juanita told him of a professor studying the bats one summer: he set up a video camera in the cave, came out and stripped off his boots and respirator, then saw that he forgot to connect a cable to the camera. He ducked back in without his respirator. He spent the next six weeks in the hospital with inflamed lungs and nasal passages and a fungal infection that nearly killed him.

You wore old clothes when visiting the cave, duds you didn't care about because the fumes would penetrate every fiber and refuse to come out after repeated washings. You washed yourself with strong lye soap and shampooed your hair two or three times to get out the smell.

Juanita did all this once or twice a week. Not to see the bats. They were an interesting sideshow that always held her attention. But her main interest was in the flesh-eating beetles that prowled through the brown piles of guano, swarming over the halt and the lame that fell from the ceilings.

She brought road kill to the cave -- squirrels, armadillos, snakes, even the occasional cow or horse carcass left by a rancher who lost some stock and knew of her artistic needs. She put the carcasses in a small pen with a locked top. There, the beetles would strip flesh from bone, leaving only gristle and the need to use a wire brush and some Clorox.

Then she worked the magic that made her a minor celebrity -- wiring snake vertebrae to the bones of an armadillo tail, making a chair out of the leg bones of a deer and a cow, making a lamp from the skull of a horse and the thigh bone of a steer.

Folk art, she called it. Gruesome bullshit was his call. But then again, she started this routine after she left him. So it wasn't his problem and damn little of his business. And like somebody once said, everybody has to have a gimmick. Trust Juanita to find a truly twisted one.

"Sweet Jesus, Big `Un, she drags those carcasses in here?"

"You bet. Right to that pen over there."

"Man, whoever said this was fun?"

"She does it for art and profit, not fun. You saw the price tags."

"If she can get that kind of money for bones, imagine what she could do selling desert up around Phoenix. You ought to marry her again and set her on the right path."

"I don't think I can keep the pace anymore."

"She says different. She says you wore her out."

"She's kind."

"You know better."

They were standing near the entrance, pulling on rubber Wellingtons. A tall white-plastic bucket held a tangle of respirators; the college boys forgot to bring them back to the trailer before they left. There was rain water in the bottom of the bucket. Burch was surprised some night critters hadn't scooted off in the brush with such bounty.

Evening was coming on. Earlier that day, Burch drove the pickup to the nearest country store with a pay phone out front. He shot a call to Juanita's. No answer. Good. He contacted Lefty Moore.

Moore would pick them up the next night, out at a small dirt strip near Segovia, less than an hour south of where they were. An hour or so later, and they'd set down at another dirt strip near Ebanito on the Mex side of the line. Lefty kept a rickety sedan locked inside a battered shed down there for those times when he wanted to hell around some border bars and brothels.

They'd fly down in Lefty's Maule, a yowling, high-winged plane built in Moultrie, Georgia, and able to leap out of barns and shoeboxes and take to the air in the shortest of takeoff distances. It was the perfect plane for hedge-hopping and border dodging.

Ten grand gave them the ride and the car. Burch liked the fact he was setting all this up with money Carla Sue had siphoned from Ross and T-Roy. Clear skies were in the forecast. And a full moon. Which was good and bad.

On his way back, Burch kept doubling back on his track, looking for tails. He drove forty miles out of his way to check the roads on the other side of the cave and the trailer. After parking the pickup, he walked through the front door and scooted out the back of the doublewide, scooping up the submachine gun with one hand, tucking a spare clip in his belt with the other.

He crept through the brush until he topped the ridge where he could cross the trail without being seen from the road or the hill on the other side of the wash. Then he circled back to a high point in the brush where he could see the road, the trail, the cave and the roof of the doublewide. He sat there most of the afternoon, sweating in the shade, watching for something he hoped wouldn't come.

It didn't.

Carla Sue stayed inside, fighting the silent, searing heat that was making her stir-crazy, cleaning the two semi-autos, the revolver and a Remington pump she found propped next to the stove. The solvent made her dizzy. Standing with her nose against a window screen, breathing hot air, didn't help.

As the sun went down, a grit-laced breeze came up -- better than still heat but not by much. Burch came back to the trailer. She needed to take a walk. The bats were beginning to stir.

They ducked out the back, picking their way through the brush the same way Burch did alone a few hours earlier.

"Damn, I'm glad to get out of that doublewide. Sweet Jesus, I don't see how anybody could stand to live in one of those things, Big 'Un. I mean to tell you, that gun solvent gave me visions of being swole up and havin' a bunch of brats hanging on me all day."

"Some hallucination. I'd be worried about the brats -- havin' some pistol packer for a mama. Might shoot 'em dead for dumpin' in their diapers."

"Right."

She punched his shoulder, then shot him one of her cold looks with those startled blue eyes.

"You weren't sleepin' out there this afternoon? Nothin's out there, right?"

"Just jackrabbits and thin cattle. Bats back this way."

"You're sure."

"Unless they chopper in here or appear out of thin air, we're all by our lonesome out here."

"Good to hear. I still don't like this."

"Just another day, slick."

He led her up over the ridgeline. She looked back once, then shrugged her shoulders and focused on his beefy frame, moving fast in the gathering darkness despite the hitch in his gait.

Across the wash, hidden in brush on the opposite ridge, a man in a mesh balaclava swept the trailer with a Starscope. Behind him, around the bend in rocky ranch track through the scrub brush, a sheriff's department Bronco pulled out from the place where it was kept hidden during the day's searing heat -- a dirt trail to a back range that was choked with thorny undergrowth and blocked by a rusty gate and a cattle guard.

A small straw-haired man with a weightlifter's build and a CAR-15 strapped across his chest got out of the Bronco and wrapped an earth-colored mesh scarf around his face and hair, tucking its ends into a gray-black battle tunic. He walked up to the man with the Starscope.

"What you got, Ray-boy? Any movement?"

A sharp, short hiss from the balaclava.

"Tole you not to call me Ray-boy, 'member asshole?"

"We still sensitive, are we? Well, pardon me all to hell and back, motherfucker."

It didn't take anything for the blood to get up and the words to get sharp between Stevie Mack Lloyd and Ray McCrary. They grew up on ranches twelve miles apart, were the only friends each other'd had as children and challenged each other each and every day they crossed paths -- from marbles and football to fistfights, beer chugging and women.

When Stevie Mack caught Ray reaching up the skirt of his girlfriend in a crowded ice house in Austin, he broke a full pitcher of Shiner bock across his best friend's skull. When Stevie Mack dealt himself a third ace during a game of Mexican stud held in the back of Steinholtz's general store, Ray declared his displeasure at his friend's attempt to deal seconds by yanking his chair out from underneath him and smashing it across his back.

Now they were deputies, bucking for rank, racing each other through SWAT training, beating on each other in sparring sessions monitored warily by a Korean karate master named Park Sung Rhee, maintaining a running argument whether they were on stakeout or in roll call.

Ray could feel Stevie Mack's tension, his rising anger at the quick shot and his refusal to answer the question. He let the silence build, sweeping the trailer and the ridgeline opposite with the Starscope. He knew Stevie Mack was boiling and knew he would rather eat a fresh cow patty than ask him again. He swept the Starscope again, then put it down and lifted the skirt of the balaclava to spit out a thick stream of Red Man.

"Nada."

"How you know they ain't left?"

"One pickup. Right there. One way out. This way."

"They could walk out?"

"Why? They ain't been spooked."

"Hell, you're so damn fiddle-fucked you could scare 'em off and never know it. You know you can't hunt deer worth a shit. Why the sergeant let you tag along on this lookout all day is bee-yond me."

"Meanin' you could do it alone."

"One riot, one Ranger."

"One fuckoff, one fuckup, more like it."

A dust-covered LTD rolled up slowly and fell in line behind the Bronco. Both vehicles sat about 150 yards from the bend in the track and a line-of-sight view of the trailer.

Three men got out of the LTD -- two in suits, one in uniform. The bright moonlight made the track at their feet look like pressed oatmeal, gray and clumped with lumps of rock. The light made dark colors black, light colors gray and bright colors a ghostly, did-I-see-that white.

A woman sat handcuffed in the back of the LTD. Half of her face was in shadow. Moonlight caught an unruly wave of black curls and a set jawline that told everyone that she was pissed off at most of the whole world.

"These are the Houston boys. They want to do this soft. Brought the man's wife along to sweet talk him. She don't look like she will but we'll bring her along. Gag her. We'll use that deer track above where the track crosses that wash. Stevie Mack, you take the point."

Stevie Mack moved forward. Five followed, one of them the woman, moving down and across the slope toward the wash. Two of the deputies had battery packs on their belts and hand-held spotlights, the kind used on deer at night from the back of a four-by with monster mud tires and a fella named Junior behind the wheel.

In the brush above, a large, dark figure in baggy black fatigues and a black windbreaker watched the group, edging along quietly, like a big cat on home turf, hunting what it hunts best, the smell of a kill humming in its blood.

No claws, though. Just an Uzi and five clips.

CHAPTER 24

Burch leaned close so he could hear her through the respirator.

"Damn, Big 'Un, these bats are the wildest things. Look at 'em."

Carla Sue whipped the beam of a flashlight across the roof of the cave. The light caught hundreds of bats in flight, heading out for a meal, heading back in to feed the pups.

She danced away, skipping across the dunes of guano, blasting sprays of brown and sugary bat droppings with her Wellingtons, almost losing her balance.

"Easy, slick."

She couldn't hear him, he was out of earshot. He wanted to go. But she was having a good time, studying the bats, exploring the cave, checking out the bones Juanita left like an offering to the flesh eaters crawling underneath their boots.

He was uneasy. She disappeared behind a boulder, moving deeper into the cave. He put a hand on the Colt that was riding his left hip, hammer cocked and locked with one round in the chamber, and wished he hadn't left that smooth, ripping German chopper back in the trailer.

Walking toward her made him sweat. His feet sank and slipped in the guano, forcing him to take short, choppy steps like he was working his way across a sandy beach. He kept an eye on her wildly swinging flashlight beam and kept his own torch dark.

Dammit to hell, she could move fast in this stuff. The bats made her giddy, made her lose that nervousness she had ever since they got to the trailer. He knew where that bad feeling wound up -- right in his gut. Right now.

He was moving toward the back of the main chamber, a deep bowl that dropped steeply from the mouth of the cave like a laundry chute in a Flintstones cartoon. Glancing over his shoulder, he could see the opening etched in the rising moonlight.

Sudden blindness from two spotlights. Like the painful white flash of a hangover jarred by loud noise and quick movement. He stumbled and his bad knee plowed up a pile of guano.

"Right where you are, mister! Hold still!"

Hold still? The words bounced and echoed over the rocks. At least the sumbitch didn't yell 'freeze!' He hated that. Back when he was a cop, he never yelled that silly word. It was always 'grab some wall' or 'grab some air.' Strong and edgy. Always up close where they could feel his bulk and know he had the big Colt ready. And know he was crazed enough to use it.

Crazed didn't count now. The Colt was sitting dumb and useless on his hip. He felt the bats whir around his head, some slapping into his chest and back, all heading toward the stabbing lights and the night sky beyond. He hoped the girl was quick enough to get lost back there. If she wasn't, she'd kill him for getting them caught.

"Hands high, mister! And step up this way!"

It was clumsy going. Whoever was working the lights was doing a good job of keeping the glare square in his eyes. He felt like a man trying to ride a bike and spin a plate on a stick.

"Where's the woman?"

"She's not here!"

"What?"

The respirator, you dumb shit. Can't talk through it. Can't be heard except close up. He waded across the guano, keeping his hands high, forcing his way through the loose footing by rolling his chest and hips from side to side.

"Where's the woman, mister?"

Jesus, who are these guys? Cheap imports or locals who never discovered the joys of the world's sixth-largest bat cave. He kept his arms up but curled one hand down, pointing twice at the goggles and double cans hanging from his face.

He was struggling up the steep slope of the bowl, heading toward the chute, the lights and the men he could hear but couldn't see. Jesus, this gig is up. Jesus, get lost, girl.

The spotlights had a halo around them, light that spilled from the sides of the beam and lit up the boulders that flanked the cave mouth. He could just make out a silhouette or two. The only sounds were the rush of flying bats, his raggy breathing and the tattoo of blood on his eardrums.

Blinding beams jerked away from his face and juked across the roof of the cave, catching the swirl of bats that seemed to drop in front of him like a drift net full of flying fish. The twitching light caught dust spraying up from the rocks and an upturned face with its mouth pitched wide open, black and full of pain. A shotgun dropped from a gloved hand that had just lost its life.

Then it hit him, like the voice of a talk-show caller on tape delay. That sound he'd heard at the Ross ranch. A long chain dropping on a cement floor. Cold, sudden and deadly. Followed by screams.

He heard the whine of a ricochet and welcomed the quick darkness that surrounded him. He scrambled toward the pen where Juanita put her road kill, hoping his eyes would adjust quick enough to find the closest cover. His hand slapped at the Colt and cleared it from leather.

Wailing from the cave mouth. High like a woman.

"Mama, mama, mama oh Jesus fuck this hurts, this hurts, this hurts, mama, mama."

Two quick shots. No more wailing. Something large and black slipping over the lip. Quicker than he could snap off a round, quicker than he could swing the Colt.

Look away from the cave mouth and the moonlight. Move toward the pen. Sweep the eyes across the darkness. Don't stare. Use the peripheral vision. Wish away a lifetime of hating carrots.

Rough wood banging into his hip with a sharp sound. Breath of pain fogs up the goggles. A half turn to get clear. Colt slams into wood, falls into darkness. Dead man, now. Flat out dead.

"Ain't too good at this, are you, man?"

High voice. Squeaky. Like a thin-necked nerd with the pocket protector. Out there in the center of the cave. Fast mover. Got the prey spotted. Play with it now. Kill it later. When bored. Do it now, willya cocksucker? No damn games.

"Don't know who I am, do you man? Don't know where I am. Know who send me, doncha? That's right. T-Roy. You gonna be dead. But you gonna be fucked up, first."

Coughing in the darkness.

"Fraid Mr. T-Roy insist on it. That's right. For doin' his woman, you gonna be fucked up before you die. Then your head gonna be on T-Roy's desk. Use your skull for an ashtray."

Keep talkin', asshole. Kneeling in the guano. Feeling for the Colt. Looking for the dark hulk with the high voice.

"I see you there. Dropped your gun, didn't you. Chump. How'd a shit like you dust Astrid?"

More coughing. A voice with a file dragging across it.

"Don' matter. Here's what's gonna happen. Shoot you in the knee first. Then walk over and start breakin' bones. Maybe carve on you a little. Make you beg to die. Think about that."

Light stabbing the eyes again. On his knees. Waiting for the wafer and the wine. Like his second ex-wife. Or was it his third? The Colt out of reach, a dull glint in bat shit.

More coughing. The voice down an octave.

"Think about this, too. Your wife was out there. Long black hair. Killer legs. Nice ass. Can you see me lookin' at her? You see that, doncha? Black man lookin' at white pussy. Piss you off, cracker?"

Well, see this -- I did her. Shot her down like a dog. That was her cryin' just now. Did the double tap."

Bile in the throat, sour and rising. Up on his feet, slogging toward the light. A grin, a gun muzzle pointing his way. Coughing and rasping behind the light. How close, motherfucker? How close before the first shot?

"You never fuck her again, man. But I might. After you gone."

Coughing. Twenty feet now. Maybe fifteen. The gun muzzle larger than a blackened cocktail coaster. Level on his churning knees. Closer, Jesus, closer. Close enough for two hands around a fat neck. No chance. Here it comes, that first shot. Got to be.

Ten feet. Nothing. Coughing and a bouncing beam. No shots. No words. Coughs and wheezes. No respirator. Nasty fumes and bad fungi doing their stuff. Big black man in black fatigues. Cut down by things he can't see. Bad enough to choke him now or kill him later. Beam bouncing to his coughs, gun dropping out of his hand.

Boom from a Colt fills the cave. Big man down on his side. A spin toward the woman as she dances across the guano, Colt leading her through the steps.

"No! Don't! Let him die this way!"

A flick of her flashlight beam across the man's face. Raspy sound from the throat. Sucking for air. Getting something far worse. Her by his side now. Both watching. She leaned close.

"Not good enough, Big 'Un."

"You right."

She slipped her Colt into his hand, hammer already back from the first round. The man was on his side, his toupee skewed, pillowing his head from the guano. A kick to the shoulder flopped him on his back. Burch standing astride him, a Wellington on either side of his chest, leaning down into his face.

"Beg."

The eyes were bulging. Anger, gunshot pain and all those fumes. The mouth was gasping. Open, then closed. Like koi.

"Beg, you cockbite motherfucker."

The eyes bulged more. Bloodshot ivory. Teeth bared. Burch rose, Colt in both hands. Two shots. One in the chest. One in the forehead. His own double tap. With hardball and a Flying Ashtray.

He handed her the Colt. He leaned down again and straightened the toupee.

"Got to look good for the beetles, slick."

CHAPTER 25

She watched him strip off his respirator, his hair slicked with sweat and twisted into devil's horns. She could smell the urine fumes coming off their clothes, strong but with a sweet and cloying backwash you didn't expect.

He limped up and over the lip of the cave, the lost Colt back on his hip. He made his way to each body, checking out the entry wounds, eyeing the angle from the killing ground to where the shooter must have stood, flying on the old automatic pilot of an ex-cop, working every spot except the one.

A fat Mex in a bad khaki suit was sprawled over another guy in a cheap, blue sportscoat. The Mex's bald head was thrown back, his mouth open, his gun still holstered. His still hands formed claws across the exit wounds on his chest.

Burch pulled the Mex down and away. There was a groan from the other suit, muffled by dirt, rock and a face turned the other way. He leaned over, grabbed a wad of sportscoat in each hand and pulled the suit into a sitting position, back against a boulder, ignoring a scream of pain.

There was a bloody welt on the man's forehead, where skull struck rock as he fell. A round had smashed into his left shoulder blade. Another had splintered his left leg below the knee, canting the limb and foot at a crazy angle that drew a wince just to look at.

Burch worked fast, rigging a tourniquet with a belt. He shucked the man's sportcoat and made a compress out of a dead man's T-shirt and two knotted bandanas.

"You know who I am, I can't say the same."

"Jones. Houston homicide."

"Doggin' me for T-Roy's skirt, right?"

"And three others. Maybe four."

Cider spoke through clenched teeth.

"Gonna bring you in, sooner or later."

"Naw, what you're gonna do is sit here and try not to die. And listen to what this one's got to say. It's a good yarn. Got all your favorite characters in it."

Burch stripped the torn khaki jacket off the Mex and waved Carla Sue to his side. She sat on her haunches and fixed the cop with those wide, cold eyes.

"Set-up deal. Burch as the patsy. Neville Ross pulling the string. Trying to get T-Roy either out in the open or killed by Burch. Made it look like Burch killed T-Roy's old lady. Lawyer up in Dallas was the middleman -- Doug Bartell. Set up Burch, set up the deal that brought the woman to Houston."

"How do you know?"

"I used to keep his bed warm."

"Ross? You there when he died?"

"Yes and yes."

"Burch kill him?"

"No."

"Who did?"

"Mister, do you really give half a fuck who iced that old pimp? If it weren't for the fireworks flippin' out the feds and John Q. Citizen, you people would be throwin' a party."

"I got four other bodies."

"Who."

"Boyfriend of one of Burch's old ladies -- head slammed through a toilet bowl. Two scumbags and a coke lawyer."

"Can't help you with the boyfriend, 'cept to tell you we been here the past two days. The lawyer, though -- that's a guy name Crutcher, right?"

"Yeah."

"Crutcher did business with T-Roy. Did business with Ross, too. He was the one on the Houston end of the set-up."

"How you know so much about T-Roy?"

"I took his money to keep tabs on Ross."

"Risky business."

"Kept life interestin.' Got one other tale to tell. That big, black cocksucker that whacked everybody out here, that's T-Roy's maximum muscle. Called him Badhair. These folks were lucky -- Badhair likes to hurt people before he kills 'em. Likes to break fingers, slice off skin, burn cigarette holes in someone's body. Likes to hear 'em scream and beg. Well, he used to."

"Dead?"

"You catch on fast. In the cave. Resting in bat shit. Stupid fucker didn't know you had to wear one of these."

She held up a respirator. Cider sucked in his breath, hit by a sudden spasm of pain. She draped the sportscoat across his chest, tucking it under his chin and under his body.

"You rest easy. If I know Big 'Un, he'll have somebody out here in a few hours to fix you up. If it was just me, you're a loose end I'd just have to tie up. But Big 'Un's still a cop at heart, so you luck out. That is, if you can stay alive. You can do that, can't you big guy?"

Her lips broke into a smile, but her eyes didn't. They were flat, icy and soulless. There was a hard line to her jaw as she looked at him. It softened slightly as she looked up, eyes on Burch standing over the fifth body.

His shoulders shook as he looked at the face of his last ex-wife. He felt like crying, but his eyes were dry and the guilt and pain he felt rising from his gut locked up his throat so he couldn't make a sound. He opened his mouth, but nothing came out.

She wasn't the one he loved the best. She wasn't the one who owned his soul. But she was the one most like him, the woman born with a roadmap to his mind and heart -- just as wounded, just as prideful, just as ornery and giving. And long gone.

He draped a bloody deputy's jacket over her ruined face to keep the buzzards from picking out her eyes. He turned and saw Carla Sue looking at him. He knew she could see the look of loss and guilt on his face. He flushed with shame.

"We gotta go, Big 'Un.'"

Her voice was sharp. He nodded once and made that quick, snapping sound -- tongue on palate -- that always set her teeth on edge. He started up the dirt path toward the trailer. She followed.

The bats whirled in and out of the cave, a stream of darting bodies and dark wings, felt more than seen until they rose above the brushline and into the moonlight.

Burch didn't look back.

CHAPTER 26

She was in her 90s and her brown, wrinkled skin, hanging in loose folds from her jaw and neck, made her look ancient and ageless. Her hair was thin and pulled tight across her tall, narrow skull -- white frost on walnut. Her eyes, once dark, deep-set and burning, were now vacant and milky.

The early morning sun felt good on her arms, her face and in her bones. Birds stirred in the low branches of trees that were beyond the reach of what was left of her sight. Swallows and a mockingbird; her ears were still that sharp. So was her mind and a soul that could see the spirit world, the shape of things to come and things past, the faces and familiars that rode with every man and woman, whether they saw them or not.

She was Cuban, of mixed blood. Her father's father had been a slave. Her mother was peasant Spanish and Indian. They were old island people, mongrels to the high Spaniards who ran the country and were afraid of being swept aside by the darker races.

The Spaniards remembered Haiti and the bloody slave revolts of the 1700s. They remembered their own island's history of violence. They brought new settlers from old Spain, white merchants and tradesmen and workers who took the jobs and places of Creoles like her father, a *tabaquero*, and her mother, a seamstress.

Bad times and blood were soon to follow. It was the early years of the new century and Cuba had her independence from Spain, but not from the *capitalistas Yanqui* and the bootheel of King Sugar and the big fruit combines. The politics of the plantation held sway; its calling cards the stooped back of cheap labor and an insatiable hunger for every plot of land.

She was young and knew little of the changes sweeping her homeland, just her mother's frown and her father's heated words with the men who wanted to buy land he didn't want to sell. She was father's *periquito* and the warmth of her mother's heart.

Her father was a *santero*, an initiate of *santeria*, that mystic amalgamation of African earth religion, with its many gods holding the power of nature, and the many saints of Catholicism, their characteristics and attributes similar to the deities of the old religion and a convenient mask for slaves who were forced to hide their old beliefs from their masters.

Her mother didn't believe in the Yoruba mysticism of her father. She worshipped in the tiny Catholic chapel down the road and didn't see an African god or goddess in the shape of St. Barnabas or St. Barbara. But she didn't interfere in her husband's ways. Nor did she prevent him from passing on these ancient ways to their daughter.

Chango, the headstrong god of thunder and fire, was her father's *orisha*. When she was very young, maybe four or five, her father took her to a *tambor*, a special party for the gods, this one a gathering of *santeros* who beat the drums and called on Chango to walk among them.

The packed earthen floor was swept. The room was crowded. A steady beat came from three drums, *batas* pounded by the palms of three black men, all *santeros*. One was a thin, bald elder with the large green eyes of her cat, Maria; another was young, dark and muscular and the third smoked a large cigar, swaying and puffing to the beat of his own hand.

She was afraid and started to whimper. Her father nuzzled her and whispered in soothing tones.

"Don't be afraid, *periquito*. I will teach you how to walk with the *santos*. They will protect you through life and give you power. That way, you will never be alone even when your father and mother are far away.

The *orishas* will love you and watch over you, just like we do. Only much better."

He led her to an old woman, her head covered with a bandana that matched the flowery print of her billowing skirt. Her father stretched out on the floor in front of the woman, flat on his stomach, his face and eyes down. This was the *foribale*, the tribute to an older *santero* or *orisha*.

The old woman held out her hand and her father rose.

"This is your child?"

"Yes, *madrina*. Give her *acuelle*, please. And tell me who her *orisha* is so that she can walk the right path."

Through the years, she could still feel the old woman's cool, wrinkled hands on her cheeks and the hold of her powerful, searching gaze. She could still feel herself drawn out of her body and into those wise eyes, brown with flecks of copper.

The old woman frowned, then looked at her father.

"What is it, *madrina*? You see *abiku*?"

Abiku, the spirit of death dreaded by every parent who followed the Yoruba ways, a wicked sprite that possessed small children and caused them to die. The old woman shook her head.

"Not that, *omo-mi*. She is strong and well. But she is not like you, she is not a child of Chango. She is a child of Alabbgwanna, the Lonely One. That is what I see, that is what is. There is more -- this child will walk with Alabbgwanna, but she will also walk with the dead. She will be a *palera*. She will wear the cuts of *palo mayombe*. She will have the power, both light and dark."

"What should be done?"

"Teach her the ways of a *santera*, *omo-mi*. Teach her to walk with the Lonely One. That is all you can do for now. One day, she will walk a way that you will not. There is nothing you can do to change that. For now, she is the child of the Lonely One and she will protect her in her way."

They talked as though she was not there. Her eyes shifted from the face of the old woman, calm and the color of coffee and milk, to the face of her father, worried and darkened by the *madrina*'s knowledge of his child.

Her father started to speak. The *madrina* cut him off with a sharp chop of the hand that caused her brass bracelets to jangle.

"It is time for Chango, *omo-mi*. Listen to what is said."

The drums were beating faster. The *santero* with the cigar was standing, his head thrown back, shoulders slack, another at his station behind one of the sacred *batas*. The *santero* stumbled forward, arms rigid and thrust outward from his chest, pushing into the crowd, forcing them to clear a rough circle in the center of the room.

"*¡Cabio Sile pa Chango!*"

As one, the crowd lifted themselves up on one foot in tribute to Chango. The *santero* spun about the room, his shoulders jerking crazily, his legs splitting out at odd angles that made it look like he was sure to fall, then snapping back quickly to keep his body upright and moving.

"*¡Cabio Sile pa Chango!*"

Again the crowd lifted themselves as one. The *santero* moved faster, his eyes rolling and unfocused, his jaw working like a man chewing a strip of dried fish. He spun, then slid to a sudden stop near a corner of the room where two, double-bit axes were stacked, their white handles trimmed with red. They were the battle weapons of Chango.

The *santero* grabbed the axes and began his terrible dance, spinning to the drumbeat, whirling the axes through the air, the whoosh of the sharp blades striking a counterpoint to the drums.

The people chanted to Chango and prayed out loud, exhorting the *orisha* to vanquish their enemies and watch over them. The *santero* stopped suddenly, banging the sides of the axe bits together with a clang that silenced the drums and struck sparks that flew up toward the dark ceiling.

He surveyed the room with wide, shining eyes. She ducked behind her father's leg, afraid of the figure with an axe in each hand, looking at every person as he slowly turned in the center of the circle. His face beaded with sweat, the *santero* pointed his axes toward the doorway.

There stood an old woman, her head covered by a black, tattered shawl, her face shadowed. She pointed a bony, gray finger at them and spoke in a hushed, raspy voice -- fine-grained sandpaper brushed over rough pine.

"She will walk many paths and see many things. She will have the power, she will be great and terrible. She will know darkness, she will know *ororo*. She will walk with *iku*. And she will live many years."

Walk with the dead, know evil. The words brought a quiet coldness into the room.

"Hear what is said. The child is mine. For now."

The old woman turned her back to the crowd, her black clothes blending into the darkness. The *santero* was curled on the floor, axes at his side, sweat drying on his body, his face relaxed in deep and sudden sleep.

Memory shifted to flames and her mother's screams in the night. Her father's hard, anguished face was bathed in flickering orange light. Through the doorway of their home, through the flames, they could see the glowing figure of a woman, reaching toward them for a brief moment.

Her father took a step toward the house, but the figure was gone. The screams stopped. The pop and crackle of fire was the only sound. His body became rigid, his face a mask of frozen anger.

He called out the name of Chango. Distant thunder answered.

He called again. More thunder, sounding from even farther away, like a man muttering an answer over his shoulder to someone he didn't want to talk to.

Father cocked his ear toward the cloud-covered sky, then fell to his knees. He looked at her.

"Chango won't come. He says it isn't his concern."

She looked away from the fire and toward the place where the pathway from their home met the dirt road to town. There stood the dark, stooped figure who spoke to them at the *tambor* many days ago, just out of reach of the light from the dying flames. A thin arm stretched out from the folds of the dark shawl, slowly beckoning.

A stillness settled over her. She looked back at her father, face down in the dirt, crying and beating the earth with his fists. She walked toward the old woman.

"You are the Lonely One."

"Yes, *omo-mi*. I watch over you. Come with me."

She peered at the shadow the shawl made, hiding the old woman's face. She heard loud music, laughter and shouts. She looked around and saw they were at a *bodega* in town. They hadn't walked; she hadn't moved her feet at all. But they were there, moving toward a table crowded with men, about ten in all, most barefoot and wearing the rough-cut cotton pullovers of cane cutters. Tucked in the rope belts of some were machetes, gleaming dully in the light of oil lamps.

The men were rolling dice for drinks, shaking the ivory cubes in a large leather cup, then banging them down with shouted oaths. The old woman pointed at two men, both light-skinned, one thin with oil-slickened hair and a drooping moustache, the other fat and bearded, his pants big enough for two men, his shirt covered with grease stains.

The old woman touched the shoulder of a tall mulatto, wearing black trousers and a vest with a faded red peasant print, standing near the table, his arms, ropy with muscle, folded across his bare chest. His body became rigid. His eyes grew bright. He smiled a tight smile and drew a machete from his belt.

The blade flashed in the lantern light in a bright arc that went toward the ceiling, then swept down and across the fat man's throat. The fat man's eyes bulged out. Gouts of blood pumped up through the matted hair of his beard. He fell across the suddenly silent table.

Flashing again, glistening with blood, the blade arced toward the thin man, catching him in the side of the neck, slicing deeply through muscle and artery. The thin man fell to the floor, his blood gushing over the feet of his companions as they pushed and scrambled away from the table and the man with the machete.

He stepped forward and swung the blade again -- this time ripping open the belly of a small black man who was backpedaling, his arms thrown up in surrender. The mulatto spun to his left and chopped the blade into the arm of a man who was swinging his own machete into action. He shouldered the man to the floor, stepping over the body of the thin man, pulling his head back by the hair, severing the head with three short, powerful chops.

He held the head aloft. The men backed away. He turned, facing the old woman. He smiled, bowed and extended the lifeless head toward her like an offering. A squat cane cutter in a straw hat stepped forward, machete in hand, and sliced his sharp blade across the back of the mulatto's neck, driving him to the floor.

The mulatto was dead before he struck the packed dirt. The head was tightly gripped in his hand.

The old woman turned to her. There was shadow where a face should be and she felt herself sucked into that darkness. The smell of blood and the swishing sound of sharp steel fell away. They were in an unlit room with a slow-turning ceiling fan. A man slept beneath mosquito netting.

A thick chord of muscle eased its way along the top edge of the footboard -- a *fer de lance*, its heavy, triangular head swaying from side to side. The snake turned toward her, its eyes locking on hers, drawing her closer.

"Don't be afraid, *omo-mi*. That one is here to do your bidding. That one is here to do harm to those who did harm to you. Touch his head."

A coldness filled her, flowing in like icy water from a deep pool. She touched the snake's head; it bowed and pushed back against her palm like a dog begging for its master's stroke.

The old woman pulled back the netting and whispered again: "This one -- he ordered the burning of your house. He had your mother killed. He has ordered the death of your father. And if his men find you, they will kill you as well. Those we saw at the *bodega* set the fire that killed your mother. They are dead. He is still alive."

Her insides felt like ice and granite. Her jaw ached with tension and something she had never felt before -- an anger that strung her tighter than a drumhead but sharpened her senses and brought a clarity to her young mind's eye. Her hand rested on the snake's head as it pressed into her palm.

She cupped its jaw and stared into its eyes. Her head tilted back. A thin wail, snapping and wolfish, flew from her lips. She flung the snake through the netting's gap, catching the man as he rose naked from deep sleep, startled by her cry, frozen by the sight of a snake on his sheets, readying its first deadly strike.

The snake lashed out, catching the man full in the throat. His eyes were wild with fear and the knowledge that he was a dead man. The snake struck again, hitting the man just below his left eye, hanging heavily by its fangs, pumping more venom. The man died without making a sound, slumping forward like a sidewalk drunk.

She looked at the old woman. Darkness surrounded by a tattered shawl. They were in the raked dirt yard where her home once stood. The old woman pointed to the closest tobacco shed. Her father's headless body hung by the heels from the rafters, spinning slowly in the night breeze.

"Others came for him. You know what you must do."

She knew darkness. She walked with evil and the dead. Through long years.

She lived with her father's people in the Sierra Maestra range and passed into the blacker side of Yoruba mysticism. She was cut in *palo*. She learned the vengeful arts of the *mayomberos*, their necromancy, their mercenary tendency to whore out to the highest bidder. This taught her commerce and its distinctive soullessness. It won her fear and the title of *La Bruja*, whispered as she passed along dusty streets.

In New Orleans, she learned *vodoun*, the ways of the *bokor* and the zombie fear that rides with the ancestors of slaves. She knew the black top hat and long-tailed suitcoat of Baron Samedi. She gulped his fiery iron jack, smoked his maduro cigars and told his lewd jokes in the trance of his possession.

Baron Samedi wanted more than jokes on a night when fog rolled in from the big river, floating like cotton past the grime-smeared windows of an abandoned warehouse where the believers met. They told her she prowled the crowded room, laughing with a deep voice and puffing a dark cigar.

She grabbed a young mulatto by the shirt, they said, ripping it open and running her tongue across his chest, puffing thick smoke into his face. She unbuckled his trousers and pushed him to the cold, concrete floor.

Her skirt bunched forward, her ass brushed by the cold, damp air, she mounted him with a grunt, her teeth tightly clenched on the dark, strong cigar favored by this randy *Guédé*, a spirit of the graveyard and sex.

The mulatto met her thrusts, their flesh clapping like cupped palms. They climaxed together, sweating in spite of the cold. The mulatto laughed and slapped her on the ass, they told her.

"We can do this again, but let's not put on such a show next time."

This drew a laugh from some, she was told. Baron Samedi was not amused. They said her eyes flared. The deep voice came from her chest. She puffed the cigar and blew more smoke in his face.

"Time is no more for you, young son. You are dead very soon."

He was found in an alley the next night.

A husband, long dead, brought her to Mexico -- Benito Obregon. She gave him six sons. He gave her the ways of Mayan and Aztec times, a sense of the need to feed and nourish the universe, maintain its precarious balance of energy. Sometimes that meant a rope of thorns drawn through the web of the hand, the blood caught in a bowl for the Vision Serpent.

Sometimes something else was called for. Her husband was a smuggler -- a hero to some because he ran guns for the Revolution, a brigand to others because he charged a high price for his weapons and later trafficked in other forms of contraband, from stolen cattle to liquor and humans.

A rival named Sanchez stole a load of her husband's liquor. Her husband caught him, killing two bodyguards with a shotgun. His men spread Sanchez across the top of a table, tearing off his shirt.

Her husband drew a hunting knife from his boot and stabbed it into Sanchez's chest, leaning over his face like a deaf man trying to read the lip movements of a dying scream.

He carved out his rival's pulsing heart, held it to the sky, then sliced off a hunk and ate it. She was horrified when he told her this. She had seen many things following the path of *vodoun* and *palo mayombe*. She had shown reverence for the dead and called on their power to help her and hurt her enemies. But passing human flesh between her lips was unthinkable.

"I did it for tribute, to keep the gods on my side and to gather the energy of my enemy for my own use."

Her husband told her about a battle between the Aztecs and the conquistadors of Cortez near the great temple on Serpent Mountain. Captured Spaniards were herded up the steps of the temple pyramid where plumes were placed in their hair and they were forced to dance before Huitzilopochtli, the god of tribute and war.

The captives were then thrown across stone altars; their chests were carved open, their hearts were cut out and offered, still quivering, to Huitzilopochtli. The dead were then pitched down the staircases and butchered. The priests gave worshipers bits of heart and flesh in a chile paste.

She was still disgusted. But as he kept talking, she began to see the parallels between her beliefs and his -- the push to replenish the energy of the universe, to draw on the power of gods and ancestors and enemies, the need to honor the forces of the underworld and the overworld, to consort with the gods themselves.

He was a willing student of her ways. He taught her about the Vision Serpent, Tlaloc the rain god, Xiuhtecuhtli the fire god and the paths between the earth, the world of the dead and the celestial home of the gods. He fed her peyote and showed her how to live the life of a coyote, a wolf or a hawk.

She taught him about the Warriors, the Lonely One, the red-eyed *loas* of the Pethro path of *vodoun*, the body cuts of *palo mayombe*, the swaying trances and the calls to the spirit world.

They developed their own ritual, one that mixed the worship of the dead and the sacrifice of the living -- a chicken or pig, perhaps; maybe their own blood and that of their sons. This was fine for the routine of life.

But to give tribute for a victory over a rival smuggler or the *federales*, only human blood would do. Sometimes her husband and her sons captured a member of a rival gang; sometimes a drifter lost his life to keep the gods happy, his parts chopped and dumped into an iron cauldron.

She learned to make the chili paste, she discovered the sickening sweet taste of human flesh and heart muscle. It had been two months since she made the paste and led her sons through solemn ceremony. And she felt the need to draw on the power of the gods.

T-Roy had promised them a special sacrifice, a man of power, a rival from the time before he came to live among them in the low, sunburned hills just south of the river. She called him Tedero and laughed to herself because it set his teeth on edge.

He had power and presence -- he could call the *orishas* and *loas*, they would answer. He possessed a cruel ability to dominate other men. He stepped into their circle and into the place her husband once held. Without effort. But he didn't believe and blinded himself to the spirits riding on his flanks.

She told him who saved him that night in Reynosa -- the Lonely One, the old woman. He smiled, but knew better than to laugh. He attended their ceremonies, but she knew better than to see him as a true believer.

They lived the life of a relaxed standoff, each profiting from the other side's particular skills and powers, but never becoming one, a family united in spirit and commerce. For a long time, this had not mattered. But now it did and she could feel it.

Her eyes were closed. The sun bathed her eyelids in an orange warmth she could see and feel. She felt something else, close by her side.

"Tedero."

She smiled as she heard him suck in his breath.

"*Madrina.*"

He kissed her outstretched hand.

"Sit."

She heard him settle on the dirt in front of her. His shadow darkened the glow warming the insides of her eyelids.

"I told you I would bring a gift, a great sacrifice that would give us power and keep the gods happy."

"I remember."

He paused. She kept her eyes closed.

"Something went wrong. I cannot give what I promised."

"I know about this. I know of your loss as well."

She heard him suck in his breath. His voice sounded strained.

"It's painful. She meant a lot to me. I need to avenge her death."

"A small matter to someone who believes."

There was a long silence. She started to enjoy the warmth of the sun again.

"I need your help. I've stirred up a hornet's nest and don't know how this will play out. There are men here and over the border who wish me dead now. Others too, from Columbia."

"It will happen the way the gods want it to."

"That's why I'm coming to you. I want the gods to want me to win."

"I can only ask for their help and a vision of what is to be."

"You can use your power."

"For my sons and me. For believers. You have never believed. Hear me -- I can protect myself and my sons. I can ask the gods about this matter. But only you can decide to walk the path or walk alone."

"As you say. There is the body of a man. I've had it placed by the cauldron."

"Lead me there."

The shed had a roof of corrugated tin, a dirt floor and thick cypress logs anchoring each corner. The walls were plywood, framed by rough pine boards. T-Roy lit an oil lamp. The body of the ex-contra, stripped and faceup, stretched the length of a thick-legged butcher's table, a blood groove running along one side of its stained, oak top.

Two men poured water into a heavy iron cauldron to the left of the table. The water hissed and steamed as it hit metal heated by a fire that burned in a pit dug beneath the cauldron.

"Leave me."

The men turned to the door. So did T-Roy.

"Stay, Tedero."

Feeling her way along the long edge of the table, she worked her way to an altar covered in oilcloth. She pulled the cloth away. Candles, a cross, the open mouths of cowrie shells with their row of tiny teeth, beads of red and yellow and several smooth stones of gray and black stood on the shelves of the altar. She lit the candles and a long double corona wrapped in dark, maduro leaf.

Puffing hard, she blew smoke onto the altar, then turned and blew smoke along the length of the dead man's body. She bent over what was left of his face and blew more smoke into his nostrils. She took a knife from the altar and held it toward the ceiling, flashing its blade in the light of the oil lamp.

With her free hand pressing down on the dead man's chest, she sawed an opening. Blood sprayed onto her blouse. She puffed more smoke into the open wound.

"Tedero, come beside me."

She told him to hold the chest open. He watched as the knife flicked around the heart, severing the arteries and veins. With a grunt, she cut the last vein and lifted the heart out of the chest cavity. Her hands were slick with blood.

"Hand me those bowls."

He reached for two wooden bowls on the altar. She placed the heart in one and drained blood from a cut in the man's neck into the other. She carried both back to the altar.

"Tedero, hand me that bottle of lamp oil."

She poured lamp oil into the bowl of blood. She sprinkled gunpowder on the slick surface. She struck a match and watched a small flame and a smoky plume rise from the bowl. Puffing hard on the cigar, she blew smoke through the plume, sending a swirl across the altar.

She held the bowl with the heart high above her head, blood inching down her arms. He was amazed how strong she seemed and how long she could hold the bowl aloft. She kept puffing the cigar.

A long, thin wail escaped her lips. Her eyes were closed. Twin jets of cigar smoke shot from her nostrils. She put the bowl back on the altar and looked at him.

"Now what happens?"

"You know what happens now. Leave me."

He moved slowly, like stitches of scar tissue pulling apart. He wanted to ask another question, one he knew she wouldn't answer. She willed him to leave, turning her back on him, waiting until she heard the shed door shut.

She reached for a small gourd of chili paste. She would taste the heart flesh and the hot, dry chili. But not for Tedero. He was alone now, as she had dreamed, as the voice of the Lonely One told her.

This was for her sons and herself.

CHAPTER 27

Mano watched T-Roy move across the dirt yard toward the porch where he sat in a wicker-bottomed chair, canted back against the adobe wall, cleaning an Uzi, taking short pulls on a bottle of mescal that caused the sweat to pop on his forehead.

Dust rose up to cover the fancy stitching of T-Roy's handmade boots as he covered the distance with a quick, choppy stride, slapping a thigh with his palm, his lips forming words that Mano couldn't hear.

Mano knew to wait. He concentrated on oiling the weapon and piecing it back together, lips pursed around the cigar, ignoring the sound of boots pacing on the porch planking beside him and the muttered curses that were starting to build in volume and intensity.

"Fuckin' dried-up crone -- tellin' me I walk alone. I been walkin' alone since I was born and I'll walk alone a long time after she's dust. I sure as hell ain't gettin' much help from a bag of bones who sits in the sun until someone gives her a stiff to do her knife work on."

T-Roy spat over the railing and ran fingers through wiry red hair.

"Fuck her and that voodoo shit. Fuck *palo* and Vision Serpent and the old woman. And fuck her sons, too. Stupid, worthless bastards -- we been carryin' them because we think they're useful. I tell you true, Mano -- they just gettin' in the way, *vato*. Just gettin' in our way and cuttin' into our action.

"We don't need 'em. We don't need her. We don't need all this weird Stephen King shit. Cut 'em loose. Let 'em drift."

Mano said nothing. He looked at T-Roy and arched an eyebrow.

"I know, I know -- it's their fuckin' *rancho*. Their fuckin' land. Their fuckin' spirits and ceremonies. Bad medicine to fuck with all that. Bad to even talk the way I'm talking. But goddam, Mano -- we lost Astrid to Ross and that Burch fuck. And that whore Carla Sue -- she been playin' both Ross and me off each other. You were right, there, man. Called that bitch a long way off.

"And I got all this heat comin' down on my ass. Can't go north because I fucked up so bad every alphabet shit the feds have got is lookin' for me. The *federales* aren't pleased to have someone so fuckin' notorious right on their front porch. And the fuckin' Cali boys don't even want to hear about the war I started in their Texas briar patch."

T-Roy paused and reached for the bottle of mescal sitting underneath Mano's chair. He tilted it back against his lips and let the liquid bubble down his throat until his eyes and nostrils burned.

"Heeeee-yahhhh, but we are truly fucked, Mano my man. We can't even get the spirit woman to sic the voodoo dogs on anyone who would do harm to my skinny ass. Here, you're workin' too hard. Have a drink. We ain't dead yet. We still got the boys. We don't need the old woman's sons. We don't need her and her spirits."

Mano took two quick pulls on the mescal, thudding the bottle onto the porch planking. He opened and closed the bolt of the Uzi, working the oil into the innards of the weapon, turning words slowly in his mind.

"We may need them more than we think, *patrón*. There aren't that many of us boys you can trust, if you think about it. Camarillo wasn't that popular with *los contras*, but he was their *jefe* and they know you iced him."

"I pay those fucks a damn good dollar. Keep 'em in tequila and pussy -- all they want."

"So we got drunks who been laid. You sure they watch your back? You sure you want them in a firefight?"

"They tore hell out of Ross's little fortress."

"Camarillo ran that show."

"What are you sayin'?"

"We need to shorten our odds and keep our friends friendly, is all. Don't need to kill any more off. And definitely don't need to get on the bad side of *La Bruja*."

Mano turned and smiled as he said these last words. T-Roy was staring at him, palm slapping thigh, the checkered grip of a Colt Python curving above his belt.

"You sayin' I was wrong to ice Camarillo?"

"Definitely not one of your better moves, *patrón*."

No words for a long time. Mano wished he had a full clip for his oiled and empty Uzi. He met T-Roy's glare, focusing his eyes on the other man's brow, an old schoolyard trick from the days of dozens and staredown.

T-Roy broke first.

"You fuck. I never could outstare you."

"*Es verdad, patrón*. But it's a small matter -- a cheap parlor trick."

"We don't need this old woman and her sons. We got the Badhair. We got money and guns and all the *anejo* we need."

"We ain't heard from Badhair in a long, long time. Not since Kenny called about the chopper ride to Uvalde. He got more gadgets than *cojones* and he calls us by now, usually."

"You got no faith in the guy. You and him never did get along."

"*Patrón* -- how to have faith in a guy who looks like he got a fuckin' poodle stuck on his head? Makes me wanna shoot it off his damn skull every time I see him. *Patrón* -- I gotta tell you -- gettin' him on this is another mistake. That guy kills first and thinks later. Bet we have bodies scattered from here to Houston by now and more fuckin' heat on our ass."

A big speech for Mano. More words than T-Roy had heard him say in ten or twelve years. He thought he saw a glitter in his friend's eye, the cold flash of a snake's gaze, a look that caused him to shudder.

"You sayin' I should let that Burch fuck live after what he did to Astrid? That what you sayin,' Mano, *mi vato*?"

"Fuck no. Should have scoped it out first, then call in a shooter. Don't leave it all to Badhair. We don't know shit about this Burch other than he was a cop and you killed his damn partner."

Another long speech. More words T-Roy didn't want to hear. Another shudder passed through T-Roy's body. He felt Mano move the eye of the snake over him.

"Astrid's dead and Burch did her. That's all I need to know. All you need to know."

"You got to let her go, *patrón*. Play it smart. Play it the way I know you can."

T-Roy's mouth broke into a grin, lips pulled back across clenched teeth. His eyes sought Mano's -- a hot, crazed glare against cool and steady sleight of eye. There it was, that cold glitter.

The only sound was T-Roy's hand whacking against his thigh. He wanted to beat that stare and hold off the shudder it sent through his body. He broke again.

"Cheap parlor tricks might get you iced one day, *vato*. Or a smart mouth. I seen you go days without sayin' dick to nobody. Barely a grunt to me. Now I can't shut you up."

"I'm sayin' stuff you need to hear. None of these other *cabrons* will tell you when you fuckin' up. And you fuckin' up, *patrón*. You losin' it. You need to get back on top of this situation and ride it, not let it ride you."

"What I just say?"

Mano held up his hand.

"I know, I know. I said it. I shut up. *Patrón* -- we're twins, joined at the hip. I saved your life. You own mine. Somebody waste me someday, but not you. Somebody waste you one day, but not me."

"You forget, my friend, but I know you now."

T-Roy was grinning again, eyes glittering. Mano smiled back, trying to figure out what was meant by that last line while watching his boss, watching how he held his hands and how close they were to the butt of his pistol.

"Let's hook 'em up again. I feel lucky. I feel strong. I feel like a snake who can watch his prey all day. I feel like you're gonna be the one that breaks first."

"Never happened before. Won't happen now. Why bother? Too fuckin' hot, *patrón.*"

They locked eyes for the third time. The gun was up and in Mano's face in the same split second he heard the heavy, metallic click of the hammer being thumbed back. It was the last sound he ever heard.

T-Roy listened to the echo of the solitary shot flatten out and spread across the dusty yard of the *rancho,* past the stable, the shed and the other outbuildings. As men started running toward the porch, he stood with his head cocked to one side, like a man watching a bank of television sets in a department store window.

One by one, the sounds and images of killing his best and only friend registered, each checking in at a slow speed and a sharp clarity -- the clatter of Mano's freshly oiled Uzi hitting the weathered planking; the blood spraying across the light tan of the adobe wall; the scuffed soles of Mano's boots, hooked up and over the cane bottom of his overturned chair.

He bent down low over the dead man, his face close to the other man's face, close enough to smell the blood pooling out from the back of his friend's head, close enough to smell his own sour breath bounce back from the skin of the dead man's ruined face. T-Roy whispered like a lover.

"I warned you, *vato.* I told you to shut up. I told you I felt lucky. I told you it was my turn to win."

He looked into Mano's eyes and felt a sudden tilt of vertigo. He would fall into that stare and lose his soul. He would tumble into those eyes and never come back. He had to break away. He had no choice.

T-Roy turned. Men crowded the top step of the porch, silhouetted by the strong sun at their back. He saw something else, quick and flashing -- the head of a snake, fangs bared, flying toward him from the sun.

"No fuckin' choice."

His words sounded thin and dry. So did his laugh. He emptied his pistol at the snake in the sky. The men scattered.

CHAPTER 28

El Paso, he said. Dump this ride, he said. She started to argue. She had her mind on a fast run to Mercedes and Lefty Moore's little tarmac airstrip. But Big 'Un wasn't someone to argue with right now.

"This is the last time I'll ever do this and this time may be enough to make me dead."

"What?"

"You heard me."

"I heard you awright, Big 'Un. But I got no goddam idea what the hell you're talkin' about."

"Just words that been runnin' through my head. Like one of those, ah -- chants -- they do."

"Who?"

"Those TM characters. Yogis."

"You mean a mantra."

"That's it. These words been runnin' through my brain, over and over again -- this is the last time I'll ever do this and this time may be enough to make me dead."

"Are you awright?"

"Shit yeah. Keep movin'."

Carla Sue didn't know which was worse -- this sudden babbling about anything that popped into Burch's head or the odd mix of sobbing and cold, brooding silence he showed during the long, nervous ride out of a rabbit hole that had turned into a trap, out toward I-10 and their sudden turn westward.

The sobbing she could take -- soft and quiet as he leaned toward the passenger side while she stared straight through the windshield, giving him as much privacy as is possible in the cab of a pickup.

The silence was another matter. It was strong and seemed like it swirled up from a hole deep inside of him, sucking all the time and sound out of the cab, leaving only heavy tension and a sense of dread. It caused the skin on the back of her neck to crawl.

She tried to shake the feeling by counting the segments of white centerline that whipped into the arc of the headlights. The silence deepened. Maybe he isn't even in the cab anymore, she thought. Maybe a black hole just ate him up. Maybe that seat is just empty now.

She glanced toward the passenger side and jerked her eyes quickly back to the road. He was staring at her, his face lit from underneath by the dashboard light, his lips pulled back across his teeth, his eyes wide and fired with hatred, looking like a killer admiring the pulsing veins of her neck for a quick bit of carving.

"We're dead, you know."

The words startled her. The truck swerved slightly. She straightened it out, anxious to fill the broken silence with her own words.

"That's not so. Not by a long shot. We get down there, we get the sumbitch, we get out."

"Won't matter. I'm dead already. You are too. We're ghosts. We ain't even here."

He laughed then. That shut her up and made things worse.

CHAPTER 29

Silva Huerta gunned a shot of well-carameled Pedro Domecq brandy with a loud smack of his lips. Old Pedro made a poor grape distillate that never saw the inside of an oak cask. Like a bottled blonde on the bad side of forty, it leaned on illusion to soften its edges -- jolts of sugar and coloring to make up for the aged attributes it didn't have.

Old Pedro did have cheap locked up. And plenty. And a presence in just about every bar, cantina and cathouse in Juarez. Good thing, Silva thought. When a man wants strong drink, he wants it now. Finish and a little false color don't matter.

With the back of one hand, he wiped beads of alcoholic sweat from his brow and nose while grabbing for an ice water chaser with the other. A nod brought the bartender shuffling over the duckboards.

Silva watched him hoist a bottle from the well. The bartender was old school -- a drooping, gray moustache waxed and parted in the middle of his lip, gray hair brush cut like a Prussian officer's, black sleeve garters on a starched white shirt that covered a hard, round belly curving out and over his black trousers. Before pouring the shot, he presented the bottle as if it were a brandy of royal lineage. He murmured: *"Otro?"*

A nod and the shot glass was filled and slipped within easy reach. Another murmur: *"Suerte, señor."*

Silva arched his back, hoping to loosen the damp cotton shirt that was stuck to his shoulder blades. It was too hot for the wrinkled linen jacket he was sweating through, but was too proud and careful to take off. His slacks were too tight around the gut. The jacket helped hide this, giving his body a thinner line. It also hid the outlines of the Browning Hi-Power stuffed in his waistband, its butt digging into his fat.

He stuck a panatela between his lips. Quick, sulfury flame flared from a kitchen match, struck on the bartender's hard thumb. Silva sucked in the fire, drawing the harsh smoke into his lungs. The bartender pinched the flame between thumb and forefinger. Silva noticed a puckered stump where a ring finger should have been. The bartender turned and Silva saw a long scar, white against brown, running from the front of the ear to the middle of the throat.

Should have noticed that right away, he thought. Should soft pedal the Old Pedro and get sharp for that meet over in Tejasland. Some bubba and his *puta* wanting to take a quiet scoot across the border and safe transport to Matamoros.

Which meant these two Anglos were hot property on both sides of the border -- American law to the north, most likely. Wasn't that always the case for the free-thinking businessmen of *El Norte*? Too many rules up there for true commerce. Too many rules for anyone who didn't already have enough money to buy a way past them.

American law was always after free-thinking men of business like himself. They weren't amused by his chosen profession. *Coyotes* -- that's what he and his brethren businessmen were called, a name that came from their own countrymen. But when it passed the lips of a Border Patrol greenshirt or a suit from *la migra*, it always had a nasty spin on it, like the man was calling him a whore or a bastard.

Coyote. The word was offensive to Silva. He saw himself as a clever operator, faster than any *federale*, but not furtive, doglike or the least bit parasitic.

His self image was made of grander, swoopier stuff. A humanitarian, that's what he was, offering opportunity to those who wanted to escape the poverty of Mexico or El Salvador or Guatemala for the dream they thought was America. Yes, that's what he did -- he gave life to their dreams.

Silva did more than run people across the border for a steep price. He was a full-service entrepreneur, working all phases of the most lucrative commerce in human flesh this side of pornography, prostitution and the old slave trade. While runaway inflation crippled his country's economy and made paupers of its people, Silva's business prospects were heightened by the resulting chaos. People were desperate to move north, pushed by civil war and poverty, pulled by dreams of more money. And the businessmen of *El Norte* were willing to hire them, motivated by the desire for ever-cheaper labor and an ever-lower bottom line.

He had recruiters working the villages of Oaxaca, Chiapas and Campeche. He had scouts sniffing the routes of travel from Central America, looking for young, strong laborers. Single men without families were targeted because wives and children meant complications and costs the businessmen of *El Norte* didn't want to pay and risks he didn't want to run as he hustled people across the border.

Silva had contacts at farms, ranches, factories and construction outfits from California to Chicago. He had forgers churning out Social Security cards and American driver's licenses. He owned safe houses and shelters on both sides of the border -- rest stops for his cargo and another place to ring up another charge on the price tag for a new life.

He had a villa in Puerto Vallarta, a home in the mountains near Guadalajara and a bone-white Lincoln Town Car with red-leather seats, a mobile phone and a TV in the dash. A twin-engined Beech Baron whisked him to rocky desert strips and busy, big-city terminals.

A silent, consumptive Texan named Slick McCoy served as his personal pilot -- thin as a communion wafer and jaundiced from too many bouts of malaria, heptitis and the clap. Referred to him by his sometime business partner, Lefty Moore, Slick was an aging action junky, a retired Army forward observer who flew L-2s in Korea and the early years of Vietnam and made opium runs in Laos for Air America.

A tidy little enterprise, all because he was a free-thinking businessman, smart enough to keep track of every phase of his operation and nervy enough to still make a lot of the border runs himself -- the best way to make sure everything was running right.

American law paid too much attention to their rules to appreciate such zeal and professionalism. Mexican authorities took a more worldly attitude as long as they got their *mordita*. He didn't mind that little bite as long as it stayed that way. When they got too frisky and wanted too much, they had to have their snouts slapped.

Mexican law sure as hell wouldn't care about *Gringo y Gringa Equis*. He'd bet on that. So, who the hell was after them on this side of the river? Or, who did *Senor y Senora Equis* not want to know they were across the border? Interesting and entertaining questions that Silva turned in his mind as he signaled the bartender for coffee, making a saucer out of one hand and raising an imaginary cup to his lips.

Interesting, entertaining and possibly profitable. Silva didn't know for sure. All he had was a time and a place to make the meet, courtesy of a call from Moore. That and the sure, easy 10 K he would pocket just for playing it straight, bringing these people across the river and quietly shepherding them to Matamoros.

Ah, but he was a free-thinking businessman, his mind warm and glowing from Old Pedro, coffee and the thought of other angles in the offing, more money for his pocket if he could find out who was interested in *Gringo y Gringa Equis* on either side of the river.

The coffee was sugary and half cut with cream. Its heat added to the flush of alcohol that was already drawing dark circles under his armpits, another beaded line across his flat, twice-broken nose and a cap of moisture that mixed with the sweet oil of his slickened black hair.

Silva had a broad forehead, bumpy with bone and a dark slash of eyebrows, like the Anglo actor, Burt Reynolds. He had heavy-lidded eyes that were out of kilter. When he got high on weed or far drunker than he was now, one eye would stay wide open while the lid of the other would droop half shut, following its own notion of the proper response to intoxication. Moore and his other Anglo business associates dubbed him Ol' Dope Eye and got a good laugh at his expense. Which was fine with Silva -- while they laughed, he took their money.

His bladder gave a call. He strolled back to the *excusado*, easing the Browning away from the spot where its butt dug into his belly. As he listened to his piss hitting the back of the galvanized trough that served as the bar's urinal, he rolled his head back and stared at the gray ceiling, thinking about who he could call to get his questions answered.

Another sometime associate came to mind. *El Rojo Loco.* Silva laughed and tucked himself back inside his slacks. That one was after everybody. All the time. Lately, everybody seemed to be after *El Rojo Loco.* And why not? The man had a habit of killing his partners. Not exactly the mark of a stable, free-thinking businessman like himself.

He walked back to his place on the bar. The bartender topped his cup and reached toward the well with a murmured *"Otro?"*

"Bastante."

A nod from the bartender and a quiet retreat to his station on the duckboards at the middle of the bar. Silva sipped more hot coffee and thought of angles, *El Rojo Loco* and the *Gringo y Gringa Equis.*

CHAPTER 30

Carla Sue watched the waves of midday heat rise from the tin roof of the barn and the flat, gray sand of the yard and the broken brush hills beyond the fenceline. This wasn't the wet 'n hot of Dallas or Houston, where prickly heat, air conditioning and a can of Desenex were the constants of suburban survival. This heat sucked a person dryer than a Baptist prayer meeting and left the body with parched lips, a layer of gritty salt on burned skin and a light head that saw visions in the shimmering bands of heated air, snaking skyward, blurring the view of the Hueco Mountains far to the north and the Finlay chain to the southeast.

She took a sip of tepid water from a Bell jar with a rusty rim. Its taste was soapy and metallic, like a trace of iron filings mixed with Ivory powder. She took another sip anyway.

She was sitting on the porch of a tarpaper shack, in the middle of a deserted ranch in the desert east of El Paso, thirty miles north of Fabens and the border. The shack once housed the *rancho's* top horseman; the corral and the barn were where the wild horses were tamed and the tamed horses housed.

Through the shack's screen door, Carla Sue could see broken bridles and worn saddles piled in the middle of the floor. A pot-bellied stove, a bunk bed, a table and two chairs and a galvanized sink with a hand pump hooked to the side made up the rest of the shack's inventory.

Bills and newspapers, yellowed with heat and age, fragile as an old man's bones, were scattered on the table. Carla Sue had browsed through them. Those that didn't crumble at her touch told her the ranch was called the Diamond R, the last wrangler was named Hub Rawlins and the subscription to the Sunday edition of the El Paso Herald-Post ran out around the time Elvis died.

She looked at the Bell jar and considered another sip. It wasn't a pleasant thought. She dumped the rest of the water over her head and shivered as it ran through her lank, blonde hair, over her face and chin and down through her open shirt and cleavage.

That felt so good she stepped into the dark, close air of the cabin and pumped up another full jar. She stood on the porch and slowly poured the water over her head, feeling a streak of electricity move from the back of her neck, down her spine and up to the base of her skull again. It made her shake like a dog.

Big 'Un had been gone since dawn, raising a streak of chalk-white dust that billowed off the ranch road in the flat, rising light and sucked up the slipstream of the white F-150 they picked up at a used car lot in Van Horn.

No Bucky Roys this time, no dances in the dirt to dodge a stream of tobacco juice, no high-spirited dickering to make her laugh. Just a simple deal with a simple little man in a plaid shirt and chinos who looked a lot like Bob Newhart.

"In'ersted in this truck?"

She nodded. He handed her the keys, shifting his gaze back and forth between her face and the broken concrete of the car lot like a dog waiting for its owner to unlatch the leash and let him get to the food dish. She took a test spin and brought the truck back into the lot.

"It'll do. Rack it up."

He nodded and shuffled off to start the paper work. Big 'Un waited at a cafe up the street -- Darly's Coffee Pot, Home of the Bottomless Cup, 35 Cents. It wasn't the popular breakfast spot. That was up by the courthouse, its parking spaces filled with pickups and squad cars. Darly's was darker and had a thinner clientele, none of them sporting suits or stars or uniforms or pistols on the hip. Some of them wore hungover faces and the dead eyes of another dull day of minimum wage.

It was a five-table-and-counter joint, full of grease and fly carcasses, squeezed between a hardware store and a discount dress shop. These were the last, threadbare outposts of the main commercial drag, out where the road changed from main artery to the quickest way to get out of town. It was a good place for one of them to hunker down, sip bad coffee and wait for the car lot to open.

The Graydog had brought them to Van Horn from Fort Stockton. Big 'Un dropped her off near the bus station with their gear, then dumped the GMC in the carport of a vacant house near the edge of town. The wait had been a long and nervy one, sitting in the station with two tickets to El Paso and a Colt in her purse and two olive drab cargo bags of automatic weapons, clothes and bundles of cash at her feet.

She leafed through a *Texas Monthly*, idly looking at pictures from the Cullen Davis murder trial, the cutlines barely registering. She wondered if Big 'Un would show up. An hour passed. Then ninety minutes. In another thirty minutes, the westbound bus would pull out. He walked in, his shirt dark with sweat, a duffle bag slung over his shoulder.

Where the hell did he get that? What the hell was he up to? She forced herself to look at the magazine. He walked up to the ticket window, passed some cash across the counter and walked away, tucking the pass into his back pocket. He glanced her way, his eyes as flat and lusterless as the black bottom of a frying pan, then took a seat at the far end of the station, picking up a discarded newspaper.

They took separate seats. She could feel him behind her, seven rows back, slumped in an aisle seat on the opposite side of the bus. She could feel that dead stare on the back of her neck, like the look of accusation from a cheated lover. It pissed her off. *You got us into this! We should be in Mexico by now, safe from the law, planning our run at T-Roy. But you had to play it safe and slow. Play it like a sucker, more like. Just where in the hell do you get off, looking at me like that? What did I do? I mean, I'm sorry your ex is dead, but at least she went quick. I'm sorry it busted you up, but it's not my fault. I'm sorry you got to suck it up or get dead or go to prison forever, but that's the way it is. Just take those eyes off me, Big 'Un. They make my skin crawl and make me feel lousy. I mean it, now. I mean it!*

She spun in her seat and started to rise, angry words in her throat. In the dim light of the Greydog's swaying interior, she could see Burch was asleep, his head canted back, his mouth open in a snore she couldn't hear. His eyes were closed.

"Sorry, m'am, was I snorin'?"

"What?"

"I said I was sorry if my snorin' disturbed you."

She looked into the watery eyes of an older man with rubbery jowls and wisps of white hair sticking out from under a Jack Daniel's gimme cap.

"No, you weren't botherin' me. Not at all."

"Ummm. Well, you spun round so quick, it gave me a start. Kinda reminded me of Myrtle elbowin' me in the ribs if I drifted off in church. She's dead now."

"Who's dead?"

"Myrtle. That's my wife. Or was. Been dead now twelve year."

"Sorry to hear that."

"Thank you, but she's been gone long enough that it don't hurt so much. And I don't miss her like I did at first. 'Cept when somethin' happens that brings her to mind real sudden. Like right now. Felt like ol' Myrtle was spinnin' round to tell me to quit snorin'. Somethin' like that happens and it's like she's right here, naggin' at me to quit smokin' or quit drinkin' or quit eatin' like a pig or somesuch nonsense. Always after me for somethin'. Told me I better take better care or I'd die of a heart attack or a cancer or a stroke."

The old man paused and snorted a short laugh.

"A cancer took her. After worryin' about my health, it gets her. Goes that way, don't it?"

"Yessir, it does. I'm sorry I startled you."

"Tell you the truth, so am I. You brought Myrtle back and I'm gettin' too damn old to keep buryin' her."

She turned back in her seat and slumped down in silence. She could hear the old man breathe then start to snore softly. Part of her wanted to spin into his face and yell: *It's Myrtle comin' at ya, old fart! Quit your damn snorin' or I'll haunt you forever!* Shake him like a rag doll, knock his damn cap off his head, cause his bald scalp to sweat and then get chilled by the draft of air conditioning passing overhead. *Make me feel like shit, old man, and you'll wish it was just Myrtle in your face instead of me. I'm a hundred times worse than bad dreams about your dead wife. You hear me or do I have to buy you a damn hearing aid, stuff it in your ear and shout!*

Wonderful. Getting all bloody-minded about a sad and polite old man. She stared out the window, watching the darkness roll by with its black shadings of things barely seen or not seen at all -- a lifeless house or an old barn; a ridge in the distance or a line of clouds; an oil pump slowly lifting up and down, attended by a cluster of tanks; a rank of old cars that would never be called on to roll again. Maybes all, shapes to guess at, their shrouded details filled in by a mind that always tries to cast light on things that would rather remain in half tones and shadows.

Too tired to snap at a harmless old man. Get a grip and enjoy the bus ride. *See America as a fugitive. Oh, yeah -- the David Janssen tour. Just where in hell is that one-armed man? And when will I get a tap on my shoulder from a cop with white hair, a beefy face and a snap-brim hat?* She kept looking out the window, feeling herself grow sleepy but refusing to give in and close her eyes. The shapes blurred into faces -- Eldon, Uncle Harlan, that black killer in the cave, his bulging-eyed rage frozen in place after Big `Un sent one into his forehead, Neville with his hair on fire, crying that death cry that just begged for leaded release. *They can't be out there, can they? I must be asleep. I can't be seeing them in the window of this bus, can I? I must be asleep. Wish I had a Myrtle to poke me in the ribs and tell me to stop snorin'. Wish I wasn't on this damn bus. Wish I was in Mexico gettin' ready to kill T-Roy.*

A fist punched her shoulder. The bus was stopped. The sky was starting to lighten with dawn, like cream slowly drizzled into coffee. Her neck was cramped. She rubbed it and rolled her head around. Her eyes focused on Big 'Un's back as he shuffled up the aisle, duffle bag hanging behind his left shoulder, bracing one of the cargo bags on his thigh, holding it in front of him so it wouldn't bang into the seat backs or the lolling heads and arms of sleeping passengers.

She shook herself awake and grabbed her purse and jacket out of the seat next to her. She swung the other cargo bag down from the rack with a grunt and moved up the aisle, choking down an urge to call out. The door to the bus station swallowed him up. She pushed past two cowboys, a mother trying to stack up a stroller with a baby in her arm and three old women gaily chatting about the joys of Metamucil.

He wasn't in the station. She hustled through the front door. He was to the left of the door, his shoulders and one boot braced against the wall behind him, his face turned away like someone looking for a ride that should be moving up the street but wasn't. The cargo bag and duffle were at his feet, two Mutt & Jeff sacks of olive drab canvas. Smoke curled up from the Lucky on his lip.

"Don't talk to me. Don't look at me. Hit the ladies room. Dig out enough cash to buy us another truck. There's a car lot two blocks the way I'm lookin'. Kill some time inside. Look like you're waiting on somebody. I'll be at Darly's."

"Where are we?"

He pushed himself away from the wall and slapped a plaque with the flat of his hand. Raised letters of tarnished brass said: "Bus Station. Van Horn, Texas. Works Progress Administration. 1937."

"Where we're at, okay?"

He hoisted the duffle over his left shoulder and bent down to pick up the cargo bag. He straightened and looked at her like she was the world's sorriest red-headed stepchild.

"You got shit for brains today, sweetcheeks. Start suckin' it up or we ain't gonna be loose and crazy much longer."

She wanted to say she was sorry, but couldn't. He made that sucking noise against his teeth, setting her nerves on edge, then turned and walked toward the cafe, leaving her standing next to the bus station door, angry with herself for feeling apologetic and with him for being such a stiff prick so early in the morning.

Bob Newhart's bubba cousin was slow with the paper work. When he finally got done, the day's heat was set to stun and the view of the brown-black spines of mountain was wavy and broken.

She drove the truck out of the lot and cruised slowly past Darly's, turning down the first side street and parking halfway down the block, next to a garage of ridged aluminum, freshly painted the color of lemon pie filling. Dark red letters above the wide, double-bay door said: Villabuena. The next line, in smaller letters: Expert Auto Mechanic.

She reached for the long, rectangular mirror that hung from a white metal rack on the truck's door. It didn't move easily. She whacked the mirror with the flat of her palm until it budged enough to give her a view of the corner behind her. With one eye on the mirror, she flipped the radio on, spinning the dial, searching for a station.

... *Now, don't it make my brown eyes*
Don't it make my brown eyes
Don't it make my brown eyes
Blu-hoo.

Jesus. Loretta's baby sister. The very essence of the limp-wristed pop sound that Nashville tried to pass off as country. No fiddles. No steel guitars. Just swish music from the same family that brought the world *You Ain't Woman Enough To Take My Man*. What in hell's hot acres ever went wrong with the gene pool of the coal miner's daughter?

She spun the dial past a livestock report, a Spanish ballad, a grocery store spot and a lot of static. She settled in on the back half of a Mel Street tune, "Borrowed Angel." She jumped when something banged into the back of the cab -- Big 'Un, slinging his duffle and cargo bag into the truck box, pulling open a passenger side door that signaled its reluctance with a loud, metallic croak.

He handed her a cardboard pop-up tray with a styrofoam cup of coffee and a sausage-and-egg biscuit wrappd in wax paper. His jeans made a soft, rippling sound, like a teen popping the pockets of air in a piece of plastic packing that cushions a new stereo receiver, as he slid his butt across the sticky red vinyl surface of the bench seat and slammed the door.

They took farm-to-market blacktop to Allamore and pulled into a small motel -- Hargrove's Motor Court, Clean & Cheap! They waited for nightfall. She slept. He cleaned their guns, stared out the window and said only enough to answer functional questions like whether he wanted a Coke or a Dr. Pepper when she went out to find them some hamburgers.

His silence was easier to manage. It no longer unnerved her and didn't seem like a finger of accusation. Maybe she was getting used to it. Maybe she didn't care. After eating the burgers, he ducked out to use a pay phone. At dusk, they loaded up their gear and pulled out. As he climbed into the truck, he broke his silence for a simple instruction.

"Drive to Fabens."

He fell into a deep sleep before they cleared town, his silence broken by his snoring.

CHAPTER 31

Brown and jagged, the Franklin Mountains thrust at the heart of El Paso like a sword from the gods. Not a Baptist god rambling on about hell's fiery furnace but something pagan, Stone Age and earthbound, forcing the town to bend around the broad, blunt point, caught between the sharp, rising rocks and the Rio Grande.

Newer subdivisions bravely terraced up the barren, sloping edges, the thickest ranks on the northeast side, next to the sprawling reservation of Fort Bliss, where Pershing launched his fruitless expedition against Pancho Villa, where the Army trained its cavalry, its tankers and its missilemen as the nation's threat shifted from the Apache and Comanche to the German and Japanese then the Russian.

North of the sword point, a well-paved road runs a pass through the crest of the mountains, linking the west side of town where it sweeps up toward New Mexico, hugging the culverted banks of the river, with the flat desert of the eastern side of town and the bleakness of Bliss, its whitewashed barracks, its earth-colored housing for married personnel.

The asphalt is smooth and black as it cranks into hairpin ascents and descents, its early sections of straightaways marked by the challenge of a suicide lane for those with strong transmissions and muscular engines. He could hear them whine as they started the long grade up the western slope, headlamps arcing up from the river valley and the city lights spreading out below him, bright and closely clustered on the American side, dimmer and scattered randomly on the Mexican side, in the town named for one of Mexico's few true democratic leaders, Benito Juarez, the country's saviour through civil wars and French intervention, the Zapotec Indian who set the mark almost none of his successors hit in the century since his death.

He was perched behind the rocks of a chimney-shaped promitory that gave him a good view of the road, the valley as it ran up toward Canutillo and La Union and the long parking lot of the scenic overlook where his pickup sat, a square of dull, white metal in the falling darkness. He got there before sunset, three hours before the meet, armed with two sliced brisket sandwiches wrapped in wax paper, two bottles of Tecate beer, a pair of Bushnell binoculars, a .45 covered by the flopping tails of his plaid rancher's shirt, a spare clip stuffed down his right boot and one of the MP-5s in the canvas duffle bag he picked up in a Fort Stockton thrift store.

To the tourists who climbed the rocks to look down at the lights and see the sun sink low over the river valley and the table of land that rose up around La Mesa, he looked like a local enjoying a private happy hour, longneck in one hand, sandwich in the other, a sweat-stained Resistol with a cattleman's crease and a dipped-down brim perched on his head, worn boots braced against the rock. He smiled and waved a longneck at some, nodding a hello as he felt the slide of the Colt wear a groove in his back.

He didn't feel a particular need to hide. His position gave him a long view of the people climbing his way. They couldn't see him until they reached the top. By that time, he had them pegged and well covered. A faint goat track fell off the rock face, hidden from the parking lot, a nice backdoor if he didn't like the looks of the Mex that was supposed to meet him here.

He didn't feel a particular need to flee. The Mex was a sometime partner of Lefty Moore, not an arc-welded guarantee, but about as good a reference as he could expect in a situation like this. Not someone to trust, but someone who knew the persuasive language of cash and the sure fact Moore wouldn't tolerate a cross. Not on this side of the border.

But that wasn't why he felt comfortable and sure, sitting on this hot bare rock, burping up beer and barbecue. He felt good with his guns and the strong will to rise up and take on anything thrown his way. He felt at ease. Not dumb and happy but alert, boosted by the job at hand and how it helped him attain his ultimate goal.

He hadn't felt this way in a long time. Not since he was working next to Wynn Moore, learning the patient cop's trade, the slow buildup of a case, the steady sifting and questioning, the grinding determination to stay on track and ride to the end of the line. It was something you never talked about, something you either had or didn't, something you recognized in others and noticed when it was absent in a man.

For years, he had operated on lukewarm substitutes for this fire -- a professional's reflexes, the routine of duty and the contrarian's stubborn desire to prove everybody wrong, from the suits who wanted to bounce him off the force to the ex-wives who discovered he wasn't the solid guy they thought they married. He did good work this way and could kid himself that he was the same badass he was before Moore got killed and the suits started chivvying his flanks. But he couldn't kid the exes and couldn't always hide the hollowness from himself in those hours when he wasn't working, when he wasn't standing with his foot on the rail at Joe Miller's or Louie's, recycling old stories and pumping Maker's Mark into his belly and bloodstream.

A man afraid of finding his foot dangling over a long drop tends to pull back and shorten his stride. He tends to narrow his scope and keep things close and simple. A small apartment. A cramped office. Thrift store furniture. A worn groove between office, home and bar. Work that doesn't challenge and doesn't force a stretch beyond that invisible border he never wants to cross again. Women who don't do the same thing.

All because he was afraid someone would crack his crusty shell and find out he was as empty as a painted Easter egg with the yoke drained out. His shell was sure shattered now, his emptiness on display for anyone who cared to look, along with signs that he was becoming seriously unhinged.

It didn't matter. No one stood up, pointed and made a loud noise about the hole where his guts and pride should be. He found out something others found out a long time ago -- a man can spend a lot of energy hiding something about himself that no one gives half a damn about.

He was on the other side of that shattered shell now, up and roving across the border again, ranging out with the cold, hard sense of purpose that left him a long time ago. After years of trying to rope off complexity and keep things simple and clear, he found himself on track toward a destination that was brutal, violent and elemental.

He hadn't dealt this play. And it wasn't a game he asked to be in. But here he was waiting on a *coyote*, a gun in the bag and one riding above the crack of his butt, with that old, icy sureness in his gut that he thought had died. It was a different feeling from the bring-it-on flush of macho he felt a few days ago, deeper and fully uncoiled by the pain of Juanita's death. It was not something that would bubble to the surface and evaporate like a slick of alcohol on the skin.

Someone had killed people dear to him. Twice. That someone had to die. Simple and clear.

He watched heat lightning flare across the northern horizon, up toward Las Cruces. The sky above him was clear and dappled with stars. Specks of light scattered across the dark bottom land below, forming a rough, imperfect mirror of the heavens. He could feel rather than see the lonely mountain humps west of the mesa, single and well-spaced domes of rock that looked like they were resting on the desert flatness, rootless and ready to be hauled away.

Headlamps drifted over the crest of the road behind him, catching his eye as the beams broke a line of darkness even with his right shoulder. The lights cut into the parking lot, leading a long white car, then swept over his pickup as the driver cut a rough S across the gravel-flecked blacktop, searching the far corners of otherwise empty blacktop.

A lone figure got out of the car, straightening his jacket, setting his shoulders, walking toward the pickup. Burch watched as the man looked in the windows of his truck. Burch checked the goat trail and the slope below him, then turned toward the man and pitched a low-toned whistle into the darkness. The MP-5 was out of the bag and leveled at the man.

"C'mon up, mister. Keep your hands out where I can see 'em."

The man waved and started striding toward the trail that led up through the rocks.

"A fine evening for such a fine view, my friend."

"I'm not here for the view, mister."

"Of course not. You're here to do business. Like me. And I can see you're a man who takes business seriously. Like me. I like that."

"You got hardware stuffed down your pants. Let's see it on the ground. Thumb and pinkie, bud. Left hand. Real slow."

The pistol was dark, slim and square as the man leaned forward and gingerly placed it on a flat rock in front of him.

"Thank you for not making me throw it into the sand. It's an old gun and I try to take care of it."

"And it will take care of you, right?"

The man smiled.

"And it will take care of me. Always. Unless the other has a bigger gun. Like you."

"Step back and to your right. That's it."

The man now stood where Burch could keep an eye on the goat trail, the slope below and most of the lot.

"Where's Huerta?"

"Right here, my friend. I don't send errand boys to do business with the friends of Lefty Moore. He is an old and trusted associate. His people I see myself."

"I appreciate the consideration."

"This is how I do business. It is how I stay on top of the heap and avoid the fall that happens to so many of my competitors. They get fat and out of touch. Their people betray them or fail them in less treacherous ways. I'm like the general who goes to the front to get the true feel of the flow of battle."

"No battle here, mister. Just business."

Burch placed the MP-5 on the rock beside him. The man grinned.

"A courtesy."

"To you and Lefty Moore."

"Of course. I understand your situation is delicate. I assume that means the law on this side of the border. And on my side? I assume the *federales* are not your problem."

"*Federales* on any side of the border are a problem."

"Not in Mexico, my friend. Not for someone who hasn't commited a crime against the ruling party. Not for someone who gives them their little bite to look the other way. Not for someone who isn't foolish enough to be on their list of undesireables to be turned over to the American DEA. Unless I am sadly mistaken, you are not a Mexican national, my friend, and you don't normally do business on my side of the border."

"True enough. Maybe."

"Come, my friend, you can see my side of the situation. I am taking a risk helping out someone who may be the sworn enemy of people who could do me great harm. I have to be prepared to meet their threat."

"It is a gamble, isn't it?"

Huerta shrugged.

"*Sí,* and one you are about to pay me well to take. But let us just say I'm curious and troubled by your need to be quietly transported down to Matamoros. If your only problem was the *federales* of my country, there are a variety of soft routes you could take on your own. You have the contacts to tell you how to get to any of them."

"And the money and guns to take care of myself and mine."

Huerta grinned.

"That is obvious. So, you make me think there is somebody after you on my side of the border. Somebody who is a great threat. To me as well as you and the woman who travels with you. As an example, there is someone near Matamoros who is very dangerous and very crazy. He is called *El Rojo Loco* by some. Like you, he is a Texan who chooses to live in my country because it is the land of the truly free. I would want to know if our business involves him in even the most tangental manner."

"I understand what you're saying, mister. Let's just say it would pay you to keep this very quiet. On both sides of the border. I have a family connection to Lefty Moore and, as you well know, he is not a nice man. Not even a little bit. You should worry about him as a threat more than anyone on your side of the border."

"Nice is not one of Señor Moore's attributes, that much is true. You don't have to spell out his guarantee in this transaction and the sanctions that will fall on me should I somehow fail to hold up my end of the deal. It hurts me that you have so little trust that you feel you must spell this out."

"No offense, mister. This is just the way I do business. Cards on the table. No guesswork. Everybody on the same page."

"The Yankee way, my friend. No serious offense taken. Nothing that cannot be smoothed over with a drink. *Con su permiso?*"

Huerta opened one side of his jacket, gesturing toward an inside pocket with a sweep of the hand. Burch eased his gun hand back toward the Colt, freeing it from his back and belt, nodding and smiling as he kept his eyes locked on Huerta's face.

"Pinkie and thumb, mister. I'm too old to take chances and trust strangers."

"I'm hurt, my friend. We have much in common. We have Lefty Moore. We should drink to his health and this deal we are about to close. Then we can work out the details about hateful things like money and time and place."

"What are we drinking, mister?"

"A modest little brandy they make on my side of the border."

Old Pedro lost none of his bite on this side of the border. And he gained no smoothness or aged charm.

Chapter 32

On the last street corner in America, the mercury-vapor lamps that arced over the bridge to Juarez and the Customs checkpoint you had to pass before you could walk free and clear into Gringoland cast a harsh yellow light on the figures moving through the early morning cold.

It was just past two but already they gathered on the corner of Sixth and El Paso, their features sharpened or shadowed by the light, huddling in small groups on the sidewalk or ducking into La Perla, an all-night coffee stand, for a small cup of caffeined warmth and some gossip washed in harsh, flourescent light.

They waited for a slow-rolling pickup and a finger pointing at them from an open window, picking them for a dawn-to-dusk day in the chile fields three hours north in New Mexico. They waited for a long ride in an old school bus and another round of stoop labor and rip-off wages that wouldn't end until ten that night.

Burch sat in an after-hours cantina two blocks north of the bridge and the waiting farm laborers. A table in back. A lukewarm bottle of Tecate and a shot of Sauza Especial for show. The Colt wedged above his butt for business.

The money Carla Sue clipped from Ross was almost gone. They needed more from her stash but couldn't get to it. Moore was playing stakehorse for them, but Moore was far away and probably being watched and Silva Huerta was a man who dealt only in cash, even when doing business with friends of old associates.

That's why he was sitting in a *cantina* on El Paso Street, waiting on a man named Angel Morales, another Moore contact, and a packet of money that would wind up in Huerta's pocket. The next best thing when Western Union wouldn't do.

He wasn't the only Anglo in the joint, but he was the only one staying put. Pool sharks, poker sharps and swing-shift zombies ducked in and out, downing quick shots or short drafts, then heading for home or the next game. The Mex regulars paid them little attention and pointedly ignored him.

A thin, sharp-featured man with a pencil moustache, a wavy pompadour and a shiny grey suit flecked with white and black strands of fabric walked in with a woman hugging his arm. The man gave short nods to the regulars, who were drinking in the woman's curves with exaggerated appreciation.

She had exaggerated curves. Hips that flared fully over well-muscled dancer's legs. Ass cheeks and breasts that pushed the limits of her white spandex dress as much as the stretchy fabric was supposed to pull against those body parts. Gold chains that dipped between cleavage deepened by the press of spandex.

Her skin was the color of whiskey held up against the soft light of an old saloon with worn brass rails and a mahogony bar. Her face was heart-shaped and dominated by slanting cheekbones that hid her black eyes when she smiled.

Wild curls framed her face and cascaded below the shoulder blades of her exposed back. The curls were black now -- natural or bottled, Burch couldn't tell. They used to be blonde -- definitely from a bottle, the same bottle used by all the girls who worked at Jimmy Carl Danmayer's joint on Harry Hines back in the D.

Jimmy C's Fabulous Ferris Wheel Club, where the fabulous Shasta did her featured number in a shower stall wheeled down the main ramp and the customers who paid a premium for their table dances were offered cozier comforts in the back rooms.

Burch was working vice back then and the woman on the dandy's arm was calling herself Amber Motion. She worked the side ramps, the tables and the back rooms, a teen runaway from the San Antonio barrio who wanted to dance on Broadway but ended up on a more sordid boulevard of lights.

He tried to nail Jimmy C for employing underaged talent, but her ID was perfect and she always looked him straight in the eye when she repeated the alias Jimmy C gave her -- Niki Delgado. Amber Motion when she hit the stage.

Burch pegged her as 16, maybe 17, back then. Her act was pure sex and energy, awkwardly punctuated with a few ballet and jazz steps that only confused the lust-stricken clientele. No polish. But all Amber needed to do was walk the ramp and roll her hips and breasts and 45-year-old married men reached for their wallets.

Fifteen years later that was still all she needed to do. She surveyed the room with a practiced eye, letting her gaze linger on this man or that, giving these random choices the false hope that they could take the dandy's place.

Burch pulled down the brim of his Resistol and leaned over his stale drinks, hoping she wouldn't catch his eye or see his face. He cursed Angel Morales for picking this place to meet. They were at the bar now, backs to the 'tender, drinks in hand, Amber leaning into the dandy's chest and thigh, absently brushing his chest with the back of her knuckles as she took a pull of Carta Blanca and scoped the room.

He saw her rap the dandy's chest and whisper, leaning her body into his, then nodding toward the table where the bar's only Anglo ex-cop sat. He watched her walk his way, drawing the eye of every man in the room. She stopped at the edge of his table and leaned across, flipping up the brim of his hat to give him a better look at the deeply-split flesh spilling from the top of her dress.

"I told Miguel it was you. I always remember a cop's face. What the hell are you doing in my town? You're a Dallas boy, right?"

"Used to be. How you doin', Amber? Sit down. Give the boys a chance to cool their action. Wave your friend over, too. I'm buyin'."

"Amber. Goddam, I haven't used that name since the Bee Gees were hip. My God, I remember you now -- the big vice cop who was always trying to find out my real name and just how underage I really was."

"Jimmy C's place. Harry Hines."

"A broken street lamp and a blow job on every corner, right *vato?*"

"The same."

She smiled and took another pull from her beer.

"If I sit down, Miguel will think he has to cut you."

She grabbed a chair and straddled it backwards, arms dangling over the ladder back, eyes hidden by a grin that caused her cheekbones to rise. She took another pull of beer then slapped the tabletop and laughed.

"I remember you now. We used to call you Professor Noble Bear because of your glasses and the way you used to shamble along. You never hit us up for a freebie. Hell, as I remember it, you never even tried to cop a feel."

"Not for lack of want to."

She drew her head back and arched a Maybellined eyebrow.

"Ohhh? Not so noble now?"

"Not a cop. And you're not a teenager no more."

"But you're still a bear. You growl like one. You got big shoulders like one. Bet you still walk like one. But I bet you're a nice bear to a mama bear. Am I right?"

She reached across the table to scratch his chest with long, red nails. He brushed her hand away and watched Miguel walk their way, his face a kiln-fired mask over a moustache and a grin.

"Has tenido tu ultima bebida y tu ultima mirada, señor. Creo que es hora de irte a otro bar donde estaras mas en casa -- un bar para maricones."

Last drink and last peek -- a warning, then an insult -- go drink someplace more homey, like a fag bar. Delivered with flashing eyes and the intent to lock him up in a staredown. No sale. Burch watched Miguel's hands. His Colt was already drawn, hammer back, held in his off-hand, his right, the one farthest away from Amber.

"Tell boyfriend to cool his jets. Tell him I meant no offense. Tell him his next drink is on me."

"I don't think Miguel wants to drink with you, Papa Bear. I think he wants to cut your cock off and stuff it down your throat."

"Tell him I wouldn't take kindly to that."

She laughed and spun toward the dandy.

"Sientate e saluda a mi primer y mejor amante. Es el que me enseno como. Hacerle el amor a un hombre. Puedes aprender algo de un hombre como este."

She laughed and ran her fingers along Burch's right arm.

"I just told him you took my cherry and were still more of a man than he is. Told him he could learn a thing or two from a *macho* like you."

"I heard."

"Oh, so Noble Bear knows Spanish now. You didn't in the old days, back when you wanted to take my cherry but were too noble to do so."

"Your cherry was long gone by the time I first slapped eyes on you."

She laughed and slapped his arm.

"The bear still growls. Ohh, I like that."

She turned to Miguel.

"Para de estar parado con esa mirada estupida. Acuchilale o sientate y bebe con nosotros."

Some choice -- have a drink with your woman's old lover or stick his ass into the next world. A switchblade flashed in Miguel's hand as he lunged across the table, slashing at Burch's face. Burch caught the dandy in the midsection with an open left hand, grabbing the front of his suit and adding to his forward momentum with a short tug and a quick pivot out of his chair.

Miguel crashed into the wall. His knife skittered across the floor. Burch slammed a knee across Miguel's chest and stuck the Colt in his face. His hat was askew, its brim badly gashed.

"Tell boyfriend I don't have to kill him, but I will."

Amber still straddled her chair, looking at Burch with an arched eyebrow. She took a final pull of beer and swung the empty bottle in a lazy arc.

"I don't think he's your biggest problem, Papa Bear."

Burch looked back and saw five *vatos* stepping his way, bottles and bats in hand. He stood up, yanked Miguel to his feet and flashed the Colt.

"Tell the boys Miguel and I are taking a short walk. Tell them he'll come back from that walk in one piece as long as I stay in one piece."

She turned to the circle of regulars: *"No creo que va a matar a Miguel o ningun otro. No tiene cojones. Si no son mujeres lo pueden tomar facilmente."*

Great – got no balls for killing, an easy mark unless the *vatos* were a bunch of women. A voice from the regulars: *"Tomale tu misma. En tu boca, en tu culo, en tu nariz. Tiene tu amante."*

Burch almost laughed -- take him yourself bitch, in your mouth, up your ass, up your nose; it's your boyfriend he's got. At least one of these slicks wasn't behind the tequila curve.

He waved the Colt: *"¡Muchachos! Les he fastidiado. Lo siento. Mi nuevo amigo y yo vamos a dar un paseo. Lo dejere sano y contento."*

An apology -- would it stick? A promise not to kill – would they believe it? A quick exit -- would he make it? Burch muscled Miguel toward the rear exit -- a firedoor propped open with a rusty length of pipe. He kicked open the door and shoved Miguel outside, leveling the Colt back on the regulars as he stepped across the threshold and slammed the door shut.

Miguel swung a punch and missed. Burch slammed his head into the door frame of a black Silverado with smoked glass and West Coast side mirrors, then wrestled him back toward the white pickup, angling away from the rear exit, eyeing it for the first sign of regulars wanting to do the Anglo stomp.

Burch shoved Miguel into the side of his pickup, watching him sprawl headfirst into the door. He fished for his keys and shot a quick glance toward the rear exit again. Out of the corner of his eye, he saw a short figure step from the shadows. He leveled the Colt at the man.

"Step on out where I can see you."

"I'm not a threat, mister, just a friend. Besides, if I'd a wanted to take you, I'd have done it a long time ago."

The man spoke in the flat sing-song of a Chicano ranch hand. The broad brim of his hat shadowed all but his mouth and jaw.

"Morales?"

"*Sí.*"

"The money?"

"Twenty grand. Already in the glove box."

"The truck was locked."

"*Sí.* So was the glove box. *No problema.*"

"Thanks, pard. Keep an eye on this guy till I get the truck fired up."

"No thanks, my friend. I have to live around here."

"A wise man. Give our friend my thanks."

"I will. He'd want me to tell you this -- for a guy on the run, you sure have a bad habit of attracting attention. Get where you're going now because you sure got the notice of some people who will make it hot for you in this town. On both sides of the law."

"You picked the place, pard. I just made the mistake of agreeing to meet you there."

"I'll tell you this from me -- you're the type who'd draw flies underwater. *Adios,* bud. Hope you live long enough to pay our friend back."

Burch fired up the truck. The rear exit of the cantina boomed open. Angel Morales disappeared quicker than the smoke from his parting shot.

CHAPTER 33

His skin was tight and hot around the stitches. His right hand and arm had four I-V needles taped down and poking into his veins. His left arm was strapped to his side, bound by the same bulging mass of gauze, tape and elastic wrapping that immobilized his bullet-shattered shoulder.

He couldn't eat. He couldn't drink. He couldn't scratch his balls. He couldn't even hold a bedpan and piss into it. If he tried to move, the bones in his shoulder ground together, causing his stomach to lurch and bile to rise in his throat.

All he could do was sit back and watch the TV shows his roomate picked -- replays of *The Andy Griffith Show*, *Green Acres* and *The Beverly Hillbillies*. On morphine, Jethro took on protean, existential overtones that rivaled Sartre and Camus. On morphine, ol' Andy seemed dark, malevolent and Machiavellian, preying on the simple, gentle souls of Mayberry. On morphine, Eb seemed Christ-like in his innocence.

The phone rang. And rang. And rang. He couldn't reach it. He yelled for a nurse. He yelled to his roomate. The phone rang. A nurse rushed in and picked it up. She held the receiver to his face.

"Cider?"

His answer sounded like a cross between a croak and a bleat. His mouth was dry. His tongue felt like sandpaper.

"Cider? Is this Detective Jones? Have I got the room of Houston Detective Cider Jones?"

He looked at the nurse with pleading eyes. She pulled the receiver to her ear.

"This is Officer Jones' room. He's unable to talk. This is his nurse, Miss Adenauer. Can I take a message?"

She listened. She nodded. He tried to watch her face, but it hurt his shoulder to turn his head toward her. She nodded again.

"I'll tell him. Thank you for calling. Yes, he's doing well for a man with a smashed shoulder. Will he what?"

She laughed and cupped the receiver.

"He wants to know if you'll ever wrestle steers again."

His eyes were flat. She shrugged.

"He's not in the mood for jokes. Thanks for calling. I'll tell him."

She hung up and shook a finger at him.

"Humor is a great healer, Officer Jones. Even bad humor."

"I'll try to remember."

A definite croak now, not a bleat.

"What was the call?"

"What?"

"The call."

"Oh. That was your lieutenant. He said to tell you they know where that criminal Burch is at. He said to tell you El Paso and the Rangers were on the way to nab him. He said you'd be glad to hear that. Is he the man who shot you?"

"No. They don't have him yet?"

"Who?"

"Burch."

"Oh. Apparently not, but he seemed to think it was a sure thing."

"Lady, there ain't been a sure thing since this whole clusterfuck started."

She flushed and put a hand over her mouth. He started to laugh, but the grating bones in his shoulder made him gag instead. His humor wasn't the healing kind.

CHAPTER 34

The Duchess hit an updraft that slammed Burch deep into his seat and made him taste bile in the back of his throat. Lightning cut a white hole in the darkness. Rain hammered the plane's thin aluminum skin.

They were at fifteen thousand feet, well above the jagged desert peaks of northern Mexico but well below the tops of the late-night thunderstorms that roamed the border sky, remnants of a Pacific storm that was riding the jet stream from Baja California up into Texasland.

Slick McCoy, Huerta's pox-ridden and opium-addicted pilot, slalomed the storm clouds, humming a toneless tune as he consulted the Stormscope to pick out the mildest rides the wild black sky had to offer.

Burch could hear Slick's humming through the lime-green Dave Clark headsets worn by each of the four people in the Duchess. Silva Huerta turned back to look at Burch and Carla Sue, bending his boom mike closer to his mouth to speak to them over the intercom. The words crackling into Burch's ear were disconnected from the movement of Huerta's mouth, adding to the jarring, disjointed feeling created by the movement of storm and plane.

"It's good you called me as soon as you did, my friend. It is a bad night for flying but a good night to get you away from your hiding place. Friends tell me the *Los Rinches* hit the ranch about an hour after you and your lady friend left."

"So this is where luck takes us."

"Don't start that death and faith crap again, Big 'Un."

Burch snapped his head around. He forgot she was there.

"It's truth and you know it. I ought to be able to tell it. I've paid enough money to say what I want in this damn plane."

Huerta knitted his brow as he listened to this, then grinned, his teeth and most of his face green in the glow of the instrument lights.

"Luck has been kind to you so far, my friend. You are lucky tonight, riding with such an experienced pilot as Slick here. Did you know he flew for Air America? He is an old and government-trained brigand, right Slick?"

Slick said nothing and reached forward to adjust the twin throttles and dial in the next fix on the plane's radio navigation receiver, a complex little black box known as a LORAN.

Looking over Slick's shoulder, when he wasn't blinded by a flash of lightning, Burch could see the needles for the each engine's oil pressure gauges and tachometers were riding in the green -- which meant they would be safe and happy if they didn't fly slap into a storm cell that put too much stress on the airframe.

"He's done this before."

"Many times, my friend. Many times."

Burch had pulled Carla Sue out of the deserted ranch house above Fabens about an hour after he bulled his way out of the *cantina*. They had called Huerta from a Shamrock gas station; he had directed them to one of his safe houses out on the desert flats east of El Paso. Slick landed the Duchess on a dirt road near the house, its packed surface maintained by Huerta's subordinates.

"This is not the way I would have moved you, my friend, but your little show in town gave us no choice. Of course, the fee will be higher."

"How much higher?"

"Three grand each for Slick and I. You are -- how does Moore put it? Ah, you are riding with the pros tonight; you have to pay the premium for the privilege."

"That sounds like Lefty. Done."

By the moonlit early hours of the next morning, they were an hour into a hike along a narrow goat track that ran through a string of low hills about forty miles below Matamoros.

Slick had flown them to a small tarmac strip just south of the city with radio-activated runway lights and a deserted hangar made of corrugated aluminum.

One of Moore's men waited to drive them deeper into Mexico and guide them into the countryside. Conjo -- fucker. Little about his look justified the name. He was a short man with shaggy hair, a dark, sharp-boned face that shielded deep-set eyes and a flattened nose that looked like it came from somebody twice as large as him.

He wore rope-soled sandals and a severely modified Ruger Mini-14 carbine -- plastic foregrip, hinged aluminum tube stock, a 30-round banana clip and a wicked-looking flash suppressor. Clothes, shoes and gun were black – flat instead of glossy. Not even his hair had a shine to it.

Conjo was Nicaraguan, one of the ex-contras brought up to the border by T-Roy. He had taken an instant dislike to his new *patrón* and *La Madrina*, drifting away from their *rancho*, hooking up with Moore's partners, rivals with a long-standing blood grudge against *La Madrina* and her sons. Something about a *patrón* having his heart cut out. Something Conjo greeted with a shudder because the same thing happened to the *jefe* who had brought them to *La Bruja's rancho* and *El Rojo Loco*.

Conjo said little as he led them along, a word or two to point out bends in the trail and treacherous footing. He didn't seem to mind Burch's babbling, words that weren't loud but were rambling. Carla Sue wondered whether the scene at the bat cave hadn't cracked Burch's egg.

"I remember this movie one time. Forget what it was all about. Anyway -- this Irish guy, some workin' stiff, got canned. He looks at the white-collar guy who's givin' him the shove and his eyes are just glaring like he wants to kill the guy on the spot. You can see all the things this guy wants to say right there in his face. He looks like he's gonna spit on the white-collar guy, then thinks better of it, like this guy isn't even worth the moisture. Not the guy, but the whole ball of wax -- the job, his life, everything. He looks him right in the eye and says -- 'You're just a petty, fookin' bee-ur-r-r-a-crat.'"

"What's your point, Big 'Un?"

"Just this -- the difference between me and you. Hate's been burnin' you up for years, but there's a lot still to burn up. You still got lots of fuel. Me -- it's different. I got my gears stripped bad by bureaucrats and wives. No fuel, nothin' left, nothin' worth the effort. Nothin' for me. Nothin' for a woman. That's what I thought. That's the way I was livin'. But I was wrong. Now I find out I got enough inside me for the hate to start burnin' one more time. Just enough for one more ride. No more, though."

"We'll just have to make that ride count then, won't we."

"Won't matter. We're dead."

"Not that shit again."

Burch said nothing. His mood had shifted. They kept walking for another hour, their breathing, the slap of brush on clothing and the calls of night animals the only sounds.

Conjo led them to a bowl-shaped hollow just beneath the brow of a hill, guiding them through a thick wall of undergrowth to a dark, rocky clearing at the base of the bowl. They were five miles from the *rancho*, three miles from T-Roy's perimeter security, manned by Conjo's former *compadres*.

"I know these men. T-Roy pays them pesos, gives tequila, women, blow. They don't give a shit for him."

Carla Sue waited for an explanation. When none came, she spurred more words out of the guide.

"He killed our *jefe*. No man like him much, but he was of us. Many do the same thing I do -- walk away."

"They do the same thing you're doin'?"

"Hey, lotta work for a man who can use a gun, lady."

"Can you get us past them?"

"Them, yes. But *El Rojo Loco* got his own men. He got heat and motion detectors. Then *La Bruja* and her sons."

Conjo told her about the *La Bruja*, his face twisting up and his voice gaining a quiet heat as he talked about the ceremonies, the cauldron and the human sacrifice.

"You mean she eats the damn heart?"

"*Si*. Her sons, too. It is something her husband did. He once cut the heart out of the *jefe* of those I work for now. For the power."

"Jesus Christ, Big 'Un, what the fuck are we walkin' into -- Nightmare on Beaner Street?"

Burch wasn't talking. He sat away from them, cleaning his .45 and that sweet German submachine gun he now called *El Niño*.

"He all there, lady? He talks too much. Now he don't say nothin.' And look at him with that gun -- I think he wants to fuck that gun."

"He'll ride the river."

"*¿Que?*"

"Don't worry about him. I'll do that. You just worry about getting us past your old compadres and into that damn *rancho*."

Daylight filtered through the thick canopy. Conjo broke out mosquito netting, sleeping mats and repellant. He gave them thick strips of jerky, then wrapped himself in netting and sat cross-legged against the trunk of a tree, falling asleep, his Ruger in his lap.

They tried to follow suit, but the air was heavy with humidity and buzzing bugs that made it hard to breathe and harder to drop off. Light dozing, punctuated by gasps and slaps, marked much of their day. Conjo snored loudly. Carla Sue wondered how many mosquitoes got sucked into his mouth.

Nightfall. More strips of jerky. Washed down by cold, bitter coffee spiked with raw sugar-cane juice. The coffee was the color of old crankcase oil and thick like a bad batch of bock beer. It snapped them awake instantly, more from fumes than caffeine and sugar.

They were stiff and tripped easily in the gray moonlight. Conjo moved like a young goat, walking them right into the guns of a squad of men hidden in the thick brush. Their first clue was the ratcheting clack of assault rifles being cocked and the sight of two men stepping onto the trail in front of them. Burch froze and started to reach for his Colt until he felt the warm muzzle of Conjo's Mini-14 press into the back of his neck.

"Not the wise choice. *Mi compadres* are trigger happy. They would rather shoot than guard you on the long walk back to the *rancho*. That would make me sad because I know your true value."

"Lefty Moore don't cotton to double crossers. He will personally take care of the matter in a way you won't like. That is, she don't get to you first."

"A woman?"

"You bet. I've seen her kill two or three men already and I know she has it in her to kill one or two more. You've just made yourself the next most likely candidate."

"You're a man who talks out of his ass a lot. I don't care about a son of bitch like Moore. I don't work for him. I work for Huerta. And he will pay me well for delivering you to *El Rojo Loco*."

"You stupid son of a bitch -- Huerta's already written you off. And you know T-Roy's crazy as shit."

Conjo shrugged.

"Not so crazy. His money spends well. I told you that other shit last night to win your trust."

"You can't lie worth shit, *compadre* -- you're scared of T-Roy."

Conjo looked away.

The two other men stood on either side of Burch. Their comrades stepped from the bush, making it a squad of six, armed with CAR-15s and M-16s. They stripped the Colts away from Burch and Carla Sue. Conjo reached forward to gently slip the strap of *El Niño* from Burch's shoulder.

They wound along the ridgeline for three hours of hard climbing and descent. Burch's damaged knee throbbed and he limped heavily, slowing the party.

The trail dropped down into a notch between two hills. As they cleared the notch, the trail widened and left the trees. It rolled through some low brush and sidled up to a dirt road, ducking toward then away from the larger path, putting off the junction like a reluctant spinster considering the qualities of a rare but not-so-welcome suitor.

Conjo signaled the other men. They faded into the brush. Carla Sue turned and arched an eyebrow at Burch.

"Checkpoint. They don't want to start a firefight. Not with this prize beef in the middle of things. I guess they don't have this wired up as tight as they'd like us to think."

Conjo smacked Burch in the face with an open hand.

"You keep your mouth shut, you fat sack of shit. I'm going to walk you in and take you to *El Rojo Loco*."

"You ain't gonna make this fly, son. You walk away from a man like T-Roy, he don't tend to forget it. You think you can waltz on in, hand us over, then waltz out again, but you can't."

"*Silencio*, fat boy."

"Brilliant line. Witty and concise. You're startin' to rattle, old chum. And you ought to. You ain't gonna live through this."

Conjo spun and kicked Burch's bad right knee. Burch fell on his side in the middle of the road. He tried to get back up, but could only hold himself up on his good leg and two arms.

Burch motioned Carla Sue to his side. She helped pull him to his feet. He draped an arm around her.

"Don't get any ideas, slick. I'm not shopping for another ex-wife. My knee feels like a coffee grinder inside."

Burch laughed and shook his head.

"Just what I need to make a first impression. Those macho fuckers will think I'm a *maricón*."

"A what?"

"A faggot. A wimp. Leanin' on a woman. No *cojones*. If I were a real man, I'd bear the pain by myself. Sooner die than lean on a damn woman."

They walked in three abreast, Conjo on the left, pointing the Ruger at them, Burch limping heavily, dragging his left foot in the dust. As they rounded the bend, Conjo called out. A man in tiger-stripe fatigues stepped out of the brush, sporting a CAR-15 across his chest and a dark blue baseball cap pulled low across his eyes.

If these guys are worth a damn, Burch thought, a machine gun, maybe an M-60, would be on the opposite side of the road, hidden in the brush, manned by at least two men. He watched that side of the road as Conjo talked to the man in the cap.

"Damn, Big 'Un, you're killin' me."

"Tough it out, slick. Make it a good show. Bitch some more, to Conjo. Make it loud."

Carla Sue turned on a pure grit accent.

"I tell you what, we oughta plug this poor cocksucker before I have to carry his sorry ass another step. All he does is limp and complain."

Conjo laughed and translated for the man in tiger stripes. The man pointed to Burch and Carla Sue.

"Si le damos un tiro a este cerdo nadie ella se cogerá a esta vieja esta noche."

Conjo translated.

"Tell him I don't have anybody to fuck me now."

She slapped Burch on the chest and spat on his boots.

"¡Maricon!"

Laughter from Tiger Stripes and from a large clump of brush just where Burch thought a machine-gun post should be.

"¡Vamos a darle un tiro al maricón! Despues nos jugamos a la vieja en la baraja."

Tiger Stripes swung the barrel of his CAR-15 toward Burch. Conjo stepped up quickly and grabbed his forearm.

"No mi amigo. El vale mucho dinero. Y a tu jefe le interesa muchisimo. El. No la chava. Si le das un tiro ahora, no recibiras nigun dinero. Si lo matas, a ti te daran un tiro."

Tiger Stripes jammed his gun barrel into Conjo's chest.

"Tal vez yo te doy el tiro a ti."

Conjo shrugged.

"Tal vez yo se algo que tu jefe necesita saber. Estos dos no le diran nada. Yo si. Ueuanos a los tres con tu jefe y ganate una lana."

Carla Sue hissed at him: "What the fuck's going on?"

"Bright Eyes can't decide whether to shoot me or our boy. And he wants to draw cards for the honor of fucking you. Our boy is talking fast, making us sound like somebody his *jefe* just has to kill in person."

"That all?"

"Nope. Bright Eyes can't decide whether you'd be a good fuck or not."

Carla Sue spun on her heel and slapped him.

"Good girl," he growled. "You were gettin' too damn friendly."

More laughter from the brush. Tiger Stripes stayed silent, staring at each of the three in turn, swinging the barrel of his gun to a stop that was leveled at the point where chest met belly.

Burch was the last in line. He could feel his sweat really start to flow.

"Bueno."

Tiger Stripes stepped up to Burch and slammed a knee into his groin. Burch fell heavily, dragging Carla Sue down into the dirt. She scrambled up, kicked him in the ribs and spat on the back of his head. Burch stayed on his hands and knees, blinking back a sharp, deep pain that caused his gorge to rise -- thin, dark gruel flecked with undigested jerky.

Conjo and Tiger Stripes stood above him, laughing. Burch kept his head hung low, spitting out vomit, letting his head clear. Carla Sue spat on him again.

"Maricon!"

Burch heard an engine fire up and a gear grind. He wished the girl knew a few more Tex-Mex slurs. Anything but faggot. Anything that didn't sound like a plateful of cookies at an old ladies' tea.

Chapter 35

"Welcome to sunny Old Mexico. I'm your humble tour guide and it is my distinct pleasure to show you around our modest little *rancho*. I think you'll find it has a few interesting features that you don't see up Dallas way. We've also got some unusual entertainment lined up for you. Been expectin' you all for days. Seemed like you'd never get down our way. Now you're here, we're all so pleased -- everybody's ready to bust a gut to make sure your stay here is a happy and pleasant event."

Dawn was three hours away. The house and yard were floodlit. T-Roy was standing on the top step of the porch where Mano died, wearing a broad-brimmed straw hat with a cattleman's crease and a white suit with a short-waisted jacket, the kind you'd see on a waiter or a *mariachi* strummer.

If he looked behind him, he could see dried splatters of blood on the adobe wall of the house. To his right, blood stained the porch planking like the shadow of an octopus. But T-Roy looked straight down at Burch, Carla Sue and Conjo, his eyes wide and wild, his arms gesturing like a revival preacher's, his voice booming like a carney barker's.

He stepped off the porch. He spread his arms open as he sauntered down to their level.

"You are my guests. We aim to make you feel right at home. But first, we got to take care of a few formalities."

T-Roy drew out this last word, chomping down on every syllable. He nodded once and men stepped up behind each of the three newcomers, pinning their arms back, forcing them to kneel in the dirt, binding them fast like rodeo ropers. Conjo started pleading his case.

"*Jefe*, I caught these two and brought them to you. I know they are worth much to you, but I want no money. Consider it a tribute, a sign I want to work for you again."

"I'm sure all that's true, pard. I'm sure comin' back to work for me is exactly why you're here. Hell, you're probably real sorry you left in the first place. Right? Tell ol' T-Roy just how sorry you are."

"It's true, *jefe*. I left because of *La Bruja*. My soul couldn't sleep."

"Well, you got somethin' there, pard. Have a tough time sleepin' myself sometimes. Lots of stuff flyin' around in the dark around here. In the daylight too. But hell, I'm interuptin'. You were gettin' set to tell me how much you miss this place. Is it the cookin'? Or maybe was it that Matamoros pussy I bring in here."

"No, *patrón*."

"So you're tellin' me the pussy ain't good enough for you and you'd like to kill the cook?"

"No, *patrón*."

"Well, maybe you'd like to make up your fuckin' mind and tell me what you do like about this wonderful *rancho* deluxe."

"The things you give us are fine to have, but I wanted to come back to work for you and be with my *compadres* again. I am lonely for home -- and this Mexico, it is many things, but it isn't home."

"A man does miss his home, that's a fact. And I do try to make things comfortable for you boys. But just why the hell would I take back a ball-less *cabron* like you, a man who would walk away from his *compadres?*"

"Because I brought you the killer of your woman."

"Is that right? Now, how's a dumbass *campesino* like you know something like that?"

"*Jefe*, the whole valley knows about the loss of your woman and this son of a whore who killed her. The price on his head. The way her death made you crazy with grief."

"And you think bringin' them here is enough to wash away your sins against me and your *compadres*? You think that?"

"*Si, patrón.* I ask your forgiveness."

Conjo touched the dirt with his forehead. As he rose up, T-Roy cupped the ex-contra's chin in one hand, leaning down, smiling and speaking softly.

"That's a real fine gesture, pard. And it touched my heart. It truly did. I wish I could find it in me to forgive and forget, but I guess I just ain't Christian enough."

Conjo looked frightened and confused. The words meant nothing to him, but the look in T-Roy's eyes did. T-Roy grabbed him by the hair and tightened his grip on Conjo's chin, giving a sharp twist to Conjo's head, working it like a balky valve wheel on a pipeline, bracing both feet wide, his face breaking into an open-mouthed leer of concentration. His long red hair shook from the effort.

Small crunching noises came first, followed by a sharp crack that caused Burch to wince. T-Roy let Conjo's twitching body drop on its side, pulling a bandana from his back pocket, tipping his hat and wiping the sweat from his face. He pointed to one of his men.

"You there -- bring me that pack. Let's see what prize these fine folk have brought us."

T-Roy rummaged through the knapsack, clucking to himself like an old woman.

"My, my -- isn't this nice," he said, pulling Carla Sue's Colt out of the pack.

He stepped in front of Burch. His voice lost all traces of studied politeness.

"This the gun you did Astrid with, you cocksucker?"

"I didn't do your ..."

A backhand slap cut Burch off. The big man spat blood in the dirt and glared at T-Roy.

"... girlfriend. Wasn't me, asshole. Ross had it done. Set me up as the patsy. Figured it might flush you from this hidey hole."

"That's an interestin' line of bullshit. Too bad I don't believe a word you say."

"Doesn't much matter if you do or don't. You got the upper hand. You gonna kill us sooner or later. I got nothin' to lose tellin' you the truth. And you know I'm way too ornery to beg for anything from a shitass like you."

Another backhand, this time with Carla Sue's pistol along for the ride. The Colt gouged a chunk out of Burch's jaw, just below his left cheekbone. He could taste more blood in his mouth. Heat and stinging pain marked where the pistol cut him.

T-Roy leaned in. His breath smelled like tequila and the inside of an unwashed jockstrap.

"You'll beg, old man. You and her will beg plenty before I'm through. But I ain't done with you yet. I got things to show you."

"Cut the drama, shithead -- I ain't interested in anything you have to show me. Heard all about this damn voodoo woman you got here. You want to hide behind her skirts, that's fine. But why don't you and me have it out. Man to man. Right here?"

"Pistols?"

"Be fine. You got a second one in that sack. It's mine -- the one I used to kill that nigger you sent. He died real pretty, right after he killed my ex."

"So, we're even."

"Not hardly. You forget Wynn Moore and the fact I didn't kill your woman. I'm one down. Killin' you would even it out, though. Maybe I can get that voodoo woman to let me do it twice. Put me ahead of the damn game. Maybe I'll get that voodoo woman to send us both to hell where I can just keep on killin' you."

"And maybe I'll just sic that voodoo woman on you. You might not like her culinary tastes."

"It won't matter what I like after I'm dead, needledick. Fact is, I'm dead already. So what you do and how you do it means about as much to me as the name of the young boy you're going to get to suck your dick tonight."

Burch shrugged as much as a bound man can.

"Pablo, Juan -- don't matter to me. It's your dick, their mouth."

Burch saw a fist and Carla Sue's Colt swinging for his head just before someone fired a flare gun behind his eyelids and he started a long fall down a very dark hole.

Chapter 36

The stench brought him back. Sweet and cloying on the surface, a gagging mix of the sewer and the morgue underneath.

He was on his side, on the dirt floor of a shed. His arms were still bound behind him. His face and forehead were on fire -- places where Carla Sue's Colt gouged grooves into his flesh, he guessed. One eye, the left one, nearest the floor, was swollen shut. With his tongue he could feel the jagged stumps of broken teeth -- four at least.

Across the room, flames licked the bottom of a fire-blackened cauldron that stood about chest high. He saw a short, barrel-chested man drop something slick and tan into the cauldron, heard that something plop into something liquid inside.

To his right, Burch saw T-Roy -- bareheaded and barechested, his face and ribcage streaked with dark wetness, his cheeks puffing in and out, forcing smoke from a large cigar into a column of smoke rising from a gourd bowl he held in front of him.

T-Roy spun to the four points of the compass, holding the bowl out and above his head, aiming the cigar smoke toward the corrugated tin roof of the shed.

He was backlit by candles burning on an altar. Light from guttering torches also flickered across his body, causing the slick, dark streaks to shine. Smoke swirled through his wiry red hair.

T-Roy placed the bowl and cigar on the altar and stepped up to a heavy, mahogany table. Burch could only see the legs and the underside of the tabletop. The legs were slick and wet, like the streaks on T-Roy's body.

His back faced Burch. The muscles of his arms and neck were corded. His right arm rocked back and forth like a man sawing hardwood or a tough cut of beef. Burch heard a wet plopping sound. T-Roy turned to face the room, holding a human heart in both hands, rubbing it across his chest, then his face.

"Sweet Jesus."

It was Carla Sue's voice -- a raspy whisper right behind him. He craned his neck back, trying to see her. She caught the movement.

"Glad you're with us. 'Fraid you might miss the show."

"Thought that might be you. Glad it isn't."

"You're sweet. It's our buddy. Hope he said his prayers last night."

"He snored, remember? What'd I miss?"

"T-Roy, playin' with his food like that. Chants and cigar smoke. Been like a hog butcherin' otherwise. Been choppin' up Conjo and slippin' him into that cauldron."

The short man handed another gourd bowl to T-Roy. He slapped the heart into the bowl, walked over and sat on his haunches in front of them. He showed them the bowl; the heart sat in the middle of a thick, greenish-brown paste that was barely liquid.

"*Chilimole.* An old Aztec recipe."

His voice was low and soft, like an accountant with bad news about taxes or the bottom line. It had the patient tone of a teacher in conference with the parents of an unruly child.

"You cut the heart, like this ..." A thin strip of muscle carved with a large hunting knife. "... then swirl it in the chilimole ..." A strip covered with goo, perched on two fingertips. "... then eat it."

T-Roy tilted his head back and dropped the strip into his mouth. He swallowed with a shudder that started at his head and traveled through his shoulders, chest and stomach.

He looked at them with blank eyes, carved and swirled again, then tilted his head back like a baby bird begging mama for a worm. The heart flesh dangled from his fingertips.

"This gives me power. Power over this man's family and friends. Power over my enemies. Power over things above and under this earth. That's what the old woman says."

"Must be a lotta power in the heart of some damn peasant *contra*."

"Just an appetizer, my friend."

T-Roy motioned to men in the far corner of the shed. They grabbed Burch, yanking him to his feet. He watched as the short man slung what was left of Conjo's body -- head, trunk and split-open chest -- onto an oilcloth behind the cauldron. They duckwalked him to the table, untying his arms and stripping his shirt off, forcing him face up onto the tabletop.

His body formed a burly bow -- arms were stretched over his head, wrists roped together and tied to a table strut. Ankles were also tied together and roped to the table. T-Roy appeared at his side, with the knife and that calm, teacher's voice.

"Just so you'll know -- I'm going to bleed you into this bowl, then burn your blood. Usually, you do this with somebody who's already dead, but I'm going to give you a special treat. I want you to see your blood burn."

T-Roy ran the knife blade under the rope binding Burch's wrists and made a deep slice on each side. Burch could feel the bite of the blade and the warm wetness spurting from the cuts, into his cupped palms and onto the floor below. T-Roy stood over him, watching the flow, watching Burch's face for a sign of fear.

"You're bleeding, old man. But that's good for you. Gets the evil humours out and puts your body into proper balance. Wards off ague and the grippe. It's good to be bled, don't you think? Just like going to one of them medieval barbers. Only I ain't gonna stop it."

Burch fought off panic that rose from his gut into his chest. He willed his body not to struggle against the ropes. He willed his eyes to return T-Roy's gaze with a flat, cold stare.

T-Roy leaned in close, resting his right ear above Burch's heart, breathing his locker room breath into Burch's nostrils.

"Damn, your ticker is doin' flip-flops. It'll make a fine meal, son. Much better than that damn ol' pissant from Nicaragua, don't you think?"

Burch said nothing.

"What's the matter, old man ..."

T-Roy rose up and brought the knife blade to Burch's chest.

"Not ..."

A flick of the blade opened an inch-long cut above his left nipple.

"... feeling ..."

Another flick, another cut above the right nipple.

"... very ..."

Flick, a long cut along the length of his sternum.

"... talkative?"

T-Roy centered the blade where Burch's chest met his belly. Resting his palm on the butt of the handle, he pushed the tip in slowly until it drew a small bubble of blood. He ran his other hand across the cuts in Burch's chest, smearing the blood across his face. In the torchlight, it took on the same rusty color as the shiny dark streaks Burch saw when T-Roy was carving on Conjo.

The room changed colors on Burch, going from flickering yellow to the tobacco-stained color of a smoker's fingertips. The edges darkened slowly, drawing in toward the center. He lost minutes and seconds of time, snapping back to a view of the room then letting it slip away again, like a deacon fighting off the Sunday sermon nods.

He saw T-Roy with a bowl in his hands. He smelled a cigar. He felt someone brush along his outstretched arms. He heard the echo of droplets hit the bottom of a bowl.

Slaps to the face then someone shoved his head up, holding him back where the hair ended and the bald pate began. T-Roy held the bowl, sprinkling dark powder like a chef adding pepper to soup. The sides of the bowl were wet and streaked. His blood, he guessed. He didn't care.

"I want you to see this, old man. See your blood burn."

T-Roy struck a match. Flames flew up from the bowl. Burch smelled the burnt powder and fuel oil, mixed with something sweet and gagging. His vision faded. He was floating in darkness. He could hear murmurs above him, like voices on the other side of a door. Smells crossed his nostrils -- burning leaves, dinner, a trash heap, a spent shotgun shell, incense? He couldn't tell and didn't care.

A long scream snapped him back into the room. It was T-Roy, perched above him with a palm on his chest and the knife above his head, ready to slash downward.

His face was in profile, tilted upward like a man looking toward the sun, eyes bulging, mouth open, tongue out, making the noise of a terrified animal. There was something up there, up in the dark, cobwebbed corner where the shed's tin roof met the rafters, something only T-Roy or a true believer could see.

"He sees the Vision Serpent. He has angered the ones he doesn't believe in."

The voice was cool, soft and old -- a wise grandmother in an antique chair. It took on a steely edge and spoke to T-Roy who was silent now, but was still looking toward the roof, palm on Burch's chest, knife held high, shaking so hard it caused Burch's belly to jiggle.

"You don't believe, yet you would do the things believers do. You mock us. You mock the gods, the *loas*, the *guédés* we believe in. You mock an old woman and the serpent that floats above you."

The shaking stopped. T-Roy looked down and gave Burch a vampish wink.

"Mock, hell -- I'm just trying to put on a good show for our guests, *madrina*."

T-Roy tensed up, raising the knife higher and pushing down on Burch's chest. He rolled his eyes toward the ceiling and started to scream.

The scream was broken by the roar of a Colt .45.

Burch could hear the bullets smack into T-Roy's skull and back. Flying Ashtrays and hardball -- he could see them punch out gobs of blood and flesh as they slammed on through T-Roy's chest and face. His head snapped downward in profile, the lifeless stare of one eye glaring at Burch like a shark or marlin brought to the side of an angler's boat to die after hours of struggle.

It is a look that says this animal still wants to fight, still wants to kill. But it can't. It is a look a man doesn't forget, one that brings on shudders in deep sleep or daydreams. Burch knew he would carry that look with him always.

"Hope you burn in hell, mister."

Carla Sue's flat, cold voice. He got to see her kill another man. Just before the room went dark again.

CHAPTER 37

In and out of the sweet nowhere that the mind uses to hide a body from a bad hurt, he saw the half light of dawn and short, muscular men in straw hats pull on the heavy rope of a hand-drawn ferry. Someone whispered *Los Ebanos*.

His jaw throbbed like someone had slammed it with a cold chisel and his tongue was so swollen he couldn't talk. He looked at his watch and saw white gauze and adhesive tape on his wrist. His head started spinning and his vision went black.

Back again, but seeing nothing. He felt the solid sway of a big car on the move and heard the sudden, whooshing sound of other cars passing by an open window. A hand stroked his head. A voice said: "Don't you die on me now, Big 'Un."

Gone again. He watched Wynn Moore order a bottle of Pearl, cup his palm on the ass of a dead whore named Candy Slice and wink at his dead aunt as she sang "... shall we gather at the river. The bee-u-tee-ful, bee-u-tee-ful a ri-iv-er ..."

He heard Shoat Nimitz, quarterback on his high school team, call his favorite play, 28-Pitch. On the deuce. Pull and get the cornerback. Make him cough blood. Smell the turf. Feel the back rip on by.

He threw a forearm. Pain snapped him awake. He saw a sign through the rear window of the car -- Pete's Paradise Motel. Faded blue on white. His vision slipped away.

He felt the cool brush of fresh sheets. She was with him again.

He could taste her musk, overripe and almost rotten, but so sweet that he arched his head off the pillow, straining the root of his tongue for more. He heard her muffled moans of approval, then a sharp yelp of pleasure as she raised her head, tossing her thick hair -- black and glossy as a Chinese girl's -- across her back, from right shoulder to left, in time with his rhythm.

"Shit, boy -- that tongue. Forgot how good -- mmmm. Shit, boy. Right -- annnhhn -- right there. Right -- annnnhhnn."

Ragged breaths. Much noise with no words. She flicked her mane faster. She cried louder. She rode him, hands planted on his soft belly, nails raking into the hair just below his chest, arching high and back, face toward the ceiling, yelling at the light, the fan and the neighbors up above.

He brushed her nipples with his fingertips, bringing her back, causing her to look down at him with a half smile, teeth just showing through her parted lips. He gave her a thrust. She hissed and pitched forward.

"No fair, boy. Get me flying and take advantage. Got to even things up. Now, what have we here?"

Her hair felt cool and heavy on his thighs and gut. She took him up slowly, pausing now and then to look at his face and run her nails through his chest hair. She grinned, then turned back to her task, taking him up and over, slurping like something starved and thirsty, riding his knee between her crotch.

She smiled her half smile. She was his first and longest love and she was with him again. He said his first words.

"Do me a favor. Don't say okra."

A loud, burring jangle -- familiar and unwanted. It wouldn't stop. Her half smile faded. So did she -- gone again and he couldn't bring her back. The jangle pulled him up and away, insistent and dragging him from a place he didn't want to leave.

He woke up. With a hard-on. And a wet spot on his sheets. With a ringing phone on the night table on his left, above his head, stabbing his ears and brain and leaving him with only one way to make it stop. He reached across his body with his right arm -- white-hot pain sliced into his ribs. He tried a blind and awkward reach with his left and knocked the handset out of the cradle with a clatter that killed the jangle. He grabbed the spiraled cord and reeled it in, tucking the business end of the blower between his jaw and shoulder, wincing with pain.

He tried to speak, but couldn't. He listened to a long-distance hiss on the line.

"Got nothin' to say, Big 'Un? That's a first. Takes a helluva lot to shut you up. Not sure you and I could stand another round of what it takes to keep you from flappin' your lips."

He tried to ask 'where are you?' It came out garbled and slurred, like slow-poured gravel from a plastic bag.

"You askin' where I'm at, I think. Better you don't know. And better if you don't try to talk. Your jaw got busted and had to be wired up. You'll be drinkin' dinner for a while. Ribs are busted, too. And we had to get your face and wrists stitched up. Your chest, too."

He looked down at his chest and saw the twin rows of stitching that closed deep cuts on either side of his sternum. He could feel the swelling along the right side of his face. He held up his right arm and turned it over, staring at the long, jagged line sewn up down the middle of his wrist. He knew it as the deep mark of a serious suicide, not a shallow, cross-cut cry for help. And not the usual choice of a killer who wanted to bleed him out.

'How?' he tried to say. More gravel poured from the bag.

"How? How are we still alive? Luck of a blind pig or more of that spooky voodoo shit. The *madrina* wanted T-Roy dead but couldn't bring herself to kill him or have her sons do it. Said the spirits told her I was the way to make that happen. Handed me the .45 just about the time T-Roy was ready to make your ticker a midnight snack. Let us go. You were a mess so her boys hauled us to a friendly *medico* on this side of the border. Motel you're in belongs to him. You're safe there -- the *madrina's* boys keep it that way and the law stays away. Paid the doc enough to keep you tended to until you mend up."

He steeled himself to punch through the gravel, one slow word at a time.

"Saw ... you ... kill ... sumbitch. Too ... fast."

"Too fast? Well fuck me runnin'. Didn't exactly have time to make it a slow, painful death, did I? I guess I should have let him cut your heart out before wastin' his sorry ass. Could've took my time that way."

"Fine ... by ... me."

"Don't give me that martyr shit, Big 'Un. We got in this together, we got out of this together. Killin' T-Roy came from the both of us. For Uncle Harlan, your partner and your ex. Don't matter who pulled the goddam trigger."

"Not ... enough."

"You're right about that. It doesn't bring them back. And it never goes away, does it? The pain of losin' them."

"No ... never ... does."

They stopped talking, the long-distance hiss the only sound between them. She broke the silence, her voice small and drained.

"This is goodbye, Big 'Un. You won't see me no more. You take care of you."

A loud click on the line. The dial tone in his ear. He looked at the scars on his chest and the wet spot on the sheets. He touched his swollen jaw and felt the pain in his ribs.

Battered but alive. Alone in a border motel.

About the Author

For more than 30 years, Jim Nesbitt was a roving correspondent for newspapers and wire services in Alabama, Florida, Texas, Georgia, North Carolina, South Carolina and Washington, D.C. He chased hurricanes, earthquakes, plane wrecks, presidential candidates, wildfires, rodeo cowboys, ranchers, miners, loggers, farmers, migrant field hands, doctors, neo-Nazis and nuns with an eye for the telling detail and an ear for the voice of the people who give life to a story. He is a lapsed horseman, pilot, hunter and saloon sport with a keen appreciation for old guns, vintage trucks and tractors, good cigars, aged whiskey and a well-told story. He now lives in Athens, Alabama. This is his first novel.

Read on for an exerpt
from Jim Nesbitt's next novel

THE RIGHT WRONG NUMBER

An Ed Earl Burch Novel

Available Summer 2016

CHAPTER 1

It wasn't San Francisco or London, but the fog was thick and flowing -- like tufts sucked from a bale of cotton, carrying the muddy tint of a used linen filter. It made him think of trench coats, lamp posts and the low warning moan of a ship's horn sounding somewhere out on the water. Rolling across the flat fields, it made dark gray ghosts of the trees that huddled along the far fence lines and left cold beads of moisture on his skin and memories of old black-and-white movies in his mind.

But there were no ships in the harbor, no waterside buckets of blood, no Rick or Ilsa. Just lightless farmhouses, barns, open-sided equipment sheds and squat corrugated feed bins for cattle, all cloaked by the fast-moving fog, glimpsed only if the wind parted the curtain of stained white wetness as you rolled by.

And it wasn't the Left Coast or Britain. It was Texas and the scrubby coastal country north of Houston, beyond the Intercontinental and its roaring planes. Take a left off the farm-market road with the four-digit number. Find the third dirt road on the left, take it for three miles. Splash through the potholes and set your teeth against tires juddering across the washboard track. Hit the T of another dirt road. Look for a faint gravel trail at your 10 o'clock. Rattle over the cattle guard. Close the gate behind you.

Easy to remember. Hard to do with visibility down to zero. Even with the window rolled down and the Beemer's fog lamps flipped on.

Nice car. Leather seats the color of butterscotch taffy. Mahogany inserts flanking the instruments and fronting the glove box. Killer sound system and a cellular phone. Shame to bang this baby along back roads, splashing mud and gravel against its polished flanks of forest green.

Not his car. Not his problem. Fog and time were. He was already a half hour behind schedule when his contact finally drove up with the car, the briefcase of bills and the directions to the meet. Fog was adding more minutes to his travel time. He had to double back when he missed one turnoff and that made him slow and leery of missing another.

Not good. Not good. Patient people weren't on the other end. They never were. But they would wait because he had the money, they had the product and both sides wanted this deal closed tonight. And if they were pissed and wanted to wrangle, he could deal with that; a matte-chrome Smith & Wesson Model 6906 with 13 rounds of 9 mm hollow-point nestled in a shoulder rig underneath his black leather jacket.

Always the chance of a wrangle on a run like this. Ripoffs were a run-of-the-mill business risk, even between long-time associates. But on this deal, the probability of gunplay was low. He was just nervous about running late. It wasn't professional. He thought about using the cellular phone but shook the idea out of his head. Not something a pro would do.

And not something his people would appreciate. They were security-conscious and worked the high-dollar end of the street. No cowboys. Pros only. Running a well-oiled machine. Not that he knew them well. He was strictly a cutout man, a well-paid delivery boy who made it his business to stay ignorant about those who hired him and their business partners.

He wasn't totally in the dark about his paymasters; no prudent pro ever was. But he kept his curiosity in check and his focus on the amount of money he was paid and the demands of the night's job.

It was a relaxing way to make a living. A phone rings. A voice on the line gives him the name of a bar or cafe. A man meets him with an envelope and instructions. And he goes where he is told -- to deliver money, to pick up a truck or car loaded with product, to put a bullet through the skull of someone he doesn't know. Command and control. Just like the Army and those over-the-border ops in Cambodia.

A sputtering string of electronic beeps startled him. The car phone. He glanced down and saw a red pin light flash to the time of the beeps. He pulled the receiver out of its cradle.

"Talk to me."

"Where the hell are you?"

"You don't want me to say."

"You're late and that's making some people nervous."

"Your man was late and this phone call is making me nervous. It's not very smart."

"We decide what's smart. We pay you to get things done and be on time. How long till you get there?"

"Ten."

"Get there."

He snapped the receiver back in place and shook his head. Not good. Not good. Lots of snoopers scanning these cellular circuits. A pro would know this and wouldn't risk a call unless the other side was making a ruckus. Made him wonder if the players in this game were as big league as he thought they were.

Those thoughts rode with him as he wheeled the Beemer down the dirt road, looking for the T intersection. There it was. He looked for the gravel trail, slowly turning the car to the left, letting the fog lamps cut a slow sweep across the far side of the road. There. At his ten o'clock. Just like he was told. He stayed alert, but his nagging nervousness and doubts started to fade.

The trail led from the gate and crossed the field at a sharp angle. He crept along, easing the car through ruts and washouts. He saw the shrouded form of a tin shed and weaved the car so the lights would pan across its open door. The yellow beams caught the wet metal of an old tractor and two men in dark slacks and windbreakers -- one tall, bald and lean; the other short, squat and slick-haired.

He stopped the car, fog lamps still on. He pulled his pistol, letting his gun hand drop to his side and rear as he stepped out, keeping his body behind the car door.

"Wanna cut the lights, guy?"

A purring voice from the short guy, coming from a full, sleek face that made him think of a seal.

"Not really. Let's keep everything illuminated. Makes me feel safe."

"You're among friends, guy. Nobody wants monkeyshines here. We just do the handoff and the call and we can get the hell out of this fog. You're late and we're cold."

"No arguments from me, my man. But let's do this by the numbers."

"Numbers it is, guy."

He stepped away from the car.

"Money's in the front seat. Have your buddy do the honors."

A nod from the talker. His companion walked to the passenger side of the Beemer and leaned in. He heard the latches of the briefcase pop open.

"Looks good to me."

"Make the call. That okay with you, guy?"

"By all means. Make that call. Tell Mabel to put a pot of coffee on."

A laugh from the talker. He could see the other guy reach for the cellular phone. Somewhere across town, a phone would ring. Assurances that the money was in hand. Somewhere else another phone would ring. Product would change hands. Then the Beemer's cellular would ring again and the night's business would be done.

He was alert but relaxed, ready to wait, the screwups behind him and the deal running smooth and professional now. He had a clear view of the talker and his companion. He had his gun in hand. He was thinking about a cup of coffee when the baseball bat cracked across the back of his skull.

"Cut those damn lights. Secure the money."

A nod from the companion. The talker moved toward the third man, the man with the baseball bat, a hulk with the arms and shoulders of a lineman and the on-the-balls-of-the-feet stance of a third baseman. They stood over the slumped body.

"Give me a hand with this sumbitch. He's heavy. Get that gun, Jack."

"Got it. Who'd this guy piss off?"

"Nobody you need to know about, guy. Or me. He's just a poor soul somebody wants whacked."

"Awful lot of trouble just to whack a guy. What the fuck are we stagin' this thing for, Louis? Why not just pop him and get it over with?"

"Not your worry, guy. Just muscle him into the driver's seat and let me dress him up pretty. Bill, did you wipe your prints?"

"Does it matter?"

A glare from Louis. The companion shrugged, pulled a bandana from his back pocket and leaned into the Beemer. When done, he hoisted the briefcase and walked back toward the shed.

Louis kept his eyes locked on the bald man as he walked away, his head swiveling like a table-top fan, his eyes popped with anger. He broke the stare and fussed with the body, pulling the head back, reaching into the mouth, then his pocket, then back into the mouth. Jack watched and shook his head.

"Bill!"

"Yo!"

"Get me that bundle, guy. The jacket and the raincoat. And bring that bag with the stuff in it."

"Yo."

Bill hustled to the car. Louis patted him on the shoulder, thanking him in that purring voice, his face soft and placid again. He turned back to the body, peeling off the leather jacket and unfastening the shoulder rig. He fished through the pockets, pulling wallet, keys and a checkbook, leaving loose change. He replaced these items with wallet, keys and a checkbook he pulled from a crumpled brown paper bag. He pulled a ring from the right hand and a fake Rolex from the left wrist, digging a wedding band, a class ring and a real Rolex -- an Oyster Perpetual Datejust -- from the bag.

The raincoat and jacket came next. Louis started to sweat as he pulled and smoothed the clothes onto the body. He unbuttoned the shirt down to the navel, then reached into the bag and pulled out a squeeze bottle, the kind with the thin nozzle that could poke through the bars of a footballer's facemask. He squeezed water onto the body's chest then reached under the dash to pop the hood of the Beemer.

"Jack -- hook up those cables, guy."

"Jesus."

"I know it's unpleasant, but just do it for me, guy."

Louis fired up the Beemer's engine then waited for Jack to hand him the twin clamps. Clamps to the body's chest. The smell of burning flesh and electrified ozone. Again. Again the smell. And again. Clamps to Jack. Engine off.

"Bill. The acid, guy."

A glass bottle of sulfuric acid. A small glass tray. Fingers and thumb from one hand in. Then the other hand. He handed the tray to Bill.

"Careful with that, guy. Dump it."

"Yo."

Louis turned back to the body. He pursed his lips as he lined up the shoulders, the head and the arms to stage the proper angles of a kill shot.

The head was the difficult part. Without a helping hand to hold it in place, it rolled about and wouldn't stay upright. Louis pulled the hips forward then shoved the shoulders deep into the folds of the leather seat, pressing them into place. The head was now resting lightly against the butterscotch leather padding of the headrest.

That's how it would line up. He stood up and pulled a .357 Colt Python from the paper bag with a gloved hand. He eyed the angle for another second then nodded Jack away.

Louis shoved the pistol into a sagging mouth, eyeing the angle one more time. He pulled the trigger, blinking at the pistol's flash and sharp report. He dropped the gun to the floor. The bullet had blown off the back of the man's skull, obliterating the pulpy mark of the baseball bat and spraying a dark stain of brains, blood and bone shards across the light-colored leather seats. The impact canted the body across the console and gearshift, head and shoulder jammed between the seats.

"Jesus, Louis."

"What?"

"Christamighty, it's one thing to whack a guy up close like that, another to do all that shit with the battery cables and the acid. But to have to fish out his dentures first? They'd have to pay me double to do that."

"They are, guy. They are."

"Whadja have to do it for?"

"They were making his gums sore. He needed a new pair."

"Like he'll need 'em where he's going."

"You never know. Blow the car, Jack. We gotta get us back on home, guy. Get us on the outside of some gumbo down to Tujague's."

"I'm for that. A shame, though. This is a nice car."

"That it is, guy. Blow her just the same. Make it burn pretty."

"Lotta noise. Lotta flash. Cops'll be here like flies on a dead fish."

"Do it quick then, guy. So we can be long gone."

Made in the USA
Middletown, DE
10 October 2022

12457212R00139